# THE
# DREAD PIRATE
# FLEUR
## & the
## Hangman's
## Noose

Also by Sara Starbuck

The Dread Pirate Fleur and the Ruby Heart

# THE DREAD PIRATE FLEUR
## & the Hangman's Noose

# SARA STARBUCK

### Illustrated by Niall Stewart Harding

RED FOX

THE DREAD PIRATE FLEUR & THE HANGMAN'S NOOSE
A RED FOX BOOK 978 1 862 30729 2

First published in Great Britain by Red Fox,
an imprint of Random House Children's Books
A Random House Group Company

This edition published 2010

1 3 5 7 9 10 8 6 4 2

Copyright © Sara Starbuck, 2010
Cover illustration copyright © Adam Relf, 2010
Inside illustrations copyright © Niall Stewart Harding, 2010

The right of Sara Starbuck to be identified as the author of this work has been
asserted in accordance with the Copyright, Designs and Patents Act 1988.

The Random House Group Limited supports the Forest Stewardship Council
(FSC), the leading international forest certification organization. All our titles that are
printed on Greenpeace-approved FSC-certified paper carry the FSC logo. Our paper
procurement policy can be found at www.rbooks.co.uk/environment.

**Mixed Sources**
Product group from well-managed
forests and other controlled sources
www.fsc.org  Cert no. TT-COC-2139
© 1996 Forest Stewardship Council

Set in 12/18pt Bembo

Red Fox Books are published by Random House Children's Books,
61–63 Uxbridge Road, London W5 5SA

www.kidsatrandomhouse.co.uk
www.rbooks.co.uk

Addresses for companies within The Random House Group Limited can be found at:
www.randomhouse.co.uk/offices.htm

THE RANDOM HOUSE GROUP Limited Reg. No. 954009

A CIP catalogue record for this book is available from the British Library.

Printed in the UK by CPI Bookmarque, Croydon, CR0 4TD

*To my mum and dad,*
*with love*

# CHAPTER 1

*The waters of Madeira, 1692*

'Well, I'll be blowed,' Tom murmured to himself as he hung from the crow's nest of the *Black Dragon*. He squinted against the sun through the lens of his telescope. 'What in the Devil's name is that?'

The Dutch flute sailed steadily on through the waves ahead of them. A large object – the one that Tom had seen tossed overboard a moment earlier – bobbed wildly in the ship's churning wake.

Tom lowered his telescope and frowned. 'That ain't normal,' he concluded, shaking his head. Then, with a fearless leap over the side of the platform, he swung nimbly onto the mast and shimmied down the smooth, worn wood. 'Jetsam on the starboard quarter!' he bellowed to all who could hear him.

Captain William Hart stood at the wheel, his broad shoulders straining against the crimson silk of his shirt. His grim expression brightened at Tom's cry. He called for a crewman to take his place at the helm, then strode across the deck to stare out over the rolling grey waves. Pulling an eyeglass from a sash at his waist, the captain studied the floating object closely, while Tom bounded over to stand at his side.

'I saw 'em toss it overboard as clear as day, sir,' Tom explained. 'Whatever it is, they didn't want to wait until they got to shore to be rid of it.'

William nodded. Box or barrel, it was odd to jettison any wood that could fuel the galley stove on a long sea crossing. He pointed over to the other ship. 'And it was definitely thrown?' he asked. 'Not dropped by clumsy hands, or lost to a slippery deck and an unlucky swell?'

''Twas quite deliberate,' Tom said firmly. 'I'm certain of it.'

William scratched his stubbled chin thoughtfully

with one end of his telescope. 'What do you think it is then, boy?' he asked at last.

Tom shrugged and scratched his own chin, mirroring the captain's movements unconsciously. 'It's a barrel, sir. That much is clear. But for firewood alone it would be worth keeping.' He paused, thinking hard. 'So I reckon there's gotta be something in that barrel. Something worth a look, maybe?'

A broad smile spread over William's craggy face. 'Aye, lad' – he nodded – 'it won't be kitchen scraps at any rate. Well spotted, Tom. You've the eyes of a kestrel. Now, let's have us a closer look.'

The captain called over to the sailor at the wheel. 'Hard to starboard,' he commanded.

'Aye, aye, Cap'n Hart.'

The ship lurched beneath them like a living thing, heaving and groaning as it fought the wind and the waves. A grave-looking Lieutenant Jack, the first mate, made his way over to them from the bridge. The rolling deck tipped and bucked beneath his feet but his steps were as steady and firm as if he were walking on solid rock. His wispy, white hair was tied back, revealing rows of heavy gold hoops in his ears and spidery black neck tattoos. Jack's blood-red albino eyes met his captain's dark ones.

'Are you sure you want to know what's in there, Cap'n?' he asked discreetly. 'I reckon they must've had good reason to get rid of it, whatever it might be.'

'Aye, mackie, perhaps. But stow that thought,' the captain replied heartily, slapping his old shipmate on the back. 'I'll warrant there's sport in it at least, or I'm a rotten mackerel. Trust me, I feel it in me bones.'

Jack rolled his eyes and sighed wearily. He pulled out a pouch of tobacco and leaned against the ship's rail. 'That's all well and good, sir,' he said, filling a small pipe as he spoke. 'But need I remind you that the last time you felt something in your bones we ended up in the Wu Dang Mountains, as prisoners of the Samurai.'

William threw back his head and laughed with gusto. 'And wasn't that fun, Jack?' he said, remembering the adventure fondly.

The first mate grinned despite himself. 'Aye, Cap'n, 'twas a riot in the end,' he admitted. 'But mark me, sir, there won't be nothing but trouble to come out of that barrel. Our course is set. Let us sail on, not slow down to invite trouble aboard.'

'Don't dampen my spirits, man,' his captain said grumpily. 'My mind's made up.' He raised his voice and barked the orders to his men. 'Shake a leg, lads. Bring her about slow and hold her steady.' He marched over to the poop deck. 'That's it, my bullies,' he cried as they bore down on the bobbing barrel. 'Heave to.' He peered over the side, his dark eyes glittering. 'Now then, drop anchor and let's see what we've won.'

The barrel thudded noisily against the hull of the *Black Dragon*. A grappling hook was lowered and several men were enlisted to heave it out of the sea.

Arthur arrived just as they were hauling the barrel over the rail. He'd grown broader and more confident since he'd first shown up on the island Fleur and William had once been marooned on, pale and nervous but with the basic training in medicine that had saved an ailing Tom.

Arthur sidled over to Tom, and both boys watched as the barrel was rolled across the deck, thundering over the wooden boards like an approaching storm.

'Go on then.' Arthur nudged his friend playfully. 'What do you reckon's in there?'

But before Tom could begin to speculate, two men stepped forward and expertly hacked away the barrel's seal with the hatchets they wore in their belts. The captain pushed them aside and flipped up the barrel's lid with the tip of his rapier. His mouth fell open in shock as he peered inside.

'Well,' he said, shaking his head slowly. 'In all my time at sea . . . Well, well, well . . .'

'What is it, Cap'n?' asked Jack urgently.

'Best have a look yourself, I reckon,' said William in dazed tones.

All the men around him surged forward at once. Jack held them off with his sword, turning to peer over his shoulder into the barrel, before meeting William's puzzled expression with one of his own. 'Well, gut me for a preacher,' he muttered. 'It's a *girl*.'

'Well, for Pete's sake, don't just stand there!' The voice, young and high-pitched but bold and clear, cut through the murmurs of the crowd like a fast ship though smooth waves. Fleur Hart elbowed a gawping crewman aside and shoved her way past Captain Hart, her uncle, to the barrel. 'Help me get her out,' she demanded, loosening her cloak and wrapping it around the shoulders of the frightened girl as she was hauled, dripping, from the barrel. 'And close your mouths, you filthy codfish,' she barked as she led her charge through the mob towards her cabin. ''Tain't like she's the first girl to come aboard – or have you forgotten about *me*?'

Fleur stuck out her jaw and glared at the men fiercely, one hand planted firmly on the butt of the dagger at her waist. With the other hand she ushered the unexpected guest inside. Then she turned for one more steely stare – the fiercest she could muster – before leading the girl below decks, slamming the door behind her.

# Chapter 2

Fleur and the mysterious new arrival sat at opposite ends of Fleur's bed. The girl was too tall and willowy for any of Fleur's clothes, so she had been wrapped in blankets while her own were drying and given a mug of hot rum to fight off the chill and shock of her dip. Several times she had been on the verge of speaking, but something had held her back, and now she had drifted into a sleep that she no doubt needed. It was all Fleur could do not to shake her by the shoulders – she was desperate to hear the strange girl's story – but she resisted the urge and, instead, allowed herself to daydream happily about her busy first month back at sea.

It had taken Fleur no time at all to fall back into her sailor's slops and the life of a pirate after her Uncle William had stormed into Cousin Myra's mansion to reclaim her. She remembered the moment she had first set eyes on the *Dragon* again, restored and repainted since the last battle with Captain Blood, snow-white sails billowing around her masts. Tom had been the first to greet her, bouncing along the gangplank with a cry of 'Ahoy, Claw-cat!' and almost bundling her to the boards of the jetty with a powerful hug. Much had changed aboard the *Dragon*, and Tom had poured out his news as fast as teeth and tongue would let him.

'She brushed up nicely, don't she! There's a new crew too. Some who came aboard to help with repairs or take the place of those we lost to Blood and his men.'

Tom had spat on the deck when he spoke his enemy's name. 'There's a few men we liberated from an African slave ship. The cap'n gave 'em their freedom but they chose to stay. They keep to themselves, most of them, but you should see 'em fight. They'd give their lives for William now, I reckon, after the kindness he showed them. There's a new bosun too – George Gates, his name is. Scary bloke with fists like loaves of bread, but a good sailor. The cap'n trusts him with security on the ship, and that's good enough for me. Then there's the surgeon,

Dubois. Jean-Baptiste Dubois. Thick grey hair and a spectacular bushy moustache. We press-ganged him into service.'

Tom had chuckled as he said this, but Fleur had felt sorry for the man. 'Found him sleeping off a bottle of gin outside a tavern in Curaçao. He ain't too happy about his new job, but at least he's got a fine apprentice in Arthur. Aye, Arthur's been training to be a proper doctor, and he ain't the only one with a new position.' Tom had puffed out his chest and shone his fingernails on his collar. 'I'm still the cabin boy, but you're only looking at the new apprentice to Sailing Master Carlton Bart too,' he told her proudly. 'And a fair student I am too, if my master's word is good.'

Fleur glowed at the memory of her friend's achievement, and the warmth of his breathless greeting. She'd missed him as much as she had William, and it was clear that he'd missed her too.

How quickly she had slotted back into life at sea! Every morning she climbed to the very top of the mainmast and watched dawn spill over the dark ocean like lava from an erupting volcano. At those moments, despite the blisters on her hands and the raw sunburn on her neck, she would close her eyes, breathe in the smell of the brine and think how lucky she was. The *Black*

*Dragon* was her home, and its motley crew, for better or worse, was her family. And now they were heading for the Americas for a season of plundering. Her uncle liked to spend his winters in the tropics and summers in New England, where the thriving maritime trade made for rich pickings. This year in particular Captain Hart hoped for a hefty haul. For while he plundered the colonies, the eyes of New England would be elsewhere. On Gallows Hill, near the town of Salem, they were hanging witches. Fleur shivered at the thought—

'Thank you.' A hoarse whisper shook her back to the present. She looked up and smiled across at her guest, who stretched out her slender arms like a cheetah in a sunny spot. The girl looked a little older than Fleur, with her long white-blonde hair and delicate rosebud lips.

'You're awake,' said Fleur warmly. 'You already thanked me when I brought you down here. No need to do it again. I'm just glad we found you alive. I'm Fleur by the way; Fleur Hart.'

'I meant thank you for letting me sleep,' said the girl. She yawned, covering her mouth daintily with a hand that looked soft and unused to hard work. 'I'm Astrid . . .' She shivered violently, her teeth chattering again.

'Um, do you want another blanket ... or some more rum, perhaps?' asked Fleur, springing to her feet so fast that the bed nearly bounced her visitor onto the floor.

Astrid smiled and opened her mouth to reply. Then she noticed Fleur's narwhal-horn staff, propped up in a corner of the cabin along with her bow, and her smile faded immediately. The ruby, set in its band of thick Inca gold, winked at the girls from the darkness.

'Astrid ... ?' Fleur prompted.

'Sorry – no thank you, Fleur,' Astrid replied curtly.

Fleur looked from the staff to the girl with a puzzled expression.

'I've seen that staff before ...' Astrid muttered before Fleur could ask the question. 'Is it yours?'

'In a way.' Fleur strode over to the legendary Hart staff and picked it up. As she did, a surge of energy coursed through her and she smiled to herself. It was so much more than just a fighting stick to her; it almost felt as if they had been carved from the very same stuff. 'There's a prophecy about it – to do with the ruby,' she said. 'It says that when the right person holds the ruby, they'll unlock the power of the ocean itself.' She turned the weapon over in her hands before propping it up against the wall again. 'Or something like that anyway,' she added, a little embarrassed at how far-fetched that sounded.

An odd expression crossed Astrid's face – a little flare of recognition perhaps; then it was gone. The old bed squeaked and groaned as she sat up and leaned against the headboard. Her whole body shuddered with a huge sigh of relief and exhaustion. Candlelight illuminated the features of her pale, delicate face. There was no denying her beauty, though it was troubling somehow, like the bright edge of a silver knife. Her long hair flowed over her pale skin like sunshine over fresh snow, but it was her large, sad eyes that were the most strange and captivating thing about her. They were precisely the colour of sweet violets. Fleur felt herself falling into Astrid's gaze, as if she were staring at her reflection in a deep pool.

'Fleur . . . ?'

'Aye.' Fleur nodded. 'That's me.'

Astrid stretched out again and wiggled her toes. 'Thank you again,' she said. 'You were the one who truly saved my life. Please don't feel nervous of me – I know people often are – for I am indebted to you for ever.'

Fleur snorted indignantly and plonked herself down on the bed again. 'It was Tom who saved you, and I'm not nervous of you,' she muttered unconvincingly. 'I just ain't got the measure of you yet. Your voice reveals nothing of your country or station.'

Astrid looked at Fleur blankly for a few moments and then shrugged forlornly.

Fleur frowned and picked at the loose threads on her worn silk bedspread. 'But everyone knows where they come from, don't they?' she asked. 'At least,' she added, thinking of her own story, 'they *think* they do.'

'Well, I don't,' said Astrid simply.

Fleur puffed out her cheeks with exasperation.

'I promise I'm not lying to you,' insisted Astrid, her eyes glazed with tears. 'All I remember is waking up on the beach one night, about a year ago. I've never lost the chill of that spiteful sea in my bones. I've travelled the world since then, surviving on my wits, but I've come no closer to knowing who I am. I have my name – that is all.'

Fleur tucked her feet up under her and nodded kindly. 'I understand a little of how you must feel,' she said. 'For a long time I didn't know who I was – not really anyway. It made me feel like a stranger to everyone, as if I didn't belong in the world at all . . . not anywhere.' She gazed out at the sea crashing beyond the cabin window and closed her eyes for a few moments. And there it was: the song of the ocean, rising like a lark from the water. She opened her eyes and breathed in the salty air. 'But now,' she sighed, 'here I am.'

'Yes, here you are,' Astrid agreed.

Fleur grinned suddenly, and her green, cat-like eyes sparkled with delight. 'Hey, I've just thought, you could be a princess. You look like one. You're pretty enough, I mean.'

Astrid chuckled at that, and both girls relaxed as a new warmth flowed between them. Fleur was about to speak again when she was interrupted by a loud rap on the cabin door.

'Who's there?' she demanded grumpily.

The door opened to reveal Tom and Arthur tumbling into the cabin. They nudged and jostled one another to get a better look at the newcomer. Arthur, Fleur noticed, had even changed into his least tattered shirt.

'What do you two want?' she snapped crossly. 'Can't you see it's ladies only in here?'

Tom snorted with laughter and plonked himself down on the bed, followed more gingerly by Arthur. 'Ladies?' he guffawed. 'You wouldn't know one if you stepped on her petticoats.'

Fleur scowled at him, but Tom just shrugged it off. Arthur nodded at Astrid and held out his hand as he cleared his throat.

'Hello,' he said politely. 'Pleased to meet you. I'm Arthur. I'm . . . um . . . the ship's doctor . . . um, well, one of them. Do you feel all right?'

Tom caught Fleur's eye and they grinned at one another. Arthur had promoted himself: he was seriously out to impress.

'I'm fine, thank you, Doctor,' said Astrid – which nearly sent Fleur and Tom off into fits of laughter. 'I'm pleased to meet you too. I'm Astrid.'

'A thoroughly suitable name,' replied Arthur. 'From the Old Norse for divine beauty, if I remember my sagas.' He blushed and pushed his spectacles back up his freckly nose.

'And I'm Tom,' Tom added. 'It's Old English for *Shut up, Arthur, you swot*.'

Everyone laughed at that, even poor red-cheeked Arthur.

'Well, I think it's pretty impressive,' said Astrid. 'In truth you know more than I do myself.'

'So what did you do to get chucked off a ship then?' Tom asked bluntly.

Astrid hugged her knees and looked nervous.

'Don't worry, Astrid,' Fleur told her reassuringly. 'You're safe with us.'

The girl swallowed hard and took a deep breath. The lantern-light fizzed while everyone waited for her to speak again. 'I was a passenger on the *Queen Mary*. I've travelled much of late and as I have no destination in mind, I simply follow the winds with a willing ship . . .' She turned from face to face, frowning.

'You say I am among friends,' she went on, 'but I do not know you, and nor you I, and what I have to tell is strange.'

'Oh, come on!' said Tom, slapping the bedclothes excitedly. 'You can't expect us to let you leave it there!'

Astrid scanned their expectant faces once more, then nodded gravely and lowered her voice. 'There are more things in this world than are dreamed of in men's understanding. I have a power . . . of sorts.'

'Is that all?' Tom grinned. 'We're well up on that sort of thing.'

Astrid looked quite crestfallen.

'Sorry,' said Fleur, shushing Tom. 'Only we do have a bit of history there. So what is it? What do you do?'

'I must say, this is all a little strange. I'm accustomed to surprise – fear even.'

'Like the *lady* says,' teased Tom; 'history.' He mimed an elaborate staff-fighting move and fell back onto the bed, chuckling to himself. 'Well? Don't keep us in suspense.'

'I see things,' said Astrid, 'in my dreams. And sometimes when I'm awake too, I sort of . . . drift off into a trance.'

'Wow,' said Arthur, enthralled. 'What do you see?'

'The truth of things,' said Astrid. 'The future,' she added softly; 'the past — sometimes as it was, not how men tell it.'

Fleur butted in as the penny dropped. She pointed to her treasured staff as she spoke. 'You had one of your visions when you came aboard, didn't you? When you saw that staff?'

'Aye, maybe.' Astrid nodded. 'But nothing I can remember.' She lowered her eyes, and Fleur knew that her guest was hiding something.

'Hmm . . . So what happened on the *Mary*?'

'A vision,' admitted Astrid, 'more powerful than any I've had before. I saw a great storm coming in a dream and warned the captain. He didn't believe me, but superstition led him to ready the ship for a tempest anyway. When it hit, we were lucky to survive, even with the sails strapped down and the cargo lashed in place. When the storm passed and the clouds parted, the crew — who had heard of my dream by that time — concluded that witchcraft was to blame, and settled on me as the likeliest source of the trouble.'

'But to throw you overboard!' Fleur protested. 'I mean, it's a terrible thing to do to someone without so much as a shred of proof.'

'Unless you really *are* a witch,' said Tom, only half joking.

'And if I were, would I not have saved myself from drowning in that barrel? I'm an ordinary girl, I swear, even though my talents are unusual,' said Astrid.

Fleur chewed her nails thoughtfully. *How could Astrid know that she wasn't a witch? After all, by her own admission she knew no more than her own name.* She kept her thoughts to herself though. After all, witch or no witch, Astrid meant them no harm, and she needed their help.

'I don't believe all that nonsense about witchcraft,' Fleur said firmly.

Tom looked at her in surprise and pointed at the Hart staff. 'Do I have to remind you about that thing?' he asked. 'There's magic in the world for good or ill, Fleur – you know that better than most.'

She glowered at him. 'You know nothing,' she snapped. 'Me and the staff, it's . . . complicated.'

Tom opened his mouth to argue, but another steely stare from Fleur stopped him dead.

She reached out and took Astrid's delicate, icy hand in hers. 'Just don't do anything . . . you know, "visionary", when we reach land,' she warned. 'At least not around the locals.'

'Why not?'

Fleur looked right into the other girl's eyes and squeezed her hand tightly. 'Because we're heading for the Massachusetts Bay Colonies, Astrid. My uncle has business in a town called Salem.'

'What's in Salem?'

'Pirates, plunder and Puritans,' said Tom, smiling at the thought of further adventure.

'Puritans?' squeaked Astrid nervously. 'There was a Brethren family bound for Pennsylvania aboard the *Queen Mary*. They were the first to damn me when the storm broke.'

'Aye, well,' said Fleur. 'You were right to fear 'em. Love of God and love of wine are much alike, my uncle says. Too much of either is a dangerous thing. And in Salem the Puritan judges have begun trying women for witchcraft. One sniff of a vision, Astrid, and they'll haul you off to the gallows.'

# CHAPTER 3

Fleur pondered for a good while before deciding to share the secret of Astrid's gift with her Uncle William. Despite the bond between them, she still feared his gruffness and – worse – his occasional cruel mockery. In the end, she decided that she might as well tell him what she had learned, if only because she was hopeless at keeping secrets from him. He was bound to pick up on any attempt to stay tight-lipped, so the secret would be out sooner or later. Better sooner, and on her terms.

'The men want me to throw her back into the sea,' said the captain. He stood with his back to Fleur as he stared out of the cabin's porthole. 'They say she has a strange look about her.'

Fleur perched on the edge of a wooden table, swallowing her nervousness. 'They're just unsettled by her presence, sir,' she replied. 'Astrid is very beautiful, after all.'

William whipped round to face her, his hands held behind his back. His face was as hard as stone. 'Are you blind, girl?' he snapped. 'I ain't never seen eyes like hers on any living thing before.' He grunted with exasperation and went to sit at his desk. 'The men say she looks right through flesh and bone to read their souls with them eyes. Stuff and nonsense, of course,' he added briskly. 'But my men are the fiercest on all the seven seas, and I won't have 'em rendered witless by a girl.' He arched an eyebrow at her, remembering the turbulent time of Fleur's arrival. 'Not twice, anyhow.'

'Hmm,' Fleur began uneasily. 'About that stuff and nonsense . . .' She paused and cleared her throat. 'Uncle . . . I think there's something you should know about Astrid . . .'

The captain listened quietly as Fleur told him all about their guest's strange clairvoyant gifts and why she'd been cast adrift in a barrel. He showed no reaction as she spoke, and when she'd finished he rocked back on the legs of his chair, crossed his hands behind his head, and frowned.

'Here's how I see it,' he said. 'We don't need another petticoat sailing with us – no offence, lassie – especially if she's stirring up the men. A female on board is bad luck at the best of times—'

'I can't believe you still think like that!' Fleur snapped, glowering fiercely. 'After all we've been through, do you still think *I'm* a blight upon your precious ship?' She planted both hands firmly on her hips, her nerves forgotten. 'And besides,' she added, 'your idiot crew are quite capable of stirring *themselves* up. They've got grog for brains, the lot of 'em.'

William held up his hands defensively. 'I'm sorry,' he said. 'An old man's habit, girl. I withdraw my slur.' However, his face hardened again immediately. 'But hold back there, Titbit,' he growled in a warning tone. 'Remember your place – you ain't the one who makes the decisions on this ship, though you always have my ear.'

Fleur blushed crimson at her uncle's rebuke. 'Sorry, Cap'n,' she mumbled, dropping her gaze.

He came to perch on the table next to her. 'I don't yet know whether we can trust this newcomer, Fleur,' he explained in a calmer tone. 'I have to put my crew's contentment first, see, and she's already making 'em edgy.

I think it best that we part ways with her without delay.'

'But you can't just chuck her back in the sea!' Fleur exclaimed. 'What do you suggest we do with her?'

William rubbed his chin and studied his niece thoughtfully. 'I'd give her the tender and some provisions to sail away with,' he said at last. 'And for all we know, that's more than she deserves.'

'You might as well toss her to the sharks in that little boat,' muttered Fleur. 'We both know she'd never find land alone.' She decided to change tack. 'Haven't you always said, Uncle, that you ask no questions about a man's past when you welcome him aboard?'

'That's right.' He nodded. 'It's what a man can do for me now that counts. The slate is wiped clean and life begins anew when you set sail with William Hart.'

'So why not show Astrid the same courtesy?' asked Fleur. 'What does it matter if her past is a mystery? That goes for half the souls aboard. As for her visions, think of the possibilities, sir. If Astrid can sense a gathering storm, what else might she forewarn us of?' She turned to her uncle with a sly smile. 'She might even lead us to treasure.'

William nodded slowly as he pulled out his pipe and stuffed it with tobacco. 'A talent like hers would indeed come in handy on any ship,' he admitted, then turned to Fleur and narrowed his eyes. 'But if Astrid stays, it'll be your job to keep an eye on her, niece. And if she brings harm to this crew, I'll send you both to the bottom of the sea in that damned barrel.'

Fleur's mouth dropped open. 'You wouldn't dare . . .'

Her uncle grinned wickedly and ruffled her hair. 'Try me,' he said.

In the end, and much to Fleur's surprise, the captain entirely came round to the idea of an onboard clairvoyant. He was quite keen to keep Astrid around in case she proved useful. But he also agreed with Fleur that it was best to keep any talents that were out of the ordinary – beyond the extraordinary fact that she'd arrived in a barrel – a secret from the rest of the crew for the time being. Only Jack, his first mate, Carlton Bart, the sailing master – and the new bosun, Gates, too, apparently – did not share the superstitious nature of the men and were to be taken into their confidence before they reached Massachusetts. Astrid was to sleep in Fleur's cabin and to make herself useful on the *Dragon*.

'You almost finished, Claw-cat?' Tom called to Fleur as he leaned against the capstan, staring out over the glassy ocean. A day had passed since their unscheduled stop to pick up Astrid, and it was all hands to the sails aboard the *Dragon* to make up for lost time.

Fleur, who was scrubbing the deck with two lumps of sandstone, paused from her back-breaking task to curl her lip at him. 'What? Does it look like it?' she snapped, gesturing at the grubby wooden boards.

Tom pointed at a pile of foul, fly-ridden fish guts left from the morning's catch. 'You want to clean up that lot before it sinks into the wood, otherwise it will stink every time we get a sunny day.' He hopped up onto the capstan. 'Where's the princess anyway?'

It hadn't taken Tom long to start with the nicknames. Fleur wiped her brow with her sleeve. The afternoon sun licked at her neck like hot treacle.

'Astrid's sleeping,' she sighed. 'She's properly done in. Probably something to do with nearly dying.'

'Fair enough,' said Tom with a smirk.

'Why?' asked Fleur, suspicious of his sly look.

He wiggled his eyebrows knowingly. 'Arthur's down in the galley making her something *special* to eat.'

'Special?' Fleur snorted with amusement. 'I wonder what he'll come up with.'

'As long as she keeps sleeping and I get to eat it, I don't care,' Tom said, rubbing his hands together. 'There was some nice hen pie left over from yesterday . . . mmm.

Or turtle stew . . .' He stared into space, drooling a little as he daydreamed about food, while Fleur went back to her scrubbing, grunting and groaning as loudly as she could in the hope of breaking his reverie. Eventually, after a particularly noisy sigh, Tom came to his senses in time to spot George Gates settling down with his back against the ship's bollard. His scalp was turning red in the intense heat.

'There's something odd about him,' Tom loud-whispered to Fleur. 'I reckon he's hiding something.'

Fleur straightened up again. 'Like a pet sparrow, you mean, in that huge beard of his,' she giggled.

'I'm serious,' Tom insisted.

They both stared over at the same time. Gates was an enormous man and cut an imposing figure on the deck of the *Dragon*. The top of his head was almost completely bald, but he had a long bushy auburn beard. He spoke like a gentleman, smoked a delicate clay pipe and was a talented fiddle player. It also transpired that he could converse with the African men in their own tongue.

'Most of the crew on this ship have their secrets, Tom,' Fleur reminded him. 'Look at Dr Dubois – I don't think I've heard him utter a word, and yet Arthur assures me that he's quick-witted and the master of several languages. What other talents ain't he sharing? Then there's Astrid, who claims to remember nothing of her past at all. But the captain wouldn't let either of them – or any man aboard – sail with us if he doubted them.'

Tom shook his head. 'The cap'n has been wrong before, as you well know,' he whispered gravely. 'I'm just looking out for him.'

'But, Tom,' said Fleur, 'the bosun is one of the most important men aboard any ship. Do you honestly think my uncle would let George Gates wield so much control if he didn't have complete faith in him? And didn't you say yourself that the captain's judgement is good enough for you?'

'But there's already questions about where Gates came from. He don't act like the rest of the men,' Tom persisted. 'He's got good manners for a start. Old Bert, the carpenter, is near convinced he's working for the King. He swears blind he's seen 'im before, and wearing navy cloth at that. He reckons Gates is spyin' on us all and will lead us to the gallows.'

Panic rose in Fleur's throat and she tried to swallow it away. She'd heard the rumours too, and noticed how Gates watched them all with cold, hawkish eyes. What if he really was a traitor amongst them?

'And look at his pipe,' Tom continued. 'Don't you think it's a bit fancy for a bosun?'

Fleur was confused. All bosuns owned a pipe of the musical variety. Sailors, like sheepdogs, were trained to respond to the bosun's pipe immediately. It was easier to hear than a shout in rough seas or stormy weather. 'What *about* his flaming pipe?' she howled with frustration.

'Next time you get a chance, have a proper look at it,' Tom replied. 'It's solid silver.'

'So?'

Tom rolled his eyes. 'Do you know nothing?' he teased. 'The pipe is a badge of rank in the King's navy. They call it the whistle of command. Gold for the lord high admiral, worn about his neck on a golden chain. Silver for the high commanders.' He peered at Gates through narrowed eyes. 'Just like the one our Mr Gates owns.'

'So?' said Fleur again. 'He might have nicked it. And since when did you know so much about the navy anyway?'

Tom just tutted and ignored her last comment. 'An officer's badge of rank,' he muttered. 'I reckon the rightful owner of that there whistle would have rather tossed it into the sea than let it fall into the hands of a filthy privateer. Unless of course the rightful owner still has it. Mark me, Claw-cat, George Gates is hiding something or I'm a pickled blowfish.'

At that moment Gates looked up and caught the two of them gazing intently at him. He shielded his eyes from the sun with one hand and stared back, frowning fiercely. Fleur nodded courteously and he returned the courtesy, but there were no smiles, and Gates continued to stare at them until they were both squirming uncomfortably. When he finally turned away, Fleur let out the breath she had been holding and exchanged knowing looks with Tom. What if the gossip was right? Even though Old Bert's bones ached when the wind grew chill, his mind and memory were as sharp as piranha teeth. And if he said that he'd seen Gates before, he had. Now Fleur was just as suspicious as her friend: either Gates was hiding something or Tom *was* a pickled blowfish. And assuming the former was true, what of the captain? Had he misjudged the new crewman, or were there deeper dealings aboard the *Dragon* than even Tom had guessed at?

# CHAPTER 4

The *Black Dragon* sailed on. The skies changed their mood incessantly. One minute the sun would be stripping the skin off their necks; the next cold rain would pelt them like musket balls. Having recovered from her ordeal, Astrid worked hard and helped wherever she could, determined to prove useful to her rescuers. The crew, for all their rough edges, were quick to acknowledge her efforts and soon accepted their strange new shipmate. Her beauty helped, as did her angelic singing voice.

The first time Astrid sang, the entire crew fell into a shocked hush. Gates had been playing his fiddle – or, more properly, *violin*, for like all his possessions it was finely made – on the prow of the ship, and at first Astrid had merely watched him. When she had begun to hum, the bosun had offered her a surprised, encouraging nod, and Astrid opened her mouth to let out a voice that would shame songbirds into silence. A crowd gathered around them immediately: even Dr Dubois stood in the shadows at a discreet distance, listening as Gates set his violin aside, leaving only Astrid's pure and simple song. Every night after that, the men would beg her to join them on the deck and sing to them. Her song was like a sky-hook connecting their creaking old ship to the stars. More than a handful of Captain Hart's battle-hardened vagabonds were utterly besotted by Astrid and she was accorded more respect than Fleur had ever been. And even though Fleur had only ever wanted to be treated as one of the men, she couldn't help feeling slightly jealous of the pretty new girl.

With less than a week to go before they reached Salem, the captain asked Fleur and Astrid to ready themselves for the trip ashore. New England ways were strict and sober, with women expected to be totally subservient to men – 'With children – especially girls – at the very bottom of the ladder,' he had explained, with a wicked glint in his eye.

'You can't expect—?' Fleur had begun furiously, but her uncle cut her off.

'Young 'uns like you are to be seen and not heard,' he had replied. 'And you can stow away your father's bow and quiver. Girls are for spinning yarn, cooking, sewing, weaving and the like. Just as it should be.' He spun on his heels and walked off, laughing at the thought of his headstrong niece playing the virtuous little Puritan girl.

Astrid still had the dress that she had arrived in: plain and simple, perfect for blending in with the locals. Fleur, on the other hand, only had the crew's ragged hand-me-downs. So William set her and Astrid the task of fashioning a new dress from whatever materials they could find on the ship.

Thus, as their long sea crossing drew to an end, the girls found themselves sitting on Fleur's bed, sewing by the flicker of candlelight. Tom was sprawled out on the floor whittling new arrows for Fleur's bow, and Arthur sat on a chair reading aloud from a book of Ben Jonson's poetry. He shared a love of books with Toby Butler, the ship's cook, who secretly dreamed of leaving the galley for the library, and Toby had recommended Jonson's love poems in the quest for Astrid's affections.

Now, as Arthur read, he gazed at her over the top of the book:

> '*Do but look on her eyes, they do light*
> *All that Love's world compriseth!*
> *Do but look on her hair, it is bright*
> *As Love's star with it riseth—!*'

Tom's exaggerated groan stopped him short. He lowered the slim volume and peered at his friend with a worried expression. 'What's wrong? Are you in pain?' he asked, concerned.

Tom clapped his hands over his ears and rolled about on the floor, wincing as if in great pain. 'Yes,' he moaned. 'I think my ears are bleeding. *Compriseth! Riseth!* Are they even words? You're making me want to puketh!'

The tips of Arthur's ears reddened and the blush spread rapidly to cover his face and neck. He cleared his throat uncomfortably. 'I thought the ladies might enjoy it,' he offered.

Fleur suppressed a giggle: in all the time they had known each other, Arthur had never offered to read *her* poetry. Neither, for that matter, had he once referred to her as a 'lady'. Astrid stayed silent, her head bent over her sewing. Her long hair veiled her face, hiding it entirely.

'Do one of your blood-and-guts stories,' suggested Tom, oblivious to the emotional drama in the room, 'or even one of those *Canterbury Tales* by Geoffrey Saucer.'

Arthur snorted. 'It's *Chaucer*, you codfish, Geoffrey Chaucer. And you said you thought it was a pile of animal dung when I tried reading it to you before.'

'Horse dung, specifically,' Tom replied, shifting his weight on the creaky floor. 'Which should give you an idea of how I feel about this sissy poetry of Fred Ronson, or whatever his name is.'

A low wail escaped from Arthur as he set aside the book, stood up, and dug his foot into Tom's ribs, hard. 'You've got no soul, Tom,' he snapped. 'You don't see the beauty in anything!'

'That's not true,' Tom retorted, clutching his side. 'I've got bucket-loads of soul and I see beauty in the world all the time. All over the place.' His eyes flicked involuntarily in the direction of Fleur. 'Only I don't see the need for harping on about it noon and night, day in, day out.' He scrambled to his feet and squared up to Arthur. 'Sissy,' he added scornfully.

'How dare you! I'm just as much a man as you. Just

because I can't swing from the rigging like a monkey and I prefer reading to . . . to flicking my bogeys all over the ship.'

'And just because I don't read books, it doesn't mean I'm stupid!' Tom retorted, just as fiercely.

Both boys glared at each other. Fleur sat back to enjoy the show. She knew that their power-play rarely led to actual fighting.

Tom jabbed a thumb in the newcomer's direction. 'Why don't we ask Astrid?' he suggested. 'Let's see if *she* thinks you're all man, shall we?'

Arthur spluttered with rage as all eyes turned to Astrid. Concentrating on her work, however, she didn't even notice them.

'Astrid?' said Fleur; then, louder, 'Astrid, are you awake?'

The other girl didn't move a muscle, so Fleur leaned across the bed and pulled back the curtain of fair hair that hid her face. Then she gasped with astonishment and stumbled backwards. Astrid was wide awake, but her eyes were empty, darting left and right at some hidden scene playing out in her mind's eye. The needle and thread fell from her hand as Fleur retreated.

'What's wrong with her?' hissed Tom urgently. 'Is she ill?'

'I don't know,' Fleur replied. 'It looks like a fit or a trance of some kind. Arthur, quickly, get over here and take a look at her.'

In two strides Arthur was at the bedside and crouching down before Astrid. He gently held the back of one hand against her forehead to check her temperature, while with the other he took her pulse. 'Her heart's racing,' he said nervously. 'Her head's burning, but her body's cold.'

Astrid continued to scan the middle distance, ignoring her companions as if she were blind to everything around her.

'She looks as if she's sort of dreaming,' said Arthur. He pushed his spectacles back up along his nose and frowned thoughtfully. 'You don't suppose it could be one of her visions, do you?'

They all stared at each other, agog, before turning back to watch Astrid.

'Should we wake her up?' asked Fleur, concerned.

'No,' Arthur replied quickly. 'The shock might kill her— Hang on though ... Look! I think she's coming round.'

Astrid shifted on the bed. She blinked, and gradually her eyes began to focus on the people and objects in the cabin once more.

'Are you all right?' Fleur asked her softly.

Astrid rubbed her eyes and nodded. She squinted in the dull candlelight as if it were as bright as the summer sun. Arthur felt her pulse again, noting that it had returned to normal, and offered her some water, which she accepted gratefully.

'You gave us quite a scare there, your majesty,' said Tom. 'Did you have another vision?'

'Tom, for goodness' sake, let the girl come back to her senses before you start bombarding her with questions,' Fleur chastized, shooing him away from the bed.

But Astrid held up a hand in a gesture of conciliation. 'It's all right,' she said quietly. 'My head hurts but I'm fine.' She nodded at Tom. 'And yes, I did have a vision of sorts. But it was different to those that have come before.'

'How do you mean?' asked Fleur.

Astrid massaged her temples and frowned. 'It wasn't a single event I saw. In fact there were too many images for me to understand. But that didn't matter because it felt as if the knowledge was being poured into my head anyway . . . from somewhere else: almost as if someone were whispering in my ear.'

Tom grinned and his eyes glittered with excitement. 'Excellent,' he barked. 'Give us the good stuff. And please tell me it included directions to buried treasure.'

Astrid remained solemn and distant. When she spoke, her voice was earnest. 'Some truths are buried because a lie is easier to bear,' she said. 'Are you sure you want to hear what I have to say, Tom?'

'Do you really need to ask that?' he replied, quite oblivious to the warning tone in her voice.

Arthur was less insensitive. 'Hang on,' he interrupted. 'Who does this vision concern?'

'All three of you,' Astrid replied. 'I'm . . . I'm so sorry, Arthur . . .' she added softly.

Arthur nervously ran his hands through his mop of chestnut hair. He looked really frightened. 'Well, now we *have* to know,' he said.

Fleur and Tom nodded in agreement.

'Go on, Astrid,' Fleur urged. 'Tell us what you saw.'

Astrid stared at each of them in turn, her violet eyes burning more brightly than ever. Finally she spoke. 'You three call yourselves orphans,' she began, 'but the title applies only to one.'

Arthur gasped and one of his hands flew to his mouth. 'Are my parents alive?' he whispered, his eyes wide. 'Please God, let it be so.'

Astrid shook her head sadly and reached out to touch

his arm. 'As I said, I am so very sorry, Arthur. You are alone in the world – as you thought.'

There was a weighted silence, and then Tom and Fleur exploded at once.

'One at a time please,' begged Astrid.

Fleur was the first to fire out her question. 'What do you mean?' she demanded. 'I saw my father murdered before me and my mother died when I was a young 'un. Stop it, Astrid – this is just cruel.'

Astrid held up her hands in defence. 'I warned you – I only tell what I see, not what others want to hear. There was more, but there are too many images in my mind to make sense of them and I do not yet understand what I have seen.'

'You must be wrong,' Fleur insisted.

Astrid bit her lip nervously. 'I'm never wrong, Fleur,' she said softly. 'Nor would I taunt you with cruel lies. Not after you have shown me such kindness.'

'But you *are* wrong.' Fleur was defiant. 'I helped to bury my father's bones. That is not something I'll forget soon.' She glanced about the room wildly and jumped to her feet, ready to storm out of the cabin.

'Have you ever been to your mother's grave?' Astrid asked quietly.

Fleur stopped dead in her tracks and considered the question for a moment. Not once had her father taken her to Rose Hart's grave – not even to leave flowers. Her father had once said something about Rose being buried in Ireland, but she had never thought to question him about it further. There had been stories – a thousand of them – which painted a portrait in Fleur's mind that was more vivid than any memory she possessed. But never so much as a mention of where her mother's body lay. As possibilities crowded her mind, Fleur felt her anger rise. Her knees felt weak and she collapsed back onto the bed. Astrid *had* to be wrong. There was *no way* her mother was alive. She would have known. She would know. She would feel it. *But then why had there been no grave to visit?*

Fleur glanced over at Arthur, who was sitting with his head in his hands. Tom was leaning against the wall, chewing on his fingernails with a strange, dark expression on his face. The tension in the room squeezed their chests.

'What do you make of this, Tom?' Fleur asked, desperate to break the mood.

Tom spat a fragment of chewed nail on the floor and shrugged. 'Nothing. My parents are as dead as ever,' he replied mechanically. He bent down and picked up his pocket knife. 'Look,' he sighed, 'I'm tired. See you in the morning.' He turned to leave.

'But don't you want to talk about this?' Fleur called out as he opened the cabin door.

'There's nothing to talk about,' he said without turning round. Then he was gone, leaving the door swinging open behind him.

'Arthur?' asked Fleur hopelessly.

Arthur raised his head, and the tears that streaked his face glinted in the candlelight. 'Look,' he began, his voice rough, 'I'd give anything to find out that one of my parents was alive, and for one moment back then I thought it might actually be so. I'm sorry, Fleur – Astrid – I can't talk about this any more. I'm going to turn in.' He nodded at them, then turned and left, closing the door behind him.

Astrid broke the silence. 'I'm sorry,' she said sincerely. 'I have no say in what is revealed to me. I didn't mean to cause any trouble.' She tugged at her long hair in frustration. 'Someone once told me that the gift of second sight is a great blessing. I call it a curse – my visions seem to cause only pain and fear.'

'Now she tells me,' Fleur muttered dully, flinching as the other girl inched towards her.

Astrid sighed and threaded her trembling fingers

together. 'I want you to understand, Fleur,' she began, 'that I do not take my visions lightly. I feel the pain of those lives I see.' Tears spilled down her pale cheeks as she spoke. 'It's so lonely. Sometimes I feel like I've lived a thousand sorrowful lives. I'm so sorry for your pain, Fleur, and I share it.'

Fleur examined her closely. She knew that this strange girl was telling the truth and suddenly she was filled with pity. 'Well, it's out now and there's nothing we can do about it.' She took a deep breath and tried a feeble smile. Then she knelt down to pick up the needles and thread scattered about the floor. 'Let's forget about visions for the time being and finish this dress. Captain's orders.'

Astrid slipped to the floor beside her and threw her slender arms around her friend. 'Thank you,' she whispered.

Fleur hugged her back, but she could not quite meet her eyes. She kept hers glued to the floor, pretending to hunt for needles. Astrid's vision had rattled her to the core. If there was any truth in it, then her entire childhood had been a lie. And what of Tom's odd reaction to the news that his parents might be alive? Had she alone seen something shifty in his response? It was almost as if he were hiding something. Only that made no sense whatever. Why would Tom conceal the truth about his parents from his closest friends? Astrid was right: ignorance was far less painful and confusing. And while Arthur mourned his family anew, Fleur found that for the first time in her life, she wished she *was* an orphan, because at least then she wouldn't be questioning everything that she had ever known.

Tom's strange dark mood continued the next day. His behaviour was so out of character that Fleur's suspicion that he was hiding something grew by the hour. At sunset she spied him in the crow's nest and clambered up to join him.

'Ahoy there, Tom,' she cried as she climbed onto the lookout platform.

Tom, who was staring blankly over the rolling waves, greeted her distractedly. 'Hoa, Claw-cat,' he mumbled, without turning to face her.

Fleur stood next to him and they stared down at the sea in silence. Two sails stood out against the darkening horizon: they looked like birds sitting on a cliff's edge. Finally Fleur broke the silence.

'Tom, I'm just going to ask you plain,' she said firmly. 'Do you think Astrid was telling the truth?'

Tom sighed deeply and carried on gazing out to sea.

A bright moon and a dusting of stars could already be seen in the gathering gloom. 'No, I think she was making it up,' he replied after a while.

'And you really are an orphan?' Fleur persisted, gripping the wooden rail.

Tom turned to face her and his blue eyes were empty. 'My parents are long dead, Fleur.'

Fleur nodded sympathetically. 'How?' she asked suddenly. 'It's just you've never spoken about them.'

'That's because I don't want to,' he snapped, looking out to sea again. 'It's no one's business but my own.'

Fleur stared at his profile, surprised: they always talked about everything.

Tom exhaled. 'Look, I don't talk about it because just thinking about them leaves me completely undone. Maybe I'll tell you one day, but not now. The past is past, Fleur. 'Tis the here and now that concerns me.' He worried the worn wooden rail with a callused finger and his voice quivered. 'My mother was the kindest lady in the world,' he stated simply. 'I'd give anything to have her back.'

Fleur's heart welled up with sadness at her friend's brave admission. She felt terrible that she had ever doubted him. She placed a hand on his shoulder and squeezed. 'Me too,' she replied in a hoarse whisper. 'Astrid must have been wrong.'

'Aye,' said Tom firmly.

But as Fleur looked out over the gleaming waves, she hoped that Astrid had been right; she would give anything to see her mother alive.

# CHAPTER 5

With the wind behind them and the waters kind, the *Black Dragon* made good time to the New England coast. And with land in sight, the atmosphere on board was rowdy and excited. Supplies were low and the crew were hungry and keen to feel ground that didn't roll and tip beneath their feet. Gates kept them all under control with a firm hand. The Hart flag fluttered boldly in the warm breeze and the captain's rapid orders boomed across the deck like rolling thunder. Fleur and Astrid were in their cabin when they heard a ruckus in the hold.

'Hold 'im, the little bleeder!' came a voice through

the wall, turning the air blue with the curses that followed. 'Stowaway!'

The girls ran to the door in time to see a small, furry shape run past with half the crew in pursuit.

''Scuse me,' said Fleur, nodding at Astrid before haring after them. When she emerged on deck, a small crowd had gathered around the mast to peer and point up at the stowaway: a wide-eyed fluffy creature that Fleur felt sure she recognized.

'Is that . . . ? It couldn't be . . .' she muttered to Arthur, who was trying to entice the animal down from the mast with a ship's biscuit.

Arthur nodded enthusiastically. 'I think it really might be,' he grinned. 'His markings are exactly the same.'

'The lemur we left behind on that island . . .' Fleur said aloud to herself, amazed.

She stared up at the animal's rusty coat and inquisitive black eyes. Surely it couldn't be the same lemur that she had played with while marooned with her uncle, Tom and Arthur.

'Must've been hiding out in the hold all the time, lassie,' called William, confirming Fleur's suspicions. 'A long way to travel just to be tonight's dinner.' He laughed long and hard at his own joke and the crew guffawed along with him.

'You wouldn't!' exclaimed Fleur, shocked.

'We ruddy would,' said Jack, still gasping from the chase. 'I found him up to his neck in our last barrel of grog. The little bleeder's already marinated.'

'That's settled it then,' said the captain. 'He's a stowaway and a rum thief, and a drunk to boot. And now he's dinner.'

A cheer went up from the assembled pirates. Fleur looked up at the cuddly lemur clinging to the mast with its long toes. Its chattering was louder now, and it was swaying dangerously from the yardarm, quite drunk.

'William the Heartless,' cried Fleur, and her voice was so stern that the cheering ceased at once. 'By the Hart flag, if you eat our new arrival I will never set foot on a ship under your command again. And you can stick your Hart staff up your—'

'All right, lassie, all right.' William laughed. 'I reckon we could do with a new mascot' – his voice dropped to a respectful murmur – 'what with Parsley the cat having fallen in battle.' He added, 'God save his flea-bitten soul. I'll make you a deal. If you gives him a name that I like, I'll see to it that he stays aboard, and out of the cook's pot.'

'Well then' – Fleur relaxed – 'that settles it.' She looked from the drunken lemur to the red-faced Jack and back again. 'We'll call him Grog.'

★

It was the end of summer in the Americas, and the fading sunlight was warm and golden. As evening drew in, the entrance to Massachusetts Bay was still teeming with ships of many shapes and sizes: English privateers, French men-o'-war, scores of high-bowed Mediterranean feluccas and piratical junks sailed side by side as they approached and left the dock. Fleur stood on the port side of the *Dragon*, fidgeting in her new dress and staring out at the unfamiliar horizon in wonder. The plain black robe, white apron and cotton bonnet felt foolish and girly. A shadow fell across her and she looked up to see William beaming as he appraised her outfit.

'Well, don't you look like a dainty bit,' he teased.

Fleur tutted and scowled up at him. 'Why have you made me put this on already? We haven't even landed yet!'

'Just in case,' he said, looking about the crowded waters shiftily. 'We don't know who we might run into.'

'I look like an idiot,' Fleur moaned, scratching at her hairline. 'This stupid bonnet itches. And how am I supposed to climb the rigging?'

'You're not!' said the captain. 'You're not to go climbing anything for the time being. Nor running, nor fighting. You'll turn heads in this town if you show 'em your true nature, Fleur. And subtlety is the order of the day, so just act the lady, if you can. We don't need any unwanted attention. Try a bit of sewing or something. Far more suited to a girl.' He chuckled.

'Pah!' Fleur spat in disgust. 'I'd like to see you trussed up like a turkey making lace doilies. Can't we just cut my hair short and call me Finn again?'

William took a swig from his flask and coughed as the harsh spirit hit the back of his throat. He frowned and stared off into the distance thoughtfully. A slithering mist had rolled in from the sea, and Fleur shivered in the sudden chill.

'No, lassie,' said William firmly. ''Tis only for a short while. I've enemies who would see me in chains. Them who live here are already stirred up by this witch-hunt nonsense. Let's not rile 'em further. We'll do what we need and clear off again as soon as we can.'

'Aye, sir.' Fleur nodded obediently.

William passed her his telescope and waved an arm at the ships to-ing and fro-ing in the harbour. 'There's rich pickings here, my girl,' he said. 'Most of it from the codfish trade. Dried fish and timber to the sugar plantations. Molasses, sugar and rum to England and the colonies. I reckon it's time those greedy merchants shared their profits a little more widely, eh?' He pointed at a row of large timber-framed mansions on the shore. 'See, some of 'em live like kings in this part o' the world.'

Their daydreams were interrupted by Jack, who burst out laughing as soon as he clapped eyes on Fleur. Fleur rolled her eyes in exasperation. 'Have you never seen a girl in a dress before, sir?' she sighed.

'Not one with so many weapons hid about her, no,' he replied with amusement.

Fleur looked down at the boarding axe, dagger and pistol hanging from her apron strings. William shook his head, chuckling. 'I didn't even notice, being so used to seeing 'em on you, Fleur. Either hide 'em properly or hand 'em over, missy,' he ordered sternly.

Fleur sighed again and began reluctantly unhooking her piratical tools of the trade from the apron. 'I'll hide them, thank you very much,' she replied icily.

Jack turned to face William, squinting and shielding his eyes from the bright glare of the sun. 'Is it north-west as usual, sir?' he asked.

William shared a smile with his lieutenant. 'Aye, Jack, to Penance Bay we go,' he replied, slapping his friend on the shoulder. 'Unless some other lucky rogue found our hidey-hole since last we visited its shores. Take her in, Jack.'

'Aye, aye, sir.' The first mate strode off to carry out his captain's orders.

William started to follow, but Fleur caught his arm. 'Where is this Penance Bay, then?' she probed.

William raised his tricorn hat and winked mysteriously. 'You'll see, lassie,' he told her. 'You'll see. Let's just say I like me privacy when I'm here.'

He turned to the main deck and bellowed above the sounds of the busy ship. 'Hard to starboard, men. Come on, you swabs, break your backs now and we'll be among the wine and the women all the sooner.'

The captain had decided that they should sail under false colours – and for good reason. The *Black Dragon* was both feared and hated all over the world. In the hold was a large collection of national flags: William had often used them to sail close to enemy ships before hoisting his true colours and sending out the raiding party. It was a neat trick, the *ruse de guerre*, but there was little hope of passing a ship like the *Dragon* off as Dutch or British. Fortunately, with long red flags bearing bold Chinese characters dancing around the masts like dragons, she could have been any Chinese junk coming ashore, with porcelain and fine silks to trade.

As they approached the shallows, Fleur stared out at the distant fields. Grog had found her alone on the deck and coiled his warm body around her cold feet. Even from a distance she could see that the land was well tended, with a host of colourful blooms. It was a huge contrast to the wild, exotic beauty of St Kitts or Madagascar, where the vegetation had been wild and chaotic: almost as if a rainbow had burst apart and scattered everywhere. For the hundredth time Fleur grinned as she thought that she was such a very long way from Cornwall.

With her nose in the air, the *Black Dragon* sailed right past the bustling port and on to a rocky cove where the waves grew treacherous and black. This was Penance Bay. No other crews dared sail in waters where the deadly current threatened to tear your ship apart. Aside from the crashing of the waves and the seagulls' taunting caws, everything was eerily silent. The *Dragon* was manoeuvred through water so shallow that at times the keel dragged along the shingle and sand. Carcasses of ships were wedged between rocky ridges; broken masts clawed at the sky like fingers, as if desperate to rise from their watery grave. Tom was keeping lookout in the crow's nest with sharpened eyes, while Gates stood on the prow, whistling careful orders.

It seemed to take for ever, but no rocks punctured the hull, and soon enough they were floating in a wide basin of water that gradually grew shallower. A barren cliff towered above a pile of boulders so huge and ordered that it looked as if a giant had left them there; at the foot was the wide mouth of a cave. Gates ordered the men to furl the sails and the *Dragon* floated into the darkness. On they sailed, deeper and deeper into the cool underworld, until the light had vanished behind them and the chill black of the cave had swallowed them completely. Lanterns blazed aboard the *Dragon*, and a strange light was cast down on the water that was as black and bottomless as a starless night. All that could be heard was the slap of the tide echoing in the yawning space. The walls were smooth, and retreated as they moved deeper into the cave. The ceiling climbed and dipped erratically; at times it seemed barely high enough for the *Dragon* to squeeze through. Tunnels branched off the sides of the cavern, creating a maze of passages. It was damp, though there were occasional blasts of sweet, fresh air, and in the distance they heard the sound of rushing water.

Even Dr Dubois ventured out of his cabin to stare at their incredible surroundings. He stood alone, with a sad faraway expression on his usually stern face. Fleur had just worked up the courage to approach him when Arthur and Astrid arrived at her side. Grog leaped onto Arthur's shoulders and started to pick through his wild chestnut hair. In the darkness of the cavern the animal's eyes seemed to radiate their own unearthly light.

Arthur, whose head always brimmed with facts and figures, examined the creature's strange glowing eyes and muttered, as if to himself, 'You know, the word lemur comes from the Latin, *lemures*: it means spirit of the night, or ghost.'

'You're so clever, Arthur,' said Astrid, reaching over to stroke Grog's soft ears. 'You soak up knowledge like sailors soak up rum.'

In the darkness Fleur could almost hear Arthur's blushes. 'This is marvellous, isn't it?' he said after a while. 'I didn't think caves as big as this existed. It feels like we're at the centre of the Earth.'

'It's so calm and still.' Astrid stood on tiptoe to look down over the side of the ship.

'Wouldn't want to fall in, mind,' said Arthur, and gingerly snaked an arm around her shoulders to pull her back.

On and on the *Dragon* slid, into the labyrinth of winding tunnels, until at last they entered a huge wide space, lit by beams of dappled golden light that poured in through cracks in the rocky ceiling high above and bounced on the surface of the water like fallen stars. On one side of the cavern, the pale green sea water thinned to reveal a wide expanse of sand as white and fine as talcum powder. Shoals of fish shimmered in the shallows, and a score of hammocks hung like smiles between posts dug into the beach. Empty grog bottles were scattered around the blackened remains of an old campfire.

'This is where we'll be staying, men,' announced William brightly, leaping up onto the poop deck to address the crew. 'Drop anchor and snap to it.'

There was a sudden burst of activity as the men set about their tasks.

'One more thing,' the captain bellowed over the din. 'Remember, you're all still under my command, but while we're here, mark me, there'll be no more orders to carry out. This is rest time – we'll go a-plundering when the mood takes us. You deserve it, my bullies.'

The cheer that erupted bounced around the cavern like bees in a bell jar.

# CHAPTER 6

The Salem landing party was split into groups. The arrival of one large pack of men would surely arouse unwanted suspicion, so they were to leave separately. Dr Dubois refused to join any group and instead stood silently on the deck until William allowed him to return to his cabin. Jack herded the hardest men together and readied them to leave. They were going that evening to fetch much-needed supplies. He marched them down the gangplank, splashed through the crystal shallows and padded across the beach to a gap in the rock face, shrouded by thick creepers and vines. Fleur, Tom, Arthur and Astrid watched them leave.

'There's a short cut that takes you right into Salem village,' Tom explained to the others, 'but you've got to take the right tunnel or you end up in the middle of the ocean or, worse, right under the town's jail.'

The men squeezed one by one through the rocky opening until the only thing left of them was footprints in the sand.

Tom yawned and stretched indulgently. 'Think I'll get a little shut-eye before we move out,' he announced. 'The cap'n'll be heading into town early in the morning, and a boy needs to look his best.'

'I'm going to read for a while,' said Arthur excitedly. 'I haven't had a proper chance for ages.'

'What about you, Astrid?' Fleur asked hopefully. 'I'm not ready to turn in. Do *you* want to explore, or something?'

'To be honest I'm exhausted, Fleur. All I want to do is get some sleep while I have the chance.' She bit her lip and curled the fingers of her hands together. 'Do you mind?'

Fleur sighed and pushed her hands into the pocket of her silly apron. 'What am I supposed to do?' she moaned. 'I feel lost now the journey's ended.'

'You could always practise doing girl things,' Tom

suggested with a wicked grin. 'Didn't the captain say something about needlework?'

That would have earned him a dead arm had Fleur not been distracted by the sound of heavy footsteps. They turned to see William standing before them in a simple cotton shirt and breeches, carrying the Hart staff in one hand and a second sturdy-looking, pale brown staff in the other.

'We're going to do some training, Fleur,' he said. 'It's been a while since you had cause to fight and I don't want you gathering barnacles. You never know when you might need to take arms again.' He tossed her the narwhal-horn staff, which she caught with one hand.

'Barnacles?' she replied, grinning back at him. 'I could beat you blindfolded, Cap'n.'

William threw his head back and laughed. 'That's as may be, missy. If I'm honest, I've got too much blood running through me veins, Fleur. I fancy a ruckus and you're the best challenge aboard. Are you game?'

'Always,' she declared, delighted to find that her uncle was feeling as fidgety as her. She looked down at her dress. 'Give me a few moments to get out of this hideous thing and I'll meet you on the sand.'

Fleur changed into her comfy old slops and hurried

down to the beach. Soon heavy clunks from their staves were echoing around the huge cave. A cluster of crewmen watched the show from the ship. Astrid had never seen Fleur in combat before; now she stood watching with undisguised awe. And what a demonstration it was. The sparring pair whirled about each other like dancers, spraying fine sand into the air with every kick. Their moves were graceful and their staves thunked together with a musical rhythm. Then the blows became faster and more furious, and soon William could barely keep up with Fleur's powerful assault. She let out a thrilling war cry that left goosebumps on every square inch of skin within earshot, and those that saw her would have sworn that it seemed to make the ruby set in the hilt of the Hart staff glow like a hot coal. Girl and weapon became a spinning blur. Fleur's face was rigid with determination and her green eyes sparked like steel on a whetstone.

The captain charged at her time and time again, sweeping and jabbing his staff with all his might, but she blocked and parried his every move effortlessly. The world around her vanished as she lost herself completely in the fight. Whether the strange legend surrounding the mighty staff was true or not, no one could doubt that the weapon had found its true mistress. It leaped and bucked in her hands as if it were alive.

At last William began to tire; Fleur spotted her opening, and with one deft flick of her wrist finally disarmed him, much to the amusement of the crew. Her uncle collapsed back into the soft sand, panting with exhaustion, and Fleur stood over him, breathing hard but smiling and ready for more. Their audience wandered away, leaving them alone. The shafts of warm light that lit the cave were fading fast and on the *Dragon* lanterns began to blaze into life.

'That's better,' Fleur said, offering a hand to William.

'Aye, lassie,' he agreed, getting to his feet and rubbing his chin thoughtfully. 'I see you've grown even stronger with the Hart staff. Tell me, girl, how long did you wait before you decided to disarm me?'

Fleur grinned. 'Do you really want me to answer that, Uncle?'

William took a deep swig from his flask and nodded.

'I could have had your staff before you laid the first blow, sir,' she replied honestly. 'But where's the fun in that?'

William laughed until his sides ached. ''Tis true, niece,'

he gasped when he'd gathered himself again. 'You are a great warrior, but you still have much to learn.'

He pointed as a small, sleek sea bird suddenly burst out from a crevice in the rock and bolted towards the silver shimmer of a shoal of fish in the nearby pool. It skimmed the surface of the water like a skipping stone, then cut through the shoal like a spear. When it rose again, a second later, a large silvery fish was skewered on its beak, three or four times the size of any fish in the shoal that they could see; the little bird struggled to carry it back to shore, then set about devouring its catch greedily.

'True warriors develop their skills by observing the world around them,' William commented. 'The behaviour of animals, birds and insects has formed the basis for many fighting systems in the Orient, y'know. The beast has a sense of his environment and acts *with* it rather than against it. See that little feller' – he gestured at the bird, happily tucking into its fish supper – 'you and I saw the shoal, but not the real prize beneath. Learn to fight like animals do and you'll have a response for every situation.'

'How do you mean?' asked Fleur.

He rubbed his hands together vigorously. The air in the cave was rapidly becoming colder. 'The tiger relies on a frontal assault,' he began, taking a stance like a boxer and curling his fingers into claws. 'It uses aggression and power. It fights fiercely, ripping and tearing. Its movements are quick and short and filled with deadly force ...Whereas the snake strikes fast at vital points, like the eyes and throat, then retreats. Snake movements flow and ripple.' He demonstrated, thrusting his fingers into the air in sharp swooping movements. 'The monkey's style will probably suit you better though, young 'un. The monkey's enemies are larger and stronger than him – or her – which is something you'll be coming across a lot. The monkey jumps, flips, climbs and rolls to avoid his attacker,' he continued.

'Or *her* attacker,' corrected Fleur. 'How do you know all this?'

Her uncle cocked his head to one side and tapped the side of his nose. 'Remember, missy, we Harts have been around a while and sailed the seven seas. Why, your forefathers trained side by side with the most remarkable warriors that ever lived. We helped their families to hide from their oppressors in the mountain tops of Japan. Their society was cloaked in secrecy, and their identities were a secret to all but the masters who could call them to battle.'

'Their masters and us,' said Fleur.

'Aye.' William nodded. 'And us. Stealth and strength must be the cornerstone of your art, Fleur, but there is one thing more that you need, and I cannot teach it. Patience,' he told her. 'Never my strong point. You rush into everything like a dog among rats and make mistakes because of it. You have to understand that haste can kill you, Fleur – and those you are fighting with, for that matter. You need control so that you can slow down sometimes and think about your next move. There is no doubt that you are a great fighter, but your hot blood sometimes needs a little time to cool.'

'So if you can't teach me,' asked Fleur grumpily, 'what am I supposed to do about it?'

'Patience comes from within, child,' William explained. 'We are not like the tides, pulled by the moon against our will. We are masters of our own minds.'

Fleur flopped back onto the sand, frowning. 'What does that mean?' she demanded.

'It means, niece, that if you want to learn patience, the first thing you need to do . . . is *be* patient.' William chuckled as he settled down beside her and pulled out his pipe and tobacco. 'Watch the world, Fleur. Try to understand your connection to things. Hone your instincts and learn to think before you act, even in the blink of an eye. The right move isn't always obvious, but if you seize the moment when it arises, your instincts will take over. Stop, think, then act. It might just save your skin.' He lit his pipe and blew a thick blue smoke ring into the air. 'Might save mine too,' he added. 'You never know when the Devil will track ye down.'

The idea of her uncle in mortal danger gripped Fleur like a python around her throat; for a moment she could neither breathe nor swallow. Since he had rescued her from a life of folding laundry at Cousin Myra's plantation, William had changed. To his men he was still the same gruff and fearsome captain, but the hell-fire of revenge and anger that had once burned behind his eyes had gone. His ruthless reputation was giving way to a new image: that of the gentleman pirate, fierce but fair, like his brother Henry had been. He had also stopped treating his niece like the hired help and more like the family she was. Though signs of real affection were few and far between, they were sincere. Fleur had quickly worked out that William had lied about needing her skills for the trip. In actual fact he'd come back for her simply because he'd missed her and wanted her with him, though she'd had to wait for Jack to confirm that. For her part, Fleur loved her uncle dearly, and now even the thought of losing him was too much to bear.

'Don't talk like that, Uncle,' she said in a panic. 'I'll

learn to be more patient, I really will. And I swear on the Hart staff that if you are ever taken I will come for you.'

William studied the plucky girl sitting beside him on the sand and smiled suddenly and brilliantly; his teeth resembled a row of broken tombstones. 'And if I'm killed?' he asked, raising an eyebrow.

'I'll avenge you, Uncle,' she said firmly.

'And I vow to do the same for you,' he replied earnestly in a rare moment of warmth. 'After all, Fleur, you and me are family. That counts for more than a hold full of diamonds and rubies in this godforsaken world.'

Fleur felt her heart swell as William reached over to squeeze her hand. Their eyes locked and they stared at each other with the same intense gaze. And though neither had ever uttered the words to the other, to both the sentiment was clear: 'I love you.'

When Fleur got back to her cabin, Astrid was sound asleep. The sun had set, and the cave was now pitch black and icy cold. Sleepy and contented after her spar with William, Fleur slipped under the covers and drifted off at once. She slept soundly, dreaming of fair winds and full sails, until she was woken by Astrid's cries.

She sat bolt upright and stared down at the girl, who, though clearly still asleep, was thrashing about as if in great pain.

'No, please, no!' Astrid cried as she tossed about, so wildly that Fleur had to pin her arms by her side to avoid a black eye – though she remembered what Arthur had said about not waking her. Instead she whispered soothing words to her, but Astrid only arched her back as if trying to fight off an attacker before suddenly falling still and silent. Fleur didn't know whether to run for Arthur or Dr Dubois, or simply to stay with her unconscious friend. Just as she had decided that calling for help would be the best course of action, Astrid's eyelids fluttered wildly, then opened wide.

'Astrid,' Fleur whispered. 'Are you awake?'

For a moment Astrid just stared straight ahead, making small whimpering sounds like a frightened animal. Fleur sat next to her, holding her hand. Loud footsteps and raucous laughter drifted down from the main deck, signalling the return of Jack and his team, laden with supplies and full of high spirits and New England.

Suddenly Astrid seemed to snap awake. She scanned the cabin fearfully, with saucer-like eyes.

'Are you all right?' asked Fleur tentatively. 'Did you have another vision? Astrid . . . ?'

The girl turned to Fleur, startled to find she had company. Even in the gloom of the cabin, Fleur could see her wide violet eyes burning like fire.

Astrid nodded, croaked and swallowed uncomfortably as if her throat was parched.

'Here, drink this.' Fleur reached for the flagon of water at the bedside and handed it to her friend, who drank deeply. The two of them sat in silence until Astrid was ready to speak.

'I felt pain this time,' she began, shuddering at the memory. 'It was as if I was seeing out of someone else's eyes; almost as if we were one and sharing the same thoughts.'

'What happened?' asked Fleur, eager to learn more.

But Astrid only shook her head and dropped her head into her hands.

'Astrid?' urged Fleur. 'Come on, tell me what happened.'

Astrid didn't look up. 'I felt the pain of a woman crushed beneath heavy rocks. Alive, but suffering terribly. I felt the breath being forced from her body and heard the blood pounding in her ears.'

'Who was she?' asked Fleur. 'What does it mean this time?'

'Fleur, I don't think—'

'Just tell me,' said Fleur fiercely, and her dark eyes fixed Astrid's pale ones with a steely glare.

Astrid sighed deeply and nodded. 'I think it was your mother.'

Fleur gasped and squeezed Astrid's hand so hard that she let out a little squeak of pain. 'I knew it,' she said to herself; then to Astrid, 'Well? What is it? The past, the present or the future? Do I mourn her passing or rush to see her?'

'Your mother lives still,' said Astrid sombrely. 'The events I saw have not yet come to pass. But they will, Fleur, and soon she will need a saviour.'

Fleur couldn't speak. Fury burned in her brain, and her heart felt fit to burst.

'Your mother really is alive . . . for now at least.' Astrid assured her. 'Someone has been lying to you.'

Fleur shook her head and tears stung her eyes. Without a word, she slid off the bed and left the cabin. It was time for William to give her some answers.

On the main deck, through the haze of tears, Fleur saw the captain sharing a drink with Jack and a few of the men. Bats swooped low over their heads. William raised his mug to greet her as she approached, but his drunken smile faded as soon as he saw her stormy, tear-streaked face. The men with him fell silent too, then took their leave and scuttled off into the bowels of the ship. Fleur stood over her uncle, staring down accusingly.

'What's wrong, girl?' he asked. He got up and rested a hand on her shoulder, but she shook him off and backed away. 'Child, tell me what's in your thoughts,' he ordered.

Fleur stood clenching and unclenching her fists. When she spoke, it was in a clear, firm voice.

'Tell me about my mother.'

# CHAPTER 7

Seated at the small table in the privacy of the captain's cabin, William puffed on his pipe and eyed his quivering, furious niece nervously. Fleur took a swig of rum from his mug, coughing violently as it burned its way down her throat.

'It gets better the more you drink,' William muttered.

Fleur pushed the cup away and tapped her foot, waiting for answers.

Her uncle cleared his throat and scratched his beard. 'Before I begin, I have to know why you're asking about Rose now and not before?'

'Astrid had a vision,' she explained flatly. 'Well, two to be precise. She says that my mother is alive but in trouble. And I believe her, though it means my father lied. And you too, Captain,' she spat. 'Tell me it ain't so, if you can.'

William drained the rum in his mug before he replied. 'Astrid is right: Rose is alive.'

For a moment his words didn't register. Whatever she had said, Fleur had been expecting him to say that her mother was indeed dead. 'Say it again,' she demanded.

William set his mug down on the table and nodded. 'Aye, she lives. 'Tis almost a relief to tell you, child, though I know it must pain you greatly. Your mother is alive, Fleur, though you'd be better off ignorant of the fact, as your father wished: I swore to keep it from you if I could.'

The walls of the cabin seemed to retreat as the truth sank in. Fleur felt as if she were falling into a black void. She gripped the table with white knuckles and held tight, as if her life depended on it. The blood drained from her face and she felt sick. William plonked an entire bottle of rum on the table and she grabbed it and took a gulp without even coughing. 'Tell me everything,' she demanded.

William sat back in his chair, studying his niece

carefully. 'Your mother, Rose,' he began, sighing heavily, 'was . . . *is* a complicated woman.'

Fleur snorted derisively.

'Hold yer tongue and hear me out, child,' he said with a flash of his old ferocity. He gathered himself quickly and continued. 'She was a landlubber when she met your father and me, that much you know.'

'An Irish farmer's daughter. Or was that a lie too?'

'No, Fleur, it's true that when Rose first ran into the Hart brothers she didn't know port from starboard. But what you don't know is that your mother took to the water like a fish to . . . well . . .' William caught Fleur by the wrist with a powerful grip. His eyes narrowed and his voice dropped to a hoarse whisper. 'God help you, Fleur, we kept the secret of your mother's fate from you for your own sake,' he hissed. 'Some stones are best left unturned and, mark me, a serpent sleeps beneath this 'un. For pity's sake, let it lie.'

'Just tell me,' said Fleur, prising her uncle's fingers from her arm.

'Very well. And don't say I didn't warn you.' William took another swig – from the bottle this time – and spoke. 'If ever Henry and I earned our reputation as the most bloodthirsty pirates on the seven seas' – he glanced at Fleur, and for a moment she thought she saw his stubbled cheeks redden with shame – 'well, we more than met our match with Rose Fitzgerald. 'Tweren't just the life of a sailor she took to; 'twas the life of a pirate too. And a mean one at that. Your mother, Fleur . . . she had a hot head and a short fuse. She used her pistols like a handshake, to say hello. And more often than not, that was the first and last thing she'd ever say to you.'

'You're lying!' shouted Fleur. 'Why would my father have fallen in love with a monster like that?'

'She wasn't always like that,' her uncle went on, 'not at first – though she learned from the scurvy crew we kept in them days. Course, she always had a fiery temper, but your father liked 'em feisty, and he was snared and hitched to her before she got a taste for . . .' He paused, leaving the sentence unfinished.

'Tell me about my birth,' said Fleur, and though it was still a demand, the fight had left her voice.

'When we found out your mother was with child, we thought it might steer her away from the bloody path she had chosen.' William sighed heavily. 'We were wrong. Rose had no desire to start a family. Family was what she'd run away from in Ireland, she said. So at first she tried pickling you in rum before you'd left her loins. We had her confined to her chambers after that, but she broke free one night, and Henry woke with the cold steel of her pistol pressed against his eye.'

Fleur gasped at the thought of her mother holding her father at gunpoint. 'What happened?'

William shrugged. 'I crept up behind her and clobbered her with a grog bottle. She weren't happy about it when she woke up.' His face darkened at a sudden memory. 'I was . . . elsewhere at the time, but I soon heard that Rose Hart had been carried in chains to England. I'm damned if they didn't have to strap her to the table even as she spat you out, else she'd have run for the first ship she saw and dropped you over the harbour wall. Henry thought she might see sense when she saw your precious face, child – but, curse her black heart, he were wrong again.'

He slapped his hands on the table and shook his head again gravely. 'She played your father for a fool, Fleur. She cooed and coddled you. She even nursed you. And when Henry thought she had settled – when he took his eyes off her, that is to say – she scarpered . . . Your father stayed ashore to raise you. I had taken my leave long ago, still hunting the Bloods for taking my own dear family from me. Our paths have never crossed since, though I've heard a tale or two. Rose Hart lives, Fleur, and sails the seas under the Jolly Roger.

And God help any man, woman or child that gets in her way.'

Fleur's head was swimming with rum and revelations. Her hand reached for the locket around her neck with the pencil sketch of Rose inside. Her uncle's words, though she knew them to be true, just didn't make sense to her. Her mother had been kind, beautiful and . . .

'Rose is clever and dangerous,' said William, seeming to read her thoughts. 'She's fierce, aye, and the life she chose will catch up with her one day, mark me. But she ain't the Devil, Fleur. She's flesh and blood with all its flaws. If you ask me, you got her good points.'

They both sat thinking their own thoughts for a while. Then Fleur stood up and started pacing around the cabin restlessly: the boards groaned beneath her bare feet. Suddenly she stopped and stared at William again. 'I can't believe she wouldn't stay,' she said sadly. 'Not even for me.'

'A caged bird cannot be happy.' William rocked back in his chair and threw his feet up on the table. 'And perhaps she loved you just enough to know that you'd be better off without her.'

Fleur slumped back down into her chair, arms stretched out on the table before her. 'Why didn't my father just tell me the truth?' she moaned, pressing her forehead against the rough wood.

Her uncle picked up the bottle and swirled the rum around in it distractedly. 'And you'd have been happier thinking your own mother was a savage pirate queen who prized the open ocean over her own child?' he asked gently.

'I don't know,' groaned Fleur. 'But how could any child be happy thinking their mother was dead?'

'Don't let it tear you apart . . .'

'I hate her.' Fleur spat out the words as if they were poison.

William winced. 'Them's big words, lassie,' he said. 'I'll agree that she's nothing but a poisonous sea-snake, but she's still your family.'

'Ha!' Fleur rose to her feet, her heart pounding and her voice trembling as her thoughts and feelings swung violently this way and that. 'She wanted nothing to do with me, and the feeling's mutual – she might as well be dead.' She strode over to the cabin door and turned to nod back at her pale-faced uncle. 'Thank you for telling me the truth.' Then she spun on her heels and left before he could reply.

Fleur couldn't sleep that night and was still reeling from the strange and terrible news the next morning. She had always thought that a mother's love was meant to be instinctive, unconditional and eternal. Well, not, it seemed, in the case of her own mother. There was no denying that Henry had been a wonderful parent to her, but she had always envied her friends their closeness with their mothers. When there were tears, it was Mother who was always there to kiss them away. When they fell, it was Mother who gathered them up and tended their bumps and grazes. A mother, Fleur had observed as a young child, is someone who never stops worrying about where you are and who you are with, what you are doing, and what will become of you. She had laughed at the mollycoddling her playmates suffered, but, even then, she knew there was a gap in her own life for just such a mother, and she felt the loss of Rose keenly.

With her father working all hours in the inn, Fleur had learned at a young age to look after herself. And when Henry's past had caught up with him, she had known the bitterness of loss once more. It had stained her life and tempered her outlook. It had made her grow up faster than she should have. In recent months, with William at her side, the thick fog of grief had slowly begun to part, revealing to Fleur a brighter future on the horizon. Now the light was fading and storm clouds gathered once again.

Dawn brought seeping golden light back into the cave. Fleur gave up on sleep entirely with the first rays of the sun and crept out of bed – quietly, so as not to disturb Astrid. She found a quiet patch on the deck above, where the snores of sleeping pirates mixed with birdsong from beyond the cavern walls, Fleur removed the precious locket from around her neck and examined the delicate sketch of Rose Hart. A memory – or a fantasy perhaps: she had been so very young – of her mother sprang into her mind. A morning, so long ago; her mother brushing her hair in front of a large, gilt mirror and bouncing a tiny girl on her lap. Fleur wondered if the scene in her mind were real: had her mother been planning her escape as she groomed her long locks?

*'How pretty you are, Fleur,' came her mother's voice faintly from the looking glass. 'Like the flowers you were named for. There is so much of your father in you, my darling, but you have my eyes.'*

*Rose laughed and her face lit up as she stared at her daughter's reflection. Then the smile faded and her eyes filled with tears.*

*'Why're you sad, Mummy?' asked the infant Fleur in the mirror, frowning seriously.*

*Rose put down the brush and wrapped her arms around her*

child. *'Because I love you so much, my little one. And I always will. Never forget that. Whenever you think you are all alone, look in the mirror and I'll be there.'*

Fleur crept back into the room as Astrid was beginning to stir. She tucked the locket away with her most precious treasures, her grandfather's astrolabe and the conch shell given to her by Tom among them.

'Out of sight,' she reasoned aloud, 'out of mind.'

If anyone noticed her tired, red-rimmed eyes that morning, they wisely chose not to tease or pry. Normally Tom would have ignored the warning signs and demanded to know what was troubling his friend. But instead he kept his own company and appeared preoccupied and anxious. Fleur knew she would have to tell him about Rose as soon as she had the chance, however raw and painful it was to talk about it. If Astrid's vision were to be believed, Tom might also have a living parent, however reluctant he was to consider the notion. Fleur did her best to push her stormy emotions aside and focus on her upcoming expedition to Salem. Her mother and everything else would have to wait.

'Eleven poor souls have hanged already,' said Jack with a theatrical flourish to his captivated audience. 'And a hundred more crowd the jail awaiting their fate.'

The first mate had returned to the *Dragon*, along with the first landing party and a fine haul of grub and grog, including several live chickens, two goats and a fat hog. Now, over a breakfast of ham and freshly baked bread, he was regaling the wide-eyed crew with tales of the strange goings-on ashore. Grog hung upside down in the rigging above their heads, chattering merrily away to himself while eating a banana.

'A witch hunt, they're calling it,' Jack muttered darkly. 'But it's sheer madness, from what me an' the lads saw. The town elders have the people worked into a lather over talk of devilry in their midst and, good Christians that they are, the fear has spread among 'em like the pox. Now they're throwing accusations about like rose-petals at a wedding. All this talk of witchcraft is bunkum. Mark me, if there's evil to be found in Salem, it comes from neighbour turning on neighbour, spreading rumours an' telling lies. That's how the Devil works in this world.'

The men grunted their agreement through mouths full of food and ale.

Jack went on, shaking his head gravely as he spoke. 'An' the poor accused prisoners – men, women and children, aye, whole families bound in chains and rotting in their own waste. Kept worse than animals, they are. And some of 'em so delirious that they actually confess to practising black magic, though their own families and friends swear it's nonsense.' He shook his head and sighed. 'They hang 'em nonetheless.' He sat back and let his gaze wander over the assembled men. 'Tell me, brothers, do you sense devilry? Or is there a human hand at work in this godforsaken town?'

'Why not devilry?' asked Tom, his eyes wide and fearful. 'We've sailed the world, sir, and seen so many strange and impossible sights.' He thought for a moment, and then went on, 'Mongolian shamans and Mexican curanderos; African witch doctors and the terrible hanged men of Haiti. Was all that power and mystery imagined, sir?'

'You've not yet been ashore, boy,' Jack reminded him impatiently.

Tom blushed and tugged at a loose thread in his breeches. 'I'm just sayin',' he murmured, 'that there's good and evil in all corners of the world, and much that we don't understand. Why *shouldn't* the whole village be tainted with witchcraft? Would it be any more surprising than another explanation?'

Jack looked down at him doubtfully, but the crowd around him began to mutter their approval. The first mate held up a hand to calm a growing sense of superstitious panic.

'You make a sound point, Tom,' he said. 'We have indeed witnessed many a strange sight. But the trouble in Salem feels all too worldly to be witchcraft. There's money or politics at the heart of the matter, or my name's not Jack Jenkins. Though I cannot figure the thinking of the silly girls who started it all.'

'Silly girls?' asked Gates, who was sitting sipping tea from his pewter mug. 'What do you mean, man?'

'I'll tell you all I know, friend,' said Jack, frowning at the harshness of the bosun's tone. 'But first, do you remember the Reverend Parris, Cap'n?' he called over to William. 'He moved to Salem with his wife and daughter and an orphaned niece several years ago.'

William blew pipe-smoke into the air. 'Aye, I remember, Jack,' he replied. 'A greedy, self-righteous cow-pat of a man, if I remember rightly, and I'm not alone in thinking it.' He grinned broadly.

. Jack nodded. 'That's the fellow. Well, his daughter, Betty, and the niece, Abigail, are the source of the madness.'

'How so, sir?' Fleur asked, her skin prickling. She knew pirates liked to pin all their troubles on the nearest female; she wanted more of an explanation.

Jack picked at his teeth and belched loudly before continuing. 'The Reverend Parris has an Indian slave,' he told her, 'named Tituba, whom he brought from the Caribbean. She was always more than happy to tell dark tales from her homeland, as I remember, and Betty and Abigail, and their giggling friends too, were tickled by her tales about sorcery and demons. They met at night to hear her, like a sort of secret club. They called it Tituba's Circle.' He took a sip from his mug of black tea, flinching as the hot liquid burned his lips. 'They played childish games and sang songs that would scandalize their elders. Told fortunes with egg whites.'

Fleur, Tom and Astrid exchanged puzzled looks.

'I've heard of that,' Arthur piped up. 'You put an egg white into a glass of water and watch to see what shapes it forms. Then you use the pictures you see to find out what the future holds. It's supposed to foretell the future like a gypsy's crystal ball. Load of rubbish, if you ask me,' he added with a quick smile.

Jack grinned. 'That's the trick, boy.'

'And what future did they see, I wonder?' asked Fleur.

'Ah,' said Jack. 'There I can help you. The tale is running riot around town: Tituba's last vision, afore they clapped her in irons along with the rest of their little gang.'

'Well?' asked Fleur impatiently. 'What was it? What did they see?'

'The gallows and a coffin lid, say the townspeople. And as we all know, both are to figure large in them poor silly girls' futures. Eleven have had their necks stretched already.' Jack fiddled nervously with one of his many gold rings. The gallows were never far from a pirate's thoughts.

'What of the Parris girls now?' asked Fleur, though she felt sure they must have been the first to feel the noose around their necks.

'They live. They saved their skins by surrendering up every girl that ever sat in on one of Tituba's tales. When they ran out of friends, they turned on the townspeople at large. They are taken by fits − or perhaps feign them − during which the names of the guilty are apparently given to them by some'−Jack waved his hands dismissively − 'higher force.'

'But that's plain madness,' protested Fleur. 'To hang a man or lock up an entire family on the whim of a . . . of a . . .' Her face reddened. She didn't want to finish her sentence.

'Of a girl? Aye, well,' said Jack, understanding Fleur's unease after here own struggle to prove herself to her shipmates; him in particular. 'Present company excepted, it is strange to see young ladies wield such power unchecked.'

'What of the law?' asked Arthur. 'Surely wisdom and caution prevail in the courtroom. Can't we talk to them or something?'

There was a burst of laughter from the men.

'Have you forgotten the company you keep nowadays, Master Arthur?' asked Jack with mock severity. 'You'd do well not to fraternize with those wicked old men of the law when you go ashore, or you'll see all the wisdom and caution they show in stringing you up. And no, in answer to your question, there's no sense coming from that corner, neither. Those damnable Puritans are lining up to do God's work, and the way they're going about it, Abby and Betty won't run out of unfortunates to deliver up till there's not a man, woman or child left in town to stand in judgement.

'Anyhow,' he went on, shifting into a more comfortable position, 'Parris asked the local churchmen to exorcize the demons he said was possessing his girls. Men from all the settlements hereabouts met in Salem to lead a day of fasting and prayer, and to quiz the girls on the root of their woes.' He rolled his eyes and couldn't keep the scorn from his voice. 'Them girls kept falling mute or claiming they were blind, then saying it was Satan's attack on 'em. They choked as if they were being strangled and twisted their bodies like fever victims. They said that evil spirits were pursuing them, threatening, biting, pinching and pricking. After that, the town went mad, with more and more girls claimin' they were bewitched an' offering up their peers for judgement.'

Troubled murmurs rippled through the listening men, but Gates cleared his throat to speak again, and they fell quiet once more. He was usually so private and reserved when he wasn't on duty that it was strange to hear him speaking so freely.

'Be wary of Puritans, men,' he urged his audience, scanning them with a fierce glare. 'It suits their faith to keep the Devil close at hand. For if Old Nick walks among them, there's more call for the Lord. A little devilry among the townspeople swells the church's coffers on Sunday, make no mistake.'

'Your feelings are clear,' said Alfredo, an Italian and one of William's finest gunners. He was clutching the gold crucifix he wore around his neck. 'But I must listen to my heart. This town has been touched by the black arts and I will not walk among the damned – present company excepted. I'll stay on the ship, *grazie, signor*.' He bowed low to Jack and strode off, leaving the crowd murmuring nervously in his wake.

The captain, who knew that superstition among the men was like a spark in a powder keg, stepped in at once to hush them. 'Look at you lily-livered spratlings. Call yourself pirates?' he roared with a shake of his massive fist. 'There's no priest on this vessel, men, and no room for one neither. Stay in the cave if you're too yellow to come ashore. We'll still bring you your meals, though I can't promise you the best cuts. But for those of you who're man enough, there's a wealthy merchant in Salem town with a warehouse full of booze, just waiting to go for a walk with us. So what'll it be? Anyone else taking holy orders, or shall we pay the locals a visit and collect our booty?'

As the cheers of the men died down, Jack nodded his respect to William and raised his voice with a final warning. 'There's sport to be had in Salem, men. But there's peril aplenty too. The greatest danger ashore ain't Old Nick, it's the hanging judge who does the bidding of those vicious maids – William Stoughton.'

Some of the pirates gasped at the name. Fleur and her friends shrugged at each other, none the wiser. 'Who's he then?' she asked.

'A man me and Jack've had dealings with before,' said William. 'Back when he did his hanging for a less pious cause. He was a mean and murderous fellow then, and he's worse now he calls himself "witchfinder" and points his finger wherever he wishes.'

'I've heard of him,' piped up Arthur. 'In London he had a reputation as a real tough nut. He'll send anyone to the gallows, even children.'

'Aye, and those who are still in their mother's bellies too. At least, the end's the same when he hangs their mothers.' The captain shook his head at the cruelty of Judge Stoughton. 'And they call *us* bad 'uns.'

'Just watch your step, lads,' said Jack as the crew finally began to disperse.

'And be careful who you talk to,' added William to a murmured chorus of 'Aye, Cap'n's.

When most of the crew had left, he came over to check on Astrid. He must have noticed her discomfort at the talk of witchfinders and hangings, and Fleur marvelled again at just how much he had changed from the black-hearted tyrant she'd first met.

'It sounds like Salem ain't a place we want to stay in for long,' he said. 'I propose we take what we need and set sail sharpish. What do you think, miss?'

Astrid nodded shyly.

'Jack here has arranged for us to pick up a horse and cart from friends – farmers called the Wardwells – so that we can travel the distance to Salem town quickly. We'll take as much rum and rye as we can carry and come straight back. In and out. How does that sound?'

There was a hearty round of 'Aye's from Fleur and her friends.

'Well then,' said the captain with a mischievous smile, 'who's coming with me? Some kiddies'll make a rogue like meself a mite more respectable, don't you think?'

# Chapter 8

Fleur and Tom, along with Gates, Jack and their shipmates Tiny Joe and Black Matt, were gathered on the main deck waiting for the captain. Tiny Joe was a giant of a man with a sweet boyish face and a mop of strawberry-blond hair. He wasn't the sharpest tool in the box, but what he lacked in brains, he more than made up for in strength and loyalty. Black Matt was one of William's finest fighters, a handsome man, with raven hair and eyes like coal, but dangerous and quick-tempered. The black tattoos inked all over his body told the story of his violent past. William had tamed him to some extent, but still he kept a very close watch on him.

Arthur paced around with his hands sunk deep into his pockets. In the end William had decided that only Fleur and Tom should accompany him – they could fight if necessary; and anyway, they were his favourites. But Arthur was fed up nevertheless and his sighs were as constant as the charging tides.

'Arthur, come here, lad,' ordered Jack, aware of his misery.

Arthur trudged over to the first mate, and Fleur watched as Jack discreetly pointed over to Astrid and murmured something in his ear. Arthur blushed and nodded immediately, happy to be entrusted with the important job of keeping an eye on the pretty young girl.

At last Captain Hart arrived with a measure of rum for every man. He held his own cup aloft and toasted the ship and its crew. 'A merry life and a short one,' he added breezily, smacking his lips.

The men downed their drinks in one, while Fleur and Tom sipped and coughed their way through theirs. Tiny Joe clutched at the wishbone necklace he wore about his neck and kissed it a couple of times before tucking it into his chemise again. It wasn't uncommon for pirates to wear the lucky charms they had collected on their travels: rabbit's feet, coins, silver bells and amulets made from solid gold. Witch fever was spreading, and the men were growing more fearful with every hour they stayed in Salem.

Fleur shifted uncomfortably in her hideous new dress, noticing that her uncle had toned down his own flamboyant clothes. A long black cape concealed his lurid tattoos and the ever-present arsenal of blades and pistols. The narwhal staff, however, he carried freely, though Astrid had wound strips of leather around it to hide the strange carvings and jewelled centrepiece.

'I'm bringing this for you, lassie,' he told his niece, tapping the shaft, 'just in case we get into a spot of bother and have need of your skills. I'll hang onto it till then – it will seem more fitting in a man's hands. And remember to leave your bonnet on, missy.' William grinned at the scowling Fleur. 'And hold your tongue, as much as you're able. Good Christian children should be seen and not heard!'

Fleur, stepping down behind her uncle, rolled her eyes and groaned. She lifted her skirts to wade through the warm water to the shore. She felt ridiculous and missed the familiar weight of her father's bow and arrows against her back. She knew that William's rules were meant to protect her, but he was enjoying them way too much, in her opinion. All along the sandy bank pirates sprawled, either swigging from flagons of ale or sound asleep and snoring. Rays of sunlight poured in through the cracks and bounced off the water like sparkling diamonds. Suddenly Grog leaped off the ship's rail and splashed through the water, screeching noisily. He clambered ashore, shook himself and jumped into Tom's arms, almost bowling him over.

'Grog wants to visit Salem too,' Tom laughed, holding the soggy animal at arm's length from his dry clothes.

'Well, he can't,' said William firmly. 'There ain't no lemurs in this neck of the woods and I don't want to draw a crowd.'

'We could try to pass him off as a cat?' joked Fleur.

'Sorry, Tiddles,' said Tom, tossing Grog back onto the gangplank, where he hung dejectedly. 'I'll get you a bowl of cream and a pinch of fresh catnip.'

The lemur scampered back up onto the junk, squawking crossly. There he found Astrid, who was waiting to say goodbye. He wound himself around her delicate ankles as she waved at them. Fleur raised her hand limply and forced a smile in return. It wasn't that she disliked Astrid; in fact she was delighted to have some female company. But the newcomer had torn her world apart with her visions, and Fleur wondered now whether the dream she'd had about her mother would come to pass. She turned her back on the ship and hurried to catch up with the others.

Gates held up his compass to get his bearings, then pointed at one of the dark crevices in the wall; soon they were crawling along a tunnel on a bed of slippery shingle. Jack set a fair pace and Fleur, at the rear, with a lantern in one hand and her skirts gathered up in the other, kept losing her grip on the loose surface of the tunnel. For a while the passage twisted and turned; the only sound was the whistling of the wind and the occasional flutter and chirp of bats. The tunnel grew smaller, and Fleur felt as if the earth above would crush them all, but then they turned a corner and daylight blinded them.

They passed through a thin curtain of hanging vegetation to emerge in the hollow heart of a great gnarled oak tree beside a small waterfall that hissed and bubbled like a kettle on the boil. The sun was warm, and every sound seemed eerily muted after the bouncing echoes of the cave. Before them, the land sloped down to a meadow with a small pond. The late summer heat had dried the water to a muddy puddle, fenced in by straggly barberry bushes. The sun was warm but a cold wind whipped past, bringing the death of summer.

Jack was surveying the scene. 'That there is called Gallows Hill,' he said, shuddering and pointing at the southern ridge of a vast mount. 'And that's why.'

Fleur followed his gaze and let out a cry of horror. On the bare grey summit of a distant hill stood a row of gallows silhouetted against the sky. Narrow wooden steps led up to the platform where the so-called witches of Salem would be made to stand. Above ran the beam strung with nooses awaiting the next poor souls to try them on. Fleur had never seen a gallows before; the sight chilled her to the bone, despite the warmth of the autumn sun.

''Tis Salem's highest point,' her uncle told her.

Gates spat on the ground and turned his back on the structure. 'Terrible deeds have been done on this hill,' he muttered darkly. 'This is a cursed place and always will be.'

'Aye,' Black Matt agreed, glancing nervously over his shoulder at the dark shape of the gallows. 'If he weren't here before, they've raised the Devil for sure.'

Fleur's heart was pounding. Evil seemed to be lying

in wait for them everywhere. Was it threatening her mother at that very point? she wondered. The bony trees on the hillside, their leaves already browning under the hot September sun, reminded her of crippled old hags and Fleur wondered fearfully what happened to this place when the sun went down. She imagined the weeping and wailing ringing out from the hangman's high vantage point, and shivered. Witches or the law, it mattered not. She wanted to leave this place as quickly as possible. Coming up alongside Tom, she slipped her hand into his.

William looked back at her and grunted. 'Right then,' he bellowed, 'I reckon we've had enough of death and devilry for the time being. No more talk of unnatural things, or you'll feel the lash of my belt. Let's hurry to our plunder, men, and make haste away from this armpit of a place.'

Having broken the mood, the captain set a brisk pace towards the village and soon Fleur was relieved to see real people bustling along the dusty streets. Here life seemed to be going on as normal, and you could almost forget the horror that Salem was living through. Some of the inhabitants were dressed in their sober Sunday best black and white garb, but most wore clothes more suited to their daily toil.

At first glance Salem village was a pretty, leafy settlement – a huge contrast to the barren pastures of Gallows Hill. The gardens were full of vibrant blooms and trees heavy with fruit; the rows of timber homes had neat thatched roofs and smoking chimneys. The captain and his first mate walked together, pointing out changes to the landscape since they had last visited. Fleur and Tom walked slightly behind, just as William had ordered. Tom was wearing his smartest clothes and had even washed his face and put on a pair of shoes for the occasion, though he walked as if they were filled with pins. They passed a huge pit over which men were sawing timber into planks with vast, two-man saws. Across the mud track sat a blacksmith's shop alongside a crowded tavern. People bustled by, busy with their duties: children peered out at them curiously from behind their mothers' mud-spattered skirts.

As they passed through Town House Square, the captain pointed to the large meeting house that acted as church, court and town hall, all rolled into one. It was a plain building with heavy oak beams and glassless windows. In front stood a row of hitching posts for the villagers' horses, each one with a stone step for dismounting. This was a farming community, and the local dwellings were scattered wide, so most of the residents rode into town for the frequent civil and religious meetings. On the green in front of the meeting house stood the pillory, stock and whipping post; the grisly tools of New England justice were no worse than those back home, Fleur reflected. Still, she shuddered when she saw them and wondered for a fleeting moment what fate was to befall her mother. Then her eyes fell upon a sight that was stranger and more terrible still. Nailed to the wall of the meeting house were two bloody wolves' heads, their cloudy eyes staring blankly, swollen tongues lolling from open jaws. Fleur cried out and then blushed at this most un-pirate-like reaction.

'Is . . . is that something to do with the witch trials?' she asked her uncle, scampering in her long skirts to match his pace.

He chuckled and patted her shoulder. 'No, child,' he reassured her. 'Wolves are a peril in these parts. There's a standing bounty on any beast that's shot or trapped. The hunters nail their trophies to the meeting-house door and write their names underneath to alert those who hold the keys to the village coffer, see?'

Fleur nodded, trying to forget her initial fright. William's explanation was some comfort, but neither the thought of marauding wolves nor the public display of their severed heads was particularly reassuring. She was beginning to realize just how close she was to the very edge of civilization.

'Mind you,' her uncle added unexpectedly, 'that's also where the names of the accused are displayed, and where the poor unfortunates are brought before the mob.' He grinned wickedly. 'Door's open – fancy a poke around? There no one here. You never know, we might find a flying broomstick.'

He and Fleur headed towards the building, curiosity soon overcoming any nerves on her part.

'Are you sure you want to go in there, sir?' Tom called out after them. His face was white and his eyes were wide. 'I ain't never seen you so keen to step inside a church or courthouse before, Cap'n – much less both at the same time.'

William turned to face Tom with a sly smile. 'And I ain't never seen you so nervous, boy. Don't let all this witchery waffle get to you. It's not like the Tom I know to come over all sparrow-like.' He paused and peered at the boy intently. 'In fact, you ain't been yourself for days. Remember what I've told you before, laddie. Face your fears without a second thought, 'cause once you've stared 'em down and come out fighting, there ain't nothing that can ever touch you again.'

'Aye, aye, Cap'n,' said Tom briskly, as if responding to an order.

'Anyway,' added the captain, glancing round the door, 'this ain't nothing but a place of gossip and nonsense. Sit outside if you like, but I'm going to have a look round.' He winked at Tom encouragingly. 'Come on, lad. Haven't you ever wondered what the House of God looks like?' He spun on his heels and strode back to Fleur's side, laughing to himself.

The first mate slapped Tom on the back. 'Come on, young 'un,' he insisted, shoving him after his captain. 'All for one . . .'

The meeting hall was empty, but it would still have seemed stark with a crowd inside. The walls were devoid of any decoration, religious or otherwise. The focal point was a simple, high pulpit, reached by a ladder. A wooden canopy hung over it to project the sound of the preacher's voice to the townspeople in the hard pews or kneeling in prayer on the rough wooden floorboards. The chill of the building was almost unbearable and services would always last a long while, no matter how cold it was.

'It's men on one side, women on the other,' said Gates, who had been looking around in silence until now. 'And children up front, near the pulpit.'

'That's right,' said William. 'And Indians and slaves up

in the rafters.' He gestured to a high gallery at the far end. ''Tain't very Christian, if you ask me.'

'What's this?' asked Tom, grabbing a long pole that was leaning against a row of pews. It had a rabbit's foot tied to one end with a leather thong, and a rabbit's tail at the other. He swished it through the air like a sword.

'That's for the tithing man, laddie,' replied Gates, taking it off him for a closer look. 'He keeps an eye out for anyone who drops off during a church service.'

'What? Does he whack 'em with it then?' Tom asked in horror. 'I thought religious folk were supposed to be kind and gentle.'

Gates and Captain Hart laughed scornfully at that comment. 'Don't count on it,' said the bosun gruffly. 'Have you not heard of the Crusades, boy? Or the Inquisition?'

Tom shrugged. Gates sighed wearily and threw the strange stick back. 'If a man nods off when he shouldn't, or a young 'un starts bleating, the tithing man deals him a sharp one to the bonce,' he explained. 'If it's one of the old dears, she gets a tickle with the tail instead. You get the picture?'

Tom leaned the stick back against the high-sided pew. Fleur wandered over to the pulpit and stood staring up at it. It was all too easy to picture a cruel judge in residence here when the hall was in courthouse mode. Fleur paced slowly around the pulpit, imagining what it must feel like to be accused of collusion with the Devil. The meeting house would be crammed to the rafters. She would be made to stand, trembling, before her judges. The accusers — girls her own age — would lead the crowd, flinging their lies about the room and collapsing in convulsions, wailing and tearing at their clothes as she tried in vain to defend herself against their accusations. And the judge, staring down at her with cold eyes; Fleur could almost hear his terrible words:

*'As these good children have witnessed and sworn by Almighty God, you are hereby found guilty of having made a contract with the Devil. You should be taken from here to a place of execution, there to be hanged by the neck until you are dead.'*

Fear coursed over Fleur like a blast of cold air and she backed away from the pulpit, panting. Astrid and Arthur were lucky not to have come to this place, she thought. Would she herself be at risk? Could she really hope to keep a low profile during their visit? The slightest disturbance would make them targets for the overzealous witchfinders. Her uncle was mad to even consider venturing into this meeting house! Fleur shut her eyes as her thoughts and fears briefly overwhelmed her. She felt someone come alongside her and turned to see that it was Gates. Surprisingly, he was a strong, calming presence, and for a while they stood together silently as Fleur gathered her senses.

'This place used to be called Naumkeag, lassie,' the bosun said after a while.

She turned, surprised that he was addressing her directly. She still had her doubts about him, but she was beginning to wonder why. The usually crabby pirate had now come out of his shell twice in one day and his respect for William seemed sincere.

'Why did they rename it?' she asked him.

'The settlers named it Salem after Shalom, the Hebrew word for peace.' He laughed bitterly and stroked his beard. 'Funny, all things considered. Don't you think?'

Fleur smiled despite herself.

Gates considered her thoughtfully. 'I hope you don't mind me saying this,' he said, 'but I think I can tell what troubles you, miss.'

Fleur looked at him doubtfully. 'I wouldn't go about reading my thoughts in this town, sir, or you'll be had up as a warlock,' she joked.

He laughed at that, surprising both of them, then

gestured to the Hart staff slung across the captain's back.

'Your abilities with that weapon are a gift, not a curse, girl, and if there's magic in you, it isn't the Devil's work. Still, you're right to feel uneasy among these people.' The bosun cut the air with the side of his hand. 'The line between good and evil is broken and fluid. One should be looking to one's own heart rather than following the mob.'

'Aye,' said Fleur. 'But dozens here have been imprisoned or worse, sir. Here the line is clearly drawn.'

'Superstition and fear. Don't let it trouble you.'

Fleur started to respond, but Gates held up a hand to silence her. 'Believe me, young 'un,' he said firmly. 'I've known Salem well over the years; it was a happy place once, but it's never been an easy one to live in. The folk here have to toil for everything they have, on land that's hard and unforgiving. A flood or a dry season can ruin a whole year's harvest. Wherever life hangs in the balance, people are apt to see the Devil in every misfortune – it's better than thinking all our hardships are down to luck or, worse still, our own failings.'

Gates brought out a pouch of his chewing tobacco and poked a wad of it into the side of his cheek. Fleur rubbed her eyes, which felt gritty and tired. She was at a loss as to what to believe about witchcraft or the trials, but she knew that the fluttering panic in her belly wouldn't go until she could feel the sea rolling beneath her feet once again. Something bad was coming; she could feel danger breathing down her neck.

'Did my uncle tell you all about me, then?' Fleur asked Gates suddenly. 'About the whole Hart staff thing, I mean?'

The bosun nodded. 'He did, miss. I hope you don't mind. There's a trust between William and me that neither of us would ever betray.'

Fleur shrugged and smoothed down her apron, spattered with mud from the cave. 'It makes no odds if I do mind, does it?' she replied eventually. 'Though I know nothing about you, do I? Not really, I mean.' She fixed him with a penetrating stare.

Gates sighed and his face grew hard again. 'Ain't much to tell,' he said flatly. 'Nothing worth hearing, anyhow.'

'I don't believe you,' said Fleur boldly. 'Everyone has a story. There's talk that you might even be a spy.'

Gates rubbed his forehead. 'Well, I'm not,' he replied curtly, and all at once turned to leave.

Before Fleur could stop him, he was striding over to William's side. 'Shall we get on, sir? Time is a-pressing,' he said, his voice ringing around the room.

The captain nodded. 'You're right, man. Let's get to our destination. This place is dampening my spirits.'

The pirates hurried out of the gloomy meeting house; its spiky coldness had sunk into their bones and the warm sun beckoned. Fleur studied Gates as he marched ahead with her uncle and resolved to discover his secret, for she was certain he had one. Every pirate did.

# CHAPTER 9

The Wardwell farm stood on the southern outskirts of the village. Tiny Joe and Black Matt peeled off to visit the nearby tavern while the others continued towards the farm.

'We've known this family for many years,' Jack explained as they headed across the pasture towards the rambling collection of barns and buildings. 'They're good people . . . I dread to think what'll happen to this place.'

Fleur was horrified – and took in her surroundings with fresh eyes. At the heart of the farm was a large black wooden house. It was a pretty building, despite the darkness of its timber, with its shake roof and wide chimney puffing out plumes of curling white smoke. On closer inspection though, Fleur noticed that the land around the house had grown wild with neglect. The outbuildings were thick with dark green moss and tangled ivy. A few lean, miserable cows huddled together under a ramshackle shelter. *The whole place has an air of hopelessness*, she thought, as her eyes settled on a notice fastened to the gate:

EXODUS 22:18: THOU SHALT NOT SUFFER A WITCH TO LIVE.

The captain ripped down the poster as they passed. He stomped up to the front door of the house and rapped on it firmly as his men gathered around him. After a moment the door was answered by a young girl, perhaps a year or two Fleur's junior. Like Fleur she wore drab skirts and a black bonnet. Her eyes widened with fear at the sight of the strange men, and she stepped back as if William were about to strike her.

'It's all right, child,' he said with what he hoped was a friendly smile. 'Don't you remember us? We ain't here to hurt ye.'

The girl frowned and nodded slowly, her eyes widening further as recognition dawned. 'Mother,' she yelled, without turning away. 'There are pirates at the door again.'

She stood staring at the motley crowd until her mother arrived, then stepped aside and continued to eyeball each one in turn, her eyes lingering on Fleur. Sarah Wardwell had been baking bread and appeared with her hands sticky with dough and her face dusted with rye flour. Her long brown hair was tied back, but whispering strands had escaped, which softened her severe appearance. She was a beautiful woman, but her cheeks were hollow, as if prematurely aged, and her eyes were dead. She wiped her hands on her apron and ushered them into the kitchen without smiling. A gaggle of young children scattered as they entered.

'Mercy, fetch refreshments for our guests,' she told the girl who had opened the door.

Mercy eyed Fleur again with a look that Fleur couldn't interpret, before nodding obediently and scampering away to the larder.

'Please, sit and rest your feet,' said Sarah, indicating the oak table and chairs that dominated the large kitchen, while in the middle burned an iron stove. The wooden floor was warm, and covered in places with soft sheepskins: jars of wildflowers sat on the windowsills. As they took their seats, Mercy returned with a jug of cider and a platter of bread and cold turkey meat. She set them down on the table and backed out of the room silently.

'It's only a little, but it's a lot of what we have,' said Sarah, blushing.

''Tis a fine feast, woman,' said William with genuine warmth. 'Thank ye kindly for your hospitality.' He shuffled his chair closer and rested his elbows on the table as he gnawed a drumstick. 'Tell me, can you contest Samuel's arrest?' he asked between mouthfuls. 'Jack 'ere has filled me in on the sad events.'

Sarah sighed as she poured out cider for her visitors. Fleur noticed that her hands were trembling. 'No, William,' she said sadly. 'Remember how Samuel always liked to tell fortunes? It was a party trick, no more than that. Parris and his ministers disagreed, and the way things are around here these days . . .' She trailed off and fell silent for a moment, then banged the empty cider jug down hard on the table. 'They say all our wealth and land comes from Samuel having made a pact with the Devil.' Her bitter laugh turned into a sob.

William frowned as he picked up his cup.

'Excuse me, gentlemen,' Sarah went on, 'but as you know, my family's money was inherited after the death of my first husband. If anyone made a pact with the Devil, it was me when I married that ornery old curmudgeon, God rest his generous soul. Still' – her eyes filled with tears – 'try telling that to William Stoughton and the other judges.' She wiped her eyes with the back of her apron and sniffed. 'Oh, I don't know. Maybe we *have* brought this on ourselves by making fun of the dark arts. Maybe God is judging us.'

'Poppycock,' said Jack firmly. 'You ain't done nothing wrong, nor has Samuel. He's a fair and decent man. None of this means a fiddler's flea coming from an old ruffian such as myself, but it's true.'

As the men around the table discussed the ongoing trials in hushed and earnest tones, Fleur and Tom sat close together, listening quietly, tucking into the fresh rolls and tender meat with relish. Every now and again, one of the many Wardwell children would poke their head into the room curiously, then dart away again at a glance from their mother. After a while Fleur's gaze began to wander. She spotted a family Bible sitting open on a chair. A pair of reading glasses rested on the open page, and a layer of dust covered the chair, book and spectacles in the otherwise spotless kitchen.

'I haven't touched that chair since the night they took him,' said Sarah suddenly, waking Fleur from her reverie. 'Makes me feel like he might walk though the door at any moment.' She gave Fleur a smile, though it didn't reach her sad eyes. 'If I clear away the signs of his last moments among us, it will mean he's gone for ever. Do you understand that?'

Fleur nodded, but she had no words to respond to such sadness. Fortunately Gates filled the silence.

'I hope I'm not speaking out of turn, as we've only just met, but Samuel isn't gone yet, Sarah,' he insisted. 'And he never will be, whatever the outcome of his trial, if you and yours keep him in your thoughts and in your hearts.'

A single tear slid down Sarah's cheek. She hid her face with shame. 'Thank you, all of you,' she said between her fingers. 'You're always welcome in our house, though I'm not sure how long we will keep this roof over our heads, or the town from tearing itself apart.' She dabbed at her eyes with her apron. 'We were a proud community once. That was our sin, perhaps. Now Salem is in ruins, though its walls are stout. The orphans of those who are hanged as witches are denied their inheritance by law. The farms lie barren, the cattle starve in the fields, and there are scarcely enough free and fit men to bring in what meagre harvest we have. And for all the hardship we have suffered, the prison fees must still be paid.'

'Fees?' asked Jack, banging his fist on the table. 'What

manner of court is this that asks payment of a man for the loss of his own liberty?'

'Aye, and on a trumped-up charge at that,' muttered William.

'We pay rent for Samuel's cell,' sighed Sarah, 'with extra for food, though the rations are poor and worm-eaten and the water is foul. Then there's the cost of the cuffs and chains and fetters that bind him. Seven shillings and a sixpence a-piece.'

The men exclaimed at the idea of paying for the pleasure of being clapped in irons, but Sarah had not finished. 'The jail keeper's fee is two pounds and eight shillings. Oh, and the trial itself costs one pound and six shillings . . .' Her words trailed away as fresh tears ran down her cheeks. She swallowed hard. 'Then, when they finally hang my darling Sam, we'll be called upon to pay for the rope and timber of the damned gallows, and the wages of the blasted hangman himself.' She slumped forward in despair, her head in her hands.

'This is intolerable,' growled William angrily. 'Though at least there we can help a little, I trust.'

'You have already done a great deal for my family. I cannot ask for charity,' Sarah replied, flushing.

William grinned and downed the rest of his drink in one. 'Charity be damned,' he bellowed. 'We've need of a stout horse and a strong cart. We'll take yours and I'll pay enough for a whole ranch of ponies.' He searched under his black cape and brought out a bulging sack of gold coins, which he plonked down on the table in front of his amazed hostess. 'And no argument,' he warned. 'We've had a fine year aboard the *Dragon* and I'm of a mind to share our good fortune.'

Fleur, who was almost as surprised as Sarah by her uncle's generosity, glowed with pride as she watched hope return to the woman's worried face.

'Keep it safe and use it wisely,' said the captain, tapping the tip of his nose with a finger. 'And for Heaven's sake, tell no one where you got the loot, or they'll know for sure you've been communing with the Devil.' He waggled his eyebrows mischievously.

Sarah reached over and squeezed his arm fondly. 'A devil you may seem to many who meet you, William Hart,' she replied with a grateful smile, 'but today, sir, you are our guardian angel.'

After a warm goodbye, Captain Hart and his crew set out in their overpriced cart. Gates took the reins – unlike the others he had a little experience with horses – and they collected a rather reluctant and slightly squiffy Black Matt and Tiny Joe from the tavern as they passed through the village. Salem town, the larger settlement to bear the name, was a seven-mile ride away but it was a pleasant afternoon and the road wasn't too bumpy beneath them. Fleur and Tom dangled their legs off the back of the cart and sucked on the sticky peppermint-scented molasses toffee that Sarah had given them as a parting gift. Shrieking gulls and red-winged blackbirds drunk on fat autumn berries soared above them, and the salty tang of the sea air drifted on the breeze, mingled with the scent of wild flowers and wood smoke. It would have been a lovely journey, but all the while Gallows Hill rose above the rolling meadows, a constant reminder of the darker side of Salem.

The scenery changed as they approached the town. Where the residents of Salem village were mostly poor farmers, the townsfolk were wealthy merchants. Salem was a prosperous port, with gravelled walkways bordered by neat flowerbeds. The townhouses had an orderly dignity, and it was easy to forget the troubles that plagued the place. William led his men towards Central Wharf, one of the largest trading posts in Salem, which was owned by a rich privateer. When a merchant ship docked, its cargo would be measured, weighed and inspected here. Once duty was paid on the goods, they were released for sale. Coffee, tea, silk, spices and ivory all passed through the wharf, and the King took his cut in taxes for every item brought ashore. Behind the wharf were the public stores, where unclaimed cargo was held until someone came up with the tax. Currently it was crammed full of liquor – a loss for the merchant who'd braved the crossing only to have his cargo taken on arrival, but a boon for an enterprising pirate captain with a few good men and a strong cart.

As they approached the town's jail, the lanes were thronged with nervous muttering crowds.

'Stop the cart,' ordered William.

Gates frowned and raised one eyebrow at him. 'Is that such a good idea, Captain?' he asked. 'Bearing in mind where we are. Let's push on, eh? We'll soon be at the docks.'

'Are you a pirate or a petticoat, man?' teased the captain. 'Are you not curious?'

'Not really, sir, no – and I *am* a pirate, sir; one who does not wish that fact to be revealed to the locals, especially when we're a stone's throw from the stocks.'

William pointed the narwhal-horn staff to a gap in the crowd. 'We'll stay in the background,' he said. 'Though if I see Samuel Wardwell being escorted out in chains, I might have to reconsider my options.'

The captain was smiling, but everyone knew he was

only half joking. Spontaneous acts of bravado were something of a Hart trademark, after all.

Fleur and Tom exchanged concerned looks with the crewmen, but no one had the courage to challenge him. Gates pulled on the reins, bringing the cart to a stop, and they clambered out and slipped in amongst the milling crowd.

They watched from a shadowy spot that had a view of the jail's heavy wooden doors. The people around them turned as a rattling bone-shaker of a cart came down the street, parting to let it through. It pulled up in front of the doors, which swung open to reveal a filthy jailer with a heavy clump of keys at his belt, and the altogether cleaner and more presentable sheriff – whose name, according to the people around them, was Corwin – with his tall staff of office. Corwin was a plump man with a ruddy face and at least three chubby chins. His long, wispy grey hair lay across his immaculate black Puritan robes.

'Bring forth the condemned,' he cried out, holding up his staff. 'Those who would converse with Satan are about to be reacquainted with their demonic master – in Hell!'

The crowd moaned and cheered in equal measure. Three women, bound with heavy chains, were shoved out through the doors and bundled into the cart. Their faces were spattered with dry blood and streaked with dirt, their clothes torn and filthy. Two of them were a picture of fear and despair, while the third hid her face with the tattered hem of her dress.

Sheriff Corwin shook his staff in the air, silencing the mob, and approached the cart. 'Show your face, witch,' he demanded of the woman hiding behind her skirts.

The prisoner made no sound or movement.

'I said *show your face*,' he bellowed. 'You vile, demonic hag.'

Fleur stood on tiptoe to get a better view of the unfolding drama.

'I'm no witch and you're a fool,' the woman replied, her voice muffled by the rags that hid her face.

The sheriff climbed onto the cart and, with one rough movement, tore the rag away, along with the woman's bonnet. Waves of fiery auburn hair tumbled down the prisoner's back and a pair of cat-like green eyes flashed with fury. The crowd gasped at her wild, beautiful appearance. Jack and the crew gasped too, but the captain groaned like a dying man and clutched his chest, feeling for his flask of spirits beneath the folds of his clothes. Fleur's eyes darted from the striking woman on the hangman's cart to her pale and shaking uncle and back again.

'What is it, Uncle?' she asked urgently as a thought took form in her mind, making her knees quiver and her hair stand on end. 'Who is that woman?'

'Who is she?' William took a gulp of rum. 'She's your bloody mother, girl.'

# CHAPTER 10

Bitter tears stung Fleur's eyes and her mind whirled as she stared at Rose Hart. Right up until that moment she had clung to a tiny shred of hope that William had been wrong about her mother. But now that hope was gone and Fleur's heart was breaking. She took a deep, shaky breath and steadied herself as the air seemed to thicken around her. Rose looked fierce and beautiful as she stared out at the crowd – a lioness carved from the coldest stone – and Fleur wondered if she'd ever loved her daughter at all. Fleur knew what love felt like. It burned and raged; it knew no laws, no fear, and it destroyed anything that got in its way. If Rose had felt like that, surely nothing could have torn her away from her daughter. Fleur squeezed her eyes shut and the tears rolled down her pale cheeks. Now that she had found her mother alive, it felt like she had finally lost her.

'We ... we have to rescue her,' she managed to stammer as the cart began its noisy journey towards Gallows Hill, with the townsfolk following behind.

William rolled his eyes and bit his tongue. It was clear that he had no great desire to risk his own skin for his brother's widow. He pointed to the armed guards positioned around the slow-moving cart. 'You have no duty to that woman,' he snapped.

'Still ...' said Fleur, her mind still reeling with conflicting emotions, her throat tight. 'We can't let her die. Not like this.'

''Twouldn't be a walk in the park, lassie. Are you sure you want to chance your life for one such as Rose Hart?'

Fleur's eyes met her uncle's with steely resolve. 'Aye, just as you would have done for Samuel Wardwell, and he ain't even kin.'

William sighed, accepting defeat, and nodded. 'Very well.' He cupped her chin with his huge hand. 'It's only right and fair that I let you fight this battle, niece. Your father would have done the same. I can't promise an easy victory, but let us ride up to Gallows Hill with them and see how it plays out.'

Gates spoke up next. 'Captain, I beg of you,' he said firmly but with deference to William's rank. 'It's too risky. I'm sorry to speak so freely, sir, but we'd be better served if we stuck to our plan.'

'Aye,' said Black Matt. 'They'll string us up for sure, Cap'n – begging your pardon,' he added quickly.

Tiny Joe, who never said much at all, nodded in agreement. Tom remained quiet; but Jack agreed with William – and addressed the men in hushed but urgent tones.

'Would you turn your backs on this child's mother?' he demanded, glancing at Rose in the retreating cart. 'It will lie heavy on your hearts for ever, however black and cold you may think 'em.'

The captain nodded at his lieutenant before turning to the rest of the crewmen. 'We won't take any – many – risks,' he assured them. 'More than we can help, at any rate.'

'For what it's worth,' said Fleur defiantly, 'I'm going with or without you.' She put her hands on her hips in the most pirate-like pose that her dress would allow.

Tom sidled alongside her. 'And I'll be going with her,' he announced bravely. 'Some help'd be nice though, or they'll likely hang the both of us.'

William beamed down at the plucky pair. 'Well, that does it then,' he said. 'I ain't prepared to lose the best fighter and the best cabin boy a captain ever had in one act of folly. We'll all be going along, men, in case they run into any trouble. Which of course they will.' He started striding back towards their horse and cart. 'Hurry to it, men,' he called out over his shoulder as he climbed aboard. 'That's an order.'

The journey to Gallows Hill was horrible. The townspeople lined the route, jeering and throwing rotten fruit at the condemned all the way. Several other carts and riders followed the procession, lashing at the prisoners with long leather whips whenever they came close enough. Jack kept away from the mob, but every now and again, through the bobbing bonnets and shaking fists, Fleur caught a glimpse of Rose's auburn hair glowing like fire in the late afternoon sunlight. She fought back the urge to cry. People were shoving and jostling all around her, but she was numb to all the digging elbows.

The road was cracked and potholed from months

of heavy use, but soon enough they were climbing the steep slope of Gallows Hill. Carts and wagons were left on the plateau below the summit and everyone continued on foot. The women prisoners were pushed and shoved at the front of the macabre parade, with the crowd still mocking and spitting at them as they trudged towards their doom. Fleur and her shipmates followed behind.

After what felt like an age, the crowd gathered around the gallows. It was a still afternoon, and the last of the sun glowed golden on the trees. A pompous official – the town's provost-marshal – demanded silence while he read out the death warrants. The two frightened young women, Martha and Mary, were to be hung within the hour, but Rose Hart, who had refused to enter a plea to the court by name, was to be interrogated first in the hope of extracting a confession. Rose spat on the marshal's feet as he paced before her and he recoiled in disgust. The guards grabbed her and threw her to the ground next to the towering scaffold. A handful of officials, Sheriff Corwin among them, stood next to the gallows wearing expressions of righteous contempt. The tallest of them, a man with a dour expression and beady black eyes, stepped forward, examining prisoners as a doctor might a cluster of plague boils. His fine, snow-white hair was carefully brushed over the shoulders of his jet-black clothes.

'That's Judge William Stoughton,' William murmured to Fleur out of the corner of his mouth; he and the first mate had tilted their hats to hide their faces as the judge surveyed the crowd. 'Remember, however things play out, he must not catch sight of me or Jack.'

'Right . . . Why?' asked Fleur vaguely, her mind wandering as she ran through a hundred fantastic rescue plans in her head. None of them, she knew, would work in the real world. Not with half a town lined up against them.

'The last time we ran into him,' the captain whispered, 'we didn't quite see eye to eye on a certain matter. Long story short, he vowed to put a noose around our necks if it were his last act in this life. So . . . best keep him at a safe distance, wouldn't you say, lassie?'

Fleur nodded distractedly, and pushed forward through the crowd to get a better view. Now a priest, who she gathered was called the Reverend Noyes, took centre-stage, standing over Rose and shaking his Bible in the air like a spear. He was a broad man, with shoulder-length brown hair and a kink in his spine from a childhood injury that gave him a slightly lopsided stoop.

'To your feet, witch,' he sneered, dragging Rose up by her hair. She snarled and writhed like a cat in a bag, but the sheriff's men stepped forward to pin her limbs to her side. The priest stood sweating before her, his eyes popping as he reached out with his stubby fingers and ripped the shoulder from Rose's ragged dress, revealing a skull-shaped birthmark. 'She bears the Devil's mark,' he roared to his congregation. 'Satan's kiss has left his foul imprint on your flesh, hag. Admit it and die swiftly with your sins absolved.'

Rose spat in Noyes's face and snapped at him like an angry terrier. He shuffled backwards in surprise, and at his signal the sheriff's men threw her to the floor like a rag doll.

'I'm no witch, you fools,' she bellowed, revealing her Irish accent. 'As you know well, priest. If I have committed any crime in this godforsaken town, then you are guilty of the same. You and your cowardly consorts.'

The Reverend Noyes narrowed his eyes as he glared down at her. His fingers fluttered over the pages of his weathered Bible and he read aloud:

'Deuteronomy, chapter thirteen, verse six . . .' He

cleared his throat theatrically. '"Any man or woman, after legal conviction, that worships any other God but the Lord God, shall be put to death."' He slammed the book shut and pointed down at her. 'You bear the mark, hag. Your name has been called out by Betty and Abigail, whom you tormented with your devilry. What's more, your neighbours, the Darbys, who are good people ...'

'Good people,' muttered the crowd obediently.

'The Darbys are willing to swear that you put a curse on their sow so that she lost a litter of piglets.'

'Then they are liars and fools too,' shouted Rose. She tried to stand up, despite the heavy chains, but Noyes planted a boot on her shoulder and pushed her back down again, laughing cruelly.

'I am innocent,' she protested, wincing at the pain. 'I am the victim of a conspiracy among the elders. Mark my words,' Rose lifted her head and cried out to the crowd, 'the men who govern this town are making fools of the lot of you. They'd see every soul here sent to the gallows to keep their own foul secrets.'

'Silence!' the priest demanded, glancing at the crowd nervously.

Again Rose tried to stand, and again she was shoved

backwards by the holy man's muddy boot. Fleur gasped and looked about the crowd, desperate for someone to come to Rose's defence. It was obvious that her mother was being set up.

'My crime was smuggling,' shouted Rose defiantly.

'Shut her up!' screamed Noyes, and a hand was clamped over Rose's mouth. She bit down hard and the guard yelped and pulled back his arm.

'The men you put your trust in have made a pretty penny out of me in recent years,' she continued. 'Now they reckon they're able to do without me and would add murder to their tally of crimes, and my share of the booty to their own coffers. Shame on Salem.'

The crowd erupted, with Fleur shouting louder than any of them.

'Lies! Damnable lies!' the Reverend Noyes roared, his face purple with rage.

Stoughton tapped him on the shoulder and took his place, his face dark and threatening. 'Silence!' he shouted to the surrounding crowds. 'I command it!'

The mob fell quiet at once. The judge looked down at Rose. 'It is my duty to cleanse Salem of the Devil's work. You *will* pay for your sins, woman.'

Rose stared up at him defiantly. 'They say a

witch can't stand to recite the Lord's Prayer
... How's this, you murderous villain?' And then she
rapidly started reciting, 'Our Father, Who art in
Heaven, hallowed be Thy name. Thy kingdom come,
Thy will—'

'Foul trickery,' said Stoughton. 'Ignore the witch.
Bring out the stones.'

Fleur, who had worked her way through to the front
of the crowd, gasped as she remembered Astrid's
premonition and realized what lay in store for her
mother. Rose was to endure the rite of *peine forte et
dure,* a horrible torture devised to extract a confession
on the promise of a swifter and less painful death. Two
strong men struggled through the crowd carrying a
heavy stone. This would be placed on Rose as she
lay pinned to the ground. Next, more heavy rocks
would be piled onto the slab until she screamed for
mercy and confessed, or her ribs cracked and her heart
was crushed. Fleur gulped as she watched Rose's captors
wrestle her onto her back. She had the feeling that
nothing could force a confession from her fearsome
mother's lips. Rose would die slowly with her pride and
reputation intact.

The guards shoved her into a shallow rectangular
pit and pinned her limbs down with their feet

while Corwin, Stoughton and Noyes hovered over her, smirking.

'Will you confess?' Sheriff Corwin demanded.

Rose said nothing.

The men with the heavy slab stepped forward and laid it on her torso. Rose grunted as she took the weight, but still she said nothing. The sheriff gave a signal, and four large rocks the size of ripe melons were thrown into the pit on top of the slab.

Fleur could not watch. She scanned the crowd instead, desperately looking for something or someone that could help her put an end to the grisly sport ... Nothing.

She pushed through the crowd until she was a few feet away from her long-lost mother. She ignored Tom's grasping hands as he tried to pull her back into the crowd. Rose was gasping for breath now as more rocks were piled on top of her chest. She turned her head to the side and Fleur saw the pain on her face. She was bright red and her eyes were bulging, then fluttering closed as the breath was slowly squeezed from her lungs.

'I am falsely accused,' she rasped.

Stoughton clicked his fingers. Noyes and Corwin

nodded their approval and the guards prepared to add yet more weight to the pile of stones.

Fleur stared hopelessly at Rose and couldn't help but cry out to her: 'Mother!'

Her sudden outburst attracted many eyes, Rose's among them. For a moment two pairs of emerald-green eyes locked together. Rose's mouth dropped open as she stared at the face in the crowd. Then she blinked a couple of times, as if waking from a dream, and mouthed Fleur's name. Fleur stood rooted to the spot, unable to move. But move she had to, and fast, or Rose Hart would surely die. She clenched her fists and gathered her resolve, then turned and pushed her way back through the baying crowd to William's side. 'I have to do this, Uncle,' she stated simply. 'Don't try to stop me.'

He frowned at her from beneath the brim of his hat. 'And what do you intend to do, young Fleur? Don't risk your life, or mine for that matter, for a woman who don't want you and never has.'

His remark cut Fleur deeply. He was right, she knew, but she had lived through the death of her mother once. She did not care to repeat the experience.

Tom approached her, brushing his hands through his hair nervously. 'What are you up to, Claw-cat?' he asked, his face pale.

Fleur looked from William to Tom, and before either of them could say another word, she snatched the narwhal staff from her uncle's side and started to barge her way back towards Rose.

'Come back, you ninny!' the captain bellowed after her. 'A thousand Rose Harts ain't worth your life, Fleur!'

But she ignored his calls. She tore the rags from the Hart staff as she pushed through the crowd. The townsfolk parted for her and were left muttering in her wake, and soon Judge Stoughton and his henchmen – along with all three prisoners – were watching her too.

'Stand aside,' said Fleur to the assembled elders as she reached the front. Noyes, disarmed by the angry girl with the big stick, did as he was told, and with deft flicks of her wrist, Fleur began knocking the rocks off the pile on Rose's chest with the tip of the staff.

'What are you doing?' said Noyes. 'Guards, arrest her.'

The sheriff's men surged forward as one and Fleur sprang into action. As the first man reached for her, she floored him with a blow to the temples, whirling the staff around her head, then crouching down on one knee, ready for her next assailant. Two came at once. She swung the staff, sending them sprawling at the feet of the astonished onlookers. As she fought, the scraps of material that had hidden the staff's finery unravelled further, revealing the glittering band of Inca gold and its brilliant ruby heart. Soon a great many of the sheriff's men were disarmed and either knocked out cold or left groaning on the floor. Judge Stoughton pointed at the weapon, and Fleur, in amazement.

'What madness has taken this girl?' barked the Reverend Noyes.

'Madness?' hissed Stoughton spitefully. 'Nay, 'tis devilry, Reverend. The girl is a witch sent straight from Hell!'

'Aye,' the crowd called out in agreement.

'Well then,' the judge went on, 'no need to waste time and the town's purse on a trial then. The evidence is irrefutable. We'll hang her now along with the rest.'

Fleur backed away as panic overwhelmed her. These men were voicing her own deepest fears: perhaps the power she felt when she fought with the staff was drawn from a darker force than she cared to think.

'No!' A voice from the back of the crowd startled Fleur and everyone present. Heads turned as one to see Tom barging his way through the mob. He pulled a knife from the folds of his coat as he approached the gallows and stood defiantly before the town's officials, his hair shining like gold amongst the sea of sombre black hats.

'Get away, Tom,' shouted Fleur, scared for her friend. 'This is my fight.'

'No it's not,' Tom insisted, his voice cracking a little as he brandished his tiny blade at Stoughton's men.

'Enough!' yelled the judge. 'Guards, seize him.'

Everyone moved at once. One guard leaped on Tom, wrestling him to the ground. Another fired his flintlock pistol into the air, sending the crowd scattering in all directions. Fleur flew into action, easily knocking aside the guards who charged at her and somersaulting through the air to avoid a volley of musket fire. In all the noise and confusion, nobody noticed Rose Hart quietly wriggling free of the remaining stones to slip away through the chaos. The townspeople had retreated, but they stayed at a safe distance to watch the show. Some of them were chanting loudly, *'Witch! Witch! Witch!'* and pointing accusing fingers at Fleur. As the sound of their mantra grew louder, one woman dropped to the ground and started writhing in pain, as if Fleur's very presence were a terrible torment.

Fleur ignored the taunts as she fought off her attackers,

thinking of nothing but the next move. Then she saw something that stopped her in her tracks: Stoughton's men were dragging Tom up the rickety wooden stairs to the gallows. Blood ran down his cheek from a wide gash and his left arm hung limp. Stoughton stood on the platform with a pair of pistols levelled at Fleur.

'Lay down your weapon, witch, or we'll stretch this lad's neck. He is your friend, I take it, and a friend to Satan too, no doubt.'

'Don't do it, Claw-cat,' Tom cried out, struggling hard against his captors' grip. 'Run for it!'

Stoughton turned from Fleur and a dozen muskets were raised at her head in place of his pistols. The judge grabbed Tom by the scruff of the neck and held up the loop of the noose in his other hand.

'Hurry up, *Claw-cat*,' Stoughton spat sarcastically. 'Unless there are any other men here who fancy mounting a rescue.' He laughed cruelly and the crowd joined in. Fleur stared up at Tom hopelessly: his face was ashen, but his eyes still shone with fighting spirit, and when she took a step towards the scaffold, he shook his head at her firmly.

A guard grabbed her roughly by the arm; she didn't struggle. *So this is it*, she thought. *It's all over.*

Then, when all seemed lost, a great commotion spread

through the spectators and a thunder of hooves split the air. The mob scattered to reveal William and Jack mounted on an enormous coal-black stallion, charging towards the gallows. The huge beast's shiny coat rippled over powerful muscles. The riders roared and rattled swords and clubs above their heads.

'Stoughton!' William cried as the black charger leaped right up onto the platform and stood there, prancing and snorting. The pirates jumped off the horse's back and brandished their weapons. 'You called for a rescue, I believe!'

'William Hart!' Stoughton roared. 'How dare you show your face! I swore at our last meeting to end your days if I ever set eyes on you again.'

'Well, now's your chance, *old friend*,' the captain sneered, prodding the judge in the stomach with the tip of his rapier. 'Have you a sword or is it fisticuffs?'

Stoughton called for a sword and a guard provided one at once. He lunged at William without warning, but the blow was parried easily and they fell on each other furiously. The clink and swish of the sharpened steel cut through the air.

Stoughton was a talented swordsman and a worthy opponent for Captain Hart. The first mate stood by with his own sword drawn, fighting off anyone who tried to intervene. Fleur stood in silent shock, a guard still clasping her arm. She scanned the crowd, searching for Rose, but her mother was nowhere to be seen. Nor was Tom, for that matter. Fleur looked up at the gallows desperately, but there was no sign of him. And now, as she turned, she saw to her horror that Jack was being held by three men, while other guards had fallen upon William. The battle-hardened pirate roared and thrashed as he was attacked from all sides, but to no avail. One guard ducked under the swinging swords of the others and plunged a dagger into William's thigh. He stumbled and sank to one knee, though he kept on swinging his rapier to bat away the approaching men. Then Stoughton caught William unawares, planting his boot on his back and sending him sprawling to the ground.

As more men piled in to pin him down, the captain called out to his niece, 'The *Dragon's* yours, lass – fair winds to ye. Now run and don't look back.'

The guard holding Fleur tightened his grip, but she wriggled sharply and flicked her staff to rap him on the head. He fell to the ground, unconscious. More guards began swarming around her, but they were no match for Fleur. She moved like a brutal ballerina: spinning, kicking and striking. It was both lethal and lovely. When the last of her attackers fell to the ground, a hush fell, and the circling group edged away fearfully.

'No, Uncle,' Fleur called back to the gallows. 'I'm going to save you.'

William laughed and spat out a loose tooth. 'Too late for that, girl,' he snarled as Stoughton grabbed him by the hair. 'Go – and if the crew give you any trouble, remind them whose blood flows through your veins.'

Stoughton burst into cruel laughter. 'Madness,' he said. 'I was under the illusion that you were the most fearsome pirate captain on the seven seas. And yet this is your heir, a mere child, a girl . . .' He curled his lip at Fleur. 'And a witch to boot.'

Then Fleur saw that Jack had been thrown onto the platform near William; both men were dragged up onto their knees and their hands tied behind their backs with chains. Jack spat at Stoughton; immediately a guard thumped him hard on the head with the hilt of his sword, and he slumped down, unconscious.

Fleur stood watching on the ground below; her despair had lifted and the staff was alive again in her hands. She twirled it in a wide arc and tossed it from hand to hand, and no one dared approach her. As the staff hummed in her palms, Fleur's eyes didn't leave her uncle's. Hot tears clouded her vision and her words almost caught in her mouth. 'Don't you dare let them take you, Captain.'

William spat more blood onto the deck of the scaffold. 'You are your father's daughter,' he bellowed. 'And I trust you above all others with the *Dragon* because you think like me. Take the wheel and honour our name.'

Stoughton's grey eyebrows rose in alarm. He peered at Fleur curiously. 'Honour?' he sneered. 'You have no honour. Satan's own blood runs in your veins.'

'If it be true, Stoughton, I'll see you in Hell,' replied the captain defiantly.

Stoughton knocked him down again and ground the heel of his boot into William's spine. 'Not so fast, Captain Hart,' he hissed. 'As much as I would love to witness your end, you have a certain celebrity that should not be wasted on so small an audience. But have no fear, you will meet your satanic master in the next life soon enough. You will be taken to Tyburn, where the whole of London will see you hang for your crimes.'

'Fleur,' William called down to her. 'Be off, girl. The judge has made his error, for I shall throw off these chains long before we reach English shores.'

'Aye, and slaughter my crew and take my ship, no doubt,' scoffed Stoughton.

'If you wish,' snarled William.

Stoughton delivered a vicious kick to his prisoner's ribs. William grunted and swore, then cried out to Fleur again. 'Neither one of us need die today, lassie. Be off, I say, and know that your uncle loves you dearly.'

Fleur's heart leaped as she heard the words she had longed for. She caught the whirling staff in both hands and planted it firmly at her feet.

'Now I *have* to rescue you,' she shouted. 'We shall be together soon, Uncle.'

'Aye, that you will,' said Stoughton, stamping his foot impatiently. He glanced around at his wounded guards with contempt, then addressed the mob. 'Good people of Salem,' he roared, 'would you suffer a witch to flee unpunished? She will leave plague and pestilence in her wake.'

The townsfolk grumbled and shuffled uncomfortably, but some of the bolder locals and the remaining guards began to push forward, slowly crowding in on Fleur.

'I don't want to hurt anybody,' said Fleur, 'and I'm not a witch, I'm a pirate. Or . . . no . . . um . . . I'm a simple Puritan girl. Damn.'

'Blasphemer!' called someone.

'Sorry,' said Fleur, holding up her hands imploringly. 'Slip of the tongue. Like I said – pirate. We can be a bit sweary. Look . . .'

Her words trailed away as sharp pain seared through her head. She raised a hand to her skull and felt a sticky wetness. Her vision began to blur and sounds became muffled. She looked at her fingertips in a daze: they were covered in blood. Fleur staggered, holding onto the Hart staff for support. A large stone whizzed past her ear. Then a second.

'Hey,' said Fleur dizzily. More and more townsfolk were casting around for missiles. 'Stop it. I—'

She didn't even feel the third stone. It put her out like a snuffed candle and she collapsed in a heap with the staff at her feet. For a moment her world was black and silent. Then the pain in her head returned, and somewhere in the distance, she thought, she heard horses and gunfire. Someone was speaking to her – shouting perhaps, though the words seemed distant and made no sense to her. She opened her eyes and the blinding light doubled the pain in her head. Then, as her sight adjusted, a face loomed over her, beautiful but wild and streaked with blood and dirt. There were more words, and this time she understood them.

'Look lively, runt! I cannot hold 'em for long. Give me your hand now.'

Fleur raised her arm feebly and her wrist was caught in a firm grasp. She felt herself being yanked up like a sack of potatoes and thrown over the broad haunches of a horse.

'Not got a thank-you for your old mum?' asked Rose Hart as she spurred the galloping beast down Gallows Hill to freedom.

But Fleur had already slipped back into unconsciousness.

# CHAPTER 11

Fleur woke in her cabin, though it took her a while to realize where she was. Lanterns flickered in the darkness, which meant that the precious sunlight had left the cave for the day. Astrid was sitting beside her on the bed, holding her hand. Grog was napping happily on her other side. Tom and Arthur were asleep on the floor, snoring.

'How are you feeling?' asked Astrid, concerned.

Fleur tried to sit up and pain flared through her head. 'Ouch!' She winced. 'Not brilliant, apparently.'

Tom yawned loudly and sat up, rubbing his eyes. His mop of hair was spiky with dried blood and he had clearly been crying. There was a nasty-looking welt on his cheek, starting at the left corner of his mouth, like a gruesome smile, and a blood-soaked bandage was wrapped around his arm. Despite his injuries, he smiled at Fleur with obvious relief and moved to join Astrid on the edge of the bed.

'Dr Dubois fixed up your head,' he told her.

Fleur rubbed her eyes as the memories of the day's events came flooding back to her jumbled mind. 'I'm sorry, Tom,' she said softly, reaching out tentatively to stroke his cheek.

''S what friends are for,' he mumbled.

Fleur studied the wide gash on his worried face and felt tears welling up in her eyes. He would never look the same again.

He shrugged. 'A scar'll make me look tougher and a sore arm means no work for a while, and that's fine by me.'

Arthur suddenly sat up bolt upright and scrambled to his feet. 'Fleur!' he exclaimed, dashing over to her bedside in a fluster. 'I didn't mean to drop off. How are you feeling?'

'My head hurts, but other than that I'm fine,' Fleur assured him. 'Thank you for looking after me.'

He smiled and placed a warm, dry hand on her

forehead to check if she were feverish. 'I'm just glad we got you back,' he said sincerely. 'I'll go and ask Toby to make you some lavender tea. It will help with the pain.'

Tom cleared his throat. 'Why don't you get *you-know-what* first, Arthur,' he said, raising his eyebrows pointedly. They exchanged knowing glances before Arthur slipped out of the room.

'What happened? How did I get back here? Where's William?' Fleur asked suddenly, the questions tumbling out.

Tom and Astrid looked at each other with concern.

'Tom . . .' demanded Fleur, struggling to sit up as her hot head pounded. 'Tell me about my uncle. And Jack too. I . . . I can't remember.'

'William is being taken to Tyburn,' he said solemnly. 'Gates followed the King's men back to Salem town and learned that they sail for London on a navy frigate called the *Triumph*.'

'No!' Fleur exclaimed with shock. 'William *always* manages to get away!'

'Not this time.'

Hot tears sprang into Fleur's eyes. 'What of Jack?' she asked in a small voice.

'Black Matt and Tiny Joe snuck up to the gallows while the crowd's attention was on you,' Tom explained.

'They couldn't get near William, but with Jack out cold no one thought to guard him. Matt and Joe snatched him off the platform and no one even noticed. He's safe. He's here.'

'Was he wounded?' asked Fleur, worried.

Tom paused and chewed on his lip.

'Tom?' snapped Fleur impatiently.

Tom sighed wearily. 'He's got a few scratches. Nothing that won't heal,' he began. 'But he ain't quite himself after that bump on the noggin'.'

'What do you mean?'

'It's best if you see for yourself . . . Arthur?' Tom called in the direction of the doorway. 'Are you back here yet with *you-know-what*?'

There was silence.

'What's going on?' demanded Fleur, looking from Tom to Astrid. 'What in Neptune's name is you-know-what?'

'I'm afraid you'll find out any moment,' said Astrid, biting on her lower lip nervously.

'Tell me now,' wailed Fleur. 'If you hadn't noticed, I'm already having a really bad day. Whatever it is, I can take it – really. Nothing could shock or shake me any more than I have been already.'

Suddenly there was a knock on the door.

'Are you ready for us?' came Arthur's voice from the passage outside.

'Bring him in,' said Tom gravely.

The cabin door creaked open and Arthur stepped inside, pushing his spectacles up on his nose and grinning nervously at Fleur.

'Hello, Fleur,' he stuttered, waving nervously. He turned round, beckoning to someone behind him. 'Come on, don't be shy.'

'Really, Master Arthur, I must object,' said Jack as he came blustering into the room.

'Jack!' cried Fleur, relieved to see him in one piece. She looked him up and down. 'Why are you standing funny? Did you hurt your leg?'

'Good morrow, miss,' said Jack with a dainty curtsey. 'My leg is fine, though I thank you for your concern. My consternation arises from quite a different source.'

'Conster-what?' asked Fleur, baffled.

'Quite how I came to be aboard this ship of rogues I do not know,' Jack continued. 'I woke in a strange bed, with a lump on my forehead as large as a robin's egg, and dressed in these ridiculous clothes.' He gestured limply at his old slops and blushed. 'A man's clothes,' he squeaked petulantly. 'It really is more than a young lady of substance can be expected to bear.'

Tom snorted and clapped his hand over his mouth. Fleur and Astrid just stared, their mouths agape.

'My dears,' Jack said imploringly, with a dainty step towards the bed, 'these brutes seem hell-bent on denying me the simplest of home comforts. I wonder, could I trouble you for a simple robe and perhaps a set of petticoats?'

'All right, that's enough for now, Jack – I mean Miss Jenkins,' interrupted Arthur. 'I need to get my patient back to bed. I'll come back soon with the lavender tea, Fleur,' he added, looking at his pale, shocked friend. 'I'll make sure Toby makes it nice and strong too.' Then he took Jack by the elbow and led him gently out of the room.

'See?' said Tom. 'Not quite himself.'

'Yes,' said Fleur, still in complete shock.

Astrid reached over and gave her hand a reassuring squeeze.

'Arthur said that Dr Dubois thinks he's got something called concussion,' she explained. 'He said it's quite normal for folk to get confused after a nasty bang on the head like that and can often start acting out of character.'

'Out of character!' exclaimed Fleur. 'But Jack's become the total opposite of himself. Will he get better?'

'Dr Dubois says yes, in a few weeks, most likely,' said Tom. 'His humours are out of balance or some such nonsense. I'm leaving him to it. Being with Jack like this gives me the heebie-jeebies. I . . . I think he fancies me.'

Despite the horrors of the day, Fleur couldn't help giggling. Tom gave in and joined her, then Astrid too, and they laughed until their sides hurt. For a few moments all their fears for William's safety and Jack's sanity were swept aside as they gripped their sides and begged one another to stop. But as their hysteria finally subsided, Fleur remembered something else from the events on Gallows Hill and her smile was wiped away in an instant.

'Rats,' she said aloud.

'What?' said Tom.

'Rose,' growled Fleur. 'Where is Rose?'

'Ah . . . yes.' Tom glanced at Astrid, then leaned in and spoke in a low voice. 'Your mother – who you should have told me about, by the way . . . Cap'n Hart told me you knew she was alive.'

'I did,' said Fleur guiltily. 'But I only just found out, and I'd planned to tell you, Tom, I promise.' She reached for his hand and smiled. 'You know what this means though, don't you?'

'What, that my parents are still dead?' Tom said flatly, his expression hardening at once.

'But, Tom,' Fleur persisted. 'What if Astrid was right about you too? What if you really do have a living parent? Aren't you curious?'

'No, Fleur,' he growled, glancing over at a cringing Astrid. 'I've said my goodbyes once, and I never want to go through that grief again.' He took a deep breath, clenching and unclenching his fists as he did so. 'Look, I don't want to talk about this,' he said firmly. 'All right?'

Both girls nodded silently.

'Anyhow,' he went on, keen to change the subject, 'Rose saved you from the townspeople, sure enough – and me too, for that matter. She shot the pistols right out of the sheriff and Stoughton's hands. Left 'em scooping up their own bloody fingers,' he added, with a smirk. 'Then she fought a fair portion of the crowd off with the help of your old staff before grabbing us both and bringing us back here on horseback. Didn't even have to ask where the ship was hidden. She must've been here before with the cap'n and your father.'

Fleur sank back onto her pillow again; too many thoughts were whirling around her mind and nothing felt real any more. Her mother was alive. She could have left Fleur to die and saved herself, but she had chosen to come back to rescue her. That had to count for something.

'Where is she now?' asked Fleur, her heart suddenly racing.

'Making herself at home in the captain's cabin,' said Tom.

'We'll see about that,' said Fleur grumpily. 'I'm grateful to her for saving my neck in Salem, but this is *my* home, not hers. And she's got a *lot* of explaining to do!'

It was all her friends could do to keep her from hobbling along to William's cabin and turfing her mother out. The cheek of it made Fleur's blood boil – even if she did owe Rose her life. Taking the captain's cabin was as good as assuming his standing aboard a pirate ship. And in William's absence the *Dragon* belonged to Fleur, not to her scheming, treacherous mother. And then there was Jack to worry about too. Only the pain in her head and the weakness in her legs as she tried to stand convinced her that staying in bed was the sensible option. She grumbled herself to sleep, and dreamed uneasily of Rose Hart poking around among her uncle's personal possessions, and of the great gallows that waited for William in London.

★

The next morning Fleur woke up feeling better. Of course, she felt the loss of her uncle like a missing limb, but she was positive that she'd find a way to get him back. Her mother was a different problem altogether; one she had no idea how to deal with. Her head still hurt and her stomach growled with hunger, but at least she could stand – though not for long. Astrid fetched some bananas, cheese, bread and fresh water, and the two girls ate breakfast in bed.

'I'm sorry about your mother, Fleur,' Astrid began cautiously. 'And that I'm the one who started all this trouble.'

Fleur shrugged and tucked into her food heartily. 'You didn't start anything. You just saw some stuff. And anyway, you were right.'

Astrid nodded as she picked at a piece of bread. 'Do *you* think the folk in Salem would hang me for a witch, Fleur?' she asked directly.

'Mm. Yes,' mumbled Fleur between mouthfuls. 'And you'd be in good company because I'm one myself, apparently.'

Astrid turned towards her friend in surprise. The two girls smiled at each other and the tension between them melted away. Astrid reached out and took Fleur's hand in hers. Her beautiful eyes glowed brightly and Fleur felt a sense of calm flood over her like gentle waves on a moonlit beach.

'You're no witch,' Astrid said, suddenly serious. 'You're something else. Something bigger. I knew it the first time I saw you with that staff of yours. I knew you were something special . . . important.'

Fleur frowned as she thought back to Astrid's first day aboard.

'In truth,' the other girl continued mysteriously, 'it was the staff that told me. It spoke to me in my dreams before I even met you. Though I'd forgotten that until I laid eyes on it.' She stared at Fleur intently. 'That staff has a spirit, Fleur, which exists outside ordinary time. It is older than the rocks on the shore. It has a purpose and a strength all of its own, and I think . . .' She sighed, aware that what she was saying must sound strange. 'I think meeting you was part of its plan.'

Fleur scoffed loudly. 'Sorry, Astrid,' she said as her friend's face fell, 'but it's probably just a stick for fighting.'

'You know that's not true!' said Astrid. 'And besides, in my dreams I have seen—'

'What?' Fleur interrupted, her eyes suddenly wide. 'Have you seen more of my future?'

Astrid let go of her hand and turned away.

'Astrid!' urged Fleur, pushing the rest of her breakfast aside.

'I have glimpsed it perhaps. But some things are hard to understand,' the girl replied, her voice a whisper. 'No one should know what lies ahead. You must live in the moment, or you're not really living at all.'

Fleur's skin prickled, and a chill swept through her bones. Something about Astrid's sudden vagueness troubled her. She leaned back and folded her arms protectively across her chest. 'It's bad, isn't it?' she asked.

Astrid smiled and shook her head. 'Nothing you can't handle. Good things and bad will come your way because of the life you've chosen, Fleur. But whether good or bad, your future is a great one. Can't you feel that?'

Fleur stared at the narwhal staff standing against the cabin wall; her green eyes glittered like jewels. 'I know there's something big waiting for me,' she mumbled. 'It's always just over the horizon, but I feel it looming fast now. It scares me, Astrid. And all this witch trial nonsense got me to thinking. If there really *is* magic locked in that staff, then where did the power come from? Perhaps I should never have meddled with it at all.'

'What does it matter where the water flows from, provided it quenches the thirst?' asked Astrid. 'And anyway, that staff found you: I'm not sure you had any choice in the matter.'

'But what if the staff is evil?' said Fleur. 'Maybe it could infect me. Turn me bad. There's a pretty dangerous streak in my family line, you must admit.'

Astrid shook her head firmly and her violet eyes seemed to flare like fire in oily water. When she spoke again, it was in such a faraway tone that Fleur wondered where she had gone.

'I promise you a marvellous future, Fleur Hart,' she began. 'Your life was written before the first man was born. Good and evil are newer ideas. In reality, they are the two sides of the same coin. They cannot be kept apart like night is from day. The narwhal staff has to contain both just to exist, and so do you. To do good or evil is a choice you make yourself.' She blinked suddenly and let out a breath.

Fleur sat up in astonishment and shook her head. 'Those words were not your own,' she gasped. 'Astrid, how do you know about such things?'

Astrid massaged her forehead with her fingertips and exhaled. 'It's like the visions,' she said, her voice normal now. 'Only quieter and calmer. If I listen carefully, there are moments when I am able to channel the world. In those moments, the words come. But I have no way of harnessing them, and if I try too hard to hear what I am saying, the whole thing falls apart ... Just as my memories fall apart when I try to remember things about myself ... my family.'

'It must be awful,' said Fleur. 'Not knowing who you are, I mean.'

Astrid's face darkened. 'Maybe it's better this way,' she said.

They were interrupted by a rap at the door. It was the bosun. 'How are you feeling, Fleur?' he asked from the doorway.

'Better,' she told him simply.

Gates had to duck as he stepped into the room. 'Young Tom has relayed the captain's orders,' he said. 'Undoubtedly he would have expected his first mate to step in had he seen him rescued, but with Jack out of action, you are to take the helm, with Bart and myself at your side for guidance, miss.'

As Fleur struggled to sit up, pain seared through her skull. She'd forgotten all about her uncle's parting commands. 'I told my uncle I wasn't ready,' she protested. 'And anyhow, I'm sure Lieutenant Jack will recover soon.'

'The first mate, or rather *Miss Jenkins*, is in no condition to take command of this ship,' said Gates firmly. 'And he won't be for a while neither by the look in his eye,' he added uncomfortably, shuddering slightly. 'So you must step up.'

'I'm too young. And I'm a girl,' Fleur argued. 'The crew won't have it.'

The bosun removed his hat and stood there awkwardly, fiddling with the brim. 'With respect, young 'un, since when has being a girl ever stood in the way of you doing precisely what you wanted?' He coughed and then blushed a little. 'Sometimes in life, responsibility is thrust upon us, Fleur. This was your uncle's wish, and he probably had good reason.' He tapped his head with a finger. 'Think about it, miss: while his heir controls his ship, no other man but his first and most trusted mate can assume the role. You're caretaking his home and he trusts you to act as he would.'

'But the men won't listen to me,' she protested.

Gates frowned at her. 'Oh, but they will, girl. Show them no fear and lead them forward. Let them know that they have a new mistress. And remember, Bart and I will help you. It takes more than a captain to keep a pirate ship asail, girl.'

Fleur narrowed her eyes and peered at him closely. 'And what of the pair of you? Will you obey my orders as your rightful captain?'

Gates looked away and cleared his throat again.

'Well, sir?' demanded Fleur. 'Tell me honestly, because I trust your counsel.'

The bosun sighed as he met her searching gaze. 'Truthfully,' he admitted, 'I think you are too young. The challenges you'll face would be too much for most full-grown men,' he told her bluntly. 'But I also know that Hart blood runs through your veins and that this is your destiny. I owe William my life and will honour his wishes. I will help you through this.'

Fleur closed her eyes and tried to ignore the pain hammering in her head. 'Thank you,' she murmured.

'But there is something that you must be aware of,' warned Gates.

Fleur snapped her eyes open again. 'What?'

He lowered his voice. 'Your mother, Rose, is quickly becoming a problem. She is vying for authority and already some of the men are falling prey to her charm and reputation. She's known and feared by many among your crew, Fleur, and I'm not sure her intentions are good. There was no love lost between William and Rose when she left your father. And it's not entirely clear that her being aboard is out of a desire to help her old brother-in-law.'

Fleur started shaking with anger. How dare her

mother show up out of the blue and try to take her place! She spoke in a low, firm voice, her fists clenched. 'That woman will not have this ship, not while I or my uncle still live,' she said. 'I have a plan, Gates. Gather the men together and tell them to be ready for me.'

# CHAPTER 12

Fleur made her way up to the main deck, and the rotund sailing master, Carlton Bart, nodded at her supportively as she headed towards Rose Hart. Her mother stood there, resplendent in clothes taken from William's trunk, regaling the men with tales of her recent imprisonment. Fleur paused for a moment, then darted behind a mast so that she could listen and watch unseen. Tom, who had spied her from his perch on top of the binnacle, hopped down to join her, with Grog clinging tightly to his shoulder as he ran.

'Why are you hiding like a stowaway, Cap'n?' he whispered.

'Don't call me that,' she hissed back. 'I ain't your captain.'

Tom raised an eyebrow and leaned against the mast. Grog leaped down from his shoulder and scampered away, tossing the core of an apple behind him. 'But you *are* captain, Fleur, in name and rank,' he tutted at her crossly. 'Don't start moaning about it – I'm too jealous to give a fig.'

'We're going to get the captain back, Tom,' said Fleur, her eyes flashing. 'Things are going to return to normal. Don't you dare leave my side through all this.'

For a split second Tom's face flashed with boyish excitement. Then the smile vanished and his expression darkened. 'You mean us to sail for London, then?'

But Fleur didn't notice her friend's sudden change of mood. Her eyes were drawn back to Rose. It was so strange to see her mother again. She was wearing William's tricorn hat; under the brim her green eyes shone cold and hard like emeralds, and her full lips were as red as blood. She was tall and lean, and her long auburn hair was tied back in a ponytail. Fleur wondered if the black hart tattooed on her neck was to remember what she had left behind. Tears clouded her eyes and she quickly blinked them away. She had often longed to have a mother, but now she felt as if she had traded William for Rose. There were countless questions that she wanted to ask, but there was also a pain and a bitterness that held her back. Fleur felt more vulnerable than ever before. William had become her family, and now he was gone and there was an imposter in his place. As she watched Rose spin her yarns to the captivated crew, Fleur's image of the sweet, loving mother was torn apart and rebuilt from scratch. She didn't recognize this wild-eyed, legendary pirate queen who had cast her aside. But she was bound to be trouble.

'The dungeons were so cold,' Rose recited theatrically. 'Hundreds of stinking prisoners crowded together on a floor covered with cockroaches.' She wrinkled up her nose with distaste. 'It was dark too, except where inmates had paid for a candle – though light only meant you could see the horrors that were better off hidden. The dungeons were near the river, and every day at high tide the foul water would flood past our ankles.' She shivered and drank deeply from a cup of rum. 'When the river rats came swimming in on the tide, looking for a nibble, we could not move in our chains, and could only curl up our toes and hope for the best. 'Twas a living hell, men.' She raised her cup and toasted them. 'But now here I am, and all my toes are intact.'

The crewmen were shouting their approval, but Fleur

could stand it no longer. 'Aye, you're here . . . praise God?' she cried out, striding forward purposefully.

Rose's face froze momentarily. 'Daughter!' she exclaimed, fixing her smile back in place.

Fleur glared at her mother coldly. 'Only in name,' she spat, and then shouldered her to one side, clambering atop a barrel to address her crew in loud, ringing tones. 'Men,' she began, 'you are all aware of Captain Hart's wishes?'

A murmur worked its way round the group, affirmative but hardly happy.

'Aye,' shouted Carlton Bart, stepping in to help Fleur. 'You are to captain the *Dragon* while William is captured.'

Fleur nodded her thanks to the portly sailing master.

'But what about Lieutenant Jack?' Black Matt shouted out. 'We brought him back to this boat. Why can't *he* take command? Surely it's his job as first mate?'

Fleur looked over at Gates, who discreetly shook his head at her. They had already decided not to tell the crew about Jack's madness: it was certain to cause unease.

'Jack was badly injured, but when he's able, he will stand at the helm. For now I am to take control . . . Will you stand by me?' she asked them, her palms sweating, her head aching and her legs a-tremble.

There were more mutterings. Fleur scanned the group nervously as her confidence began to slip away. Rose Hart, however, was a stranger to stage-fright. Plonking herself at Fleur's feet with her hands on her hips, she used the lull to address the crew again.

'Men, what do your instincts tell you?' she asked, tossing her red hair.

'Silence,' ordered Gates. 'You are not crew – you haven't signed the articles and you have no rights here, woman.'

'I want to hear what she says,' shouted Peter Fenn, one of the gunners. There was a chorus of agreement.

Rose glanced at Fleur and smiled coyly. 'All I'm saying is that if we're to elect a captain—' she began.

'We're *not* electing a captain,' said the sailing master impatiently. 'William has named Fleur as she is his blood heir; you ruffians have no say in it.'

'And when William dies he will have no more say in the matter either,' hissed Rose angrily.

'*If* he dies,' said Fleur, staring down at her mother's fiery curls.

Rose eyed her daughter suspiciously, then spun on her heel and began to make her way through the crowd.

'All I'm saying is, for a captain to be great, he – or *she* – must have certain skills. A captain must be learned, bold and brilliant, and above all command respect. A proper captain is the finest sailor and the fiercest fighter among his men.' She stopped and turned to Fleur, flashing a smile. 'Now, if that's my daughter, so be it. You all know her better than I. But if you are merely caught up in William's fondness for the girl, well . . . you would be fools. Word's already out that William the Heartless has gone soft. Would he make you all a laughing stock too? And mark me, his misplaced faith could mean the death of his beloved niece, and every man jack of you too. Let that be on your consciences.'

There was uproar as the crew all started shouting at once. Fleur looked around the sea of troubled faces and panicked. Someone barged into the barrel she stood on, making it wobble dangerously: Rose was right, she thought desperately. She was already losing control. She found Gates among the upturned faces and gazed at him imploringly. This was the moment when she discovered whether he was truly on her side. He held her eyes for a moment; then, without warning, he drew his pistol and fired into the air.

'Silence, you thugs!' he shouted. 'I still wield the whip aboard this ship and will not tolerate this behaviour.

Fleur here has a plan. You will listen to it. And if any of you ruffians has a problem with that, I dare say the good folk of Salem'll be happy to take you in. There's room in Stoughton's jailhouse for starters.'

He nodded over at Fleur to continue. She swallowed down her nervousness and began to speak again.

'I understand your reservations, truly I do,' she said firmly, waving a hand over her slight frame. I hope those who've fought by my side have more faith though. Either way, men, this is a temporary measure. Our true captain lives and breathes, and while I have command of the *Dragon*, by God, this ship and her crew will be dedicated to keeping him in that state. Now, we have a rescue to organize. Are you with me?'

This time a cheer broke out, to Rose's obvious dismay. Her smile vanished as she turned from man to man, snorting and shaking her head dismissively.

'No captain can achieve greatness without the right crew to sail under him,' Fleur continued, staring pointedly at Rose. 'Men, we are the wild things that good people fear and run from in their dreams. We're the greatest pirate crew in the world!'

A roar of approval went up – at which Rose wrinkled her nose in disgust.

'We'll outrun the navy to England and snatch William

– and to Hell with all the King's men.' Fleur paused, staring at the crew with the same intensity that William himself possessed. 'I need the help of every man who's up for the task,' she said solemnly. 'If anyone dares challenge me, do it now. Leave or fight me – either way, you are no longer welcome on this ship.'

The men cheered again. Their support for Fleur's plan was apparently unanimous. Rose began to make her way back to the cabin she had claimed.

'Ready this ship to leave,' Fleur commanded boldly, buoyed by the crew's support. 'Time is short and the crossing long and hard. But first,' she added, spotting her mother as she tried to slip away, 'I have something to take care of.'

'How dare you presume to come aboard this ship!' shouted Fleur. 'And take the captain's cabin, no less!'

Mother and daughter sat facing each other across the table in William's cabin. As Fleur had feared, Rose had clearly been sifting through her brother-in-law's belongings, and Fleur vowed to turn out her mother's pockets before they parted ways again.

'You rescued me!' Rose replied.

Fleur let out her breath and placed cool hands on her hot cheeks. 'I couldn't just leave you to die . . . I . . . I couldn't lose you again . . .' Her throat tightened and her words tailed off. Bitter tears fell onto the table. Suddenly she felt very young again: simply being in her mother's presence made her feel smaller somehow; more vulnerable.

'I had no idea,' said Rose and reached out a hand, but Fleur recoiled as if bitten. She sighed deeply. 'I saw you fight with the Hart staff, child,' she said. 'Your father taught you well. You've clearly inherited his skills in combat. I was impressed . . . thank you for rescuing me.'

Fleur laughed bitterly, and gulped back the tears. 'Yeah, well, that was before I saw for myself what a wicked, scheming hellcat you were.'

'But I'm your mother,' said Rose, hurt. 'I carried you in my belly and suckled you.'

Fleur shook her head. 'No, you severed that bond when you left me to follow your own path. There is nothing left between us. We are strangers.'

Rose stared at her daughter with her beautiful cold eyes. 'You were with me all the time, Fleur. I never stopped loving you.' She reached for the locket around her neck and flipped it open to reveal a tiny pencil sketch of Fleur as a little girl. 'You had a locket of your own with a picture of me.'

Fleur nodded. Her face was hard, but her entire body

was shaking. 'Aye,' she said. 'And I wore it every day of my life until the day I learned the truth of your betrayal.' She studied her mother closely, trying to gauge her sincerity. Rose tried to reach out for her daughter's hand, and though Fleur longed to feel her mother's arms around her, she pulled away again.

'There were many reasons why I left,' Rose explained, clipping her locket shut and tucking it away. 'I knew that if I stayed I would be a terrible mother – worse than none at all. And you deserved better, Fleur. Can you understand? I left to make things better for you, girl. It was the hardest decision that I ever took, but I did it for you. I did what I thought was best.'

'By leaving Father and me to cope on our own,' muttered Fleur bitterly.

'Aye,' Rose replied. 'But I checked up on you both from time to time. I knew you were doing all right.'

'And did you know then that my father – your husband – was murdered in front of my eyes?' Fleur snarled accusingly.

Rose swallowed uncomfortably and shook her head. 'Not for a long time,' she said quietly. 'I had a crew and a fine ship. We were making a name for ourselves in Pacific waters. I'd had no news from English shores for a while . . .' She trailed off, her eyes damp with tears.

'Don't you know how much we both loved you?' said Fleur, her voice cracking with emotion. 'My father never wanted anyone but you. I don't think he ever stopped hoping that you would come home.' She twisted her father's ruby ring round her finger and felt the resentment rise in her throat like bile. 'We needed you. If you'd truly loved us, you could never have walked away so easily.'

Rose laughed bitterly. 'I told you, Fleur,' she said. 'It was the single hardest thing I've ever had to do. But I couldn't stay. Every day on dry land shrivelled my spirits and I died a little more with every dawn. I started to resent the life I'd been led to, and I couldn't stand the notion of that resentment being turned on those I loved most.'

'So you ran,' spat Fleur. 'You could have tried harder. Think what my father gave up. Why couldn't you do the same for him? Or for me? You are weak, selfish and unworthy of your husband's name, Rose Fitzgerald!'

Her mother flinched at the sound of her maiden name and her eyes filled with tears. 'Don't hate me, please,' she begged. 'There were other reasons too. You're too young to understand.'

'I was too young to be abandoned by you,' replied Fleur curtly. 'I missed you every day of my life, *Mother*.'

She tossed her head and laughed bitterly. 'You know, I used to talk to you at night thinking you might hear me from the heavens. I wished on every shooting star that I might one day see you again.'

'Then surely your wish has been granted?'

Fleur pursed her lips and narrowed her eyes, crushing any hope Rose might have had that her words would soften her daughter. 'I never wished for you to spring from nowhere and hijack my life. As captain I could easily have you thrown off this ship, y' know.'

Rose sighed with exasperation and her expression hardened again. 'I'm not trying to usurp you, you silly girl,' she said in exasperation. 'I just don't want you killed, that's all.'

'Ha!' snapped Fleur. 'Don't lie. You want this ship. It's obvious.'

Rose leaned back in her chair and shrugged. 'Aye, fair enough. I'll admit that I've taken to harder ways since we last met, daughter. I've half an eye on any prize that ain't chained down or rooted to the spot. If I see something I want, I take it. Which ain't actually out of step with the notion of the pirate life, after all. Coming to which, it strikes me that you're not quite ready to captain a ship if the notion of plunder gives you the wobbles – whereas I'm a dab hand on a ship that needs a strong arm at the helm.' She looked around William's cabin. 'This one will do nicely.'

Fleur slammed her fist down on the table. 'Over my dead body!' she roared.

Their eyes met and sparked, like clashing blades.

'I don't want you dead, girl, I've already made that clear.' Rose leaned forward and her face was a mask of iron. 'But mark me, daughter, the *Black Dragon* will be mine.'

# CHAPTER 13

Fleur wasted no time weighing anchor and leaving Salem as quickly as possible, with a muttered vow never to return again. With all able men on deck, the *Dragon* was carefully navigated out through the labyrinthine tunnels that had hidden them. Gates stood on the poop deck whistling his orders, and Carlton Bart took the wheel. Tom's arm was still too sore for the climb up to the crow's nest so, armed with a torch, Fleur clambered up in his place to keep a lookout. The Hart flag hung from the mainmast, limp and lifeless in the airless cave; a good reflection of the crew's spirits, thought Fleur with a flash of self-doubt.

Soon, though, they emerged into a bright morning. The sails caught a favourable wind and they raced out of Penance Bay and into the Atlantic, where they saw a horizon dotted with the masts of merchant ships. Fleur screwed up her eyes, hoping to catch a glimpse of the departing *Triumph*. But as she concentrated on the distant sails, she heard a deep guttural moan in the churning waters below and watched as Grog scampered along the ship's rail to peer inquisitively over the side. With squeals of alarm he leaped away and bolted below deck.

Fleur scanned the waves and spotted the huge tail of a humpback whale as it slid gracefully beneath the surface to starboard. More haunting, primal calls issued from the water and she watched in awe as three whales breached the surface together. They slapped down on their backs, revealing their mottled black and white bellies and sending up a spray that started a chorus of oaths from the men on deck. Fleur glanced down at the dripping crew and let out a hearty laugh, then turned back in time to see the whales vanish beneath the bubbling foam again. Their song remained on the air long after they had disappeared, booming and resonating around the ship's wooden flanks. And, as she listened to it, a strange feeling came over Fleur. It was as if the eerie song of the whales was meant for her; as if they had a message to impart.

Fleur thought back to that time when she had dived into the sea, determined to find Jack's precious black pearls. How long ago it seemed now. Then the shark had seemed to awaken the song of the ocean itself. Fleur closed her eyes and listened for the deep note that hummed beneath everything else. Her mind buzzed; it was as if she was immersed in a pool of warm light. And there it was – the low, lulling song of the ocean itself, harmonizing with the whales' cries; and to Fleur's surprise, she suddenly began to understand what they were saying to her:

'*There is trouble ahead, Fleur Hart. Trouble ahead,*' they moaned mournfully. '*Remember who you are, Heart of the Ocean. Your course is set. Stay strong and true, Fleur Hart. Strong and true.*'

And then it was gone; the song, the message and almost the memory. Fleur nearly toppled out of the crow's nest in shock as she gathered her thoughts and struggled to hold onto words she was already unsure she had heard. Had those whales really been speaking to her? Or had she just spent too much time in the sun? She blinked, shook her head and waggled her fingers in her ears to make sure nothing was lodged in there. Maybe the bump on her head had done more damage than anyone had noticed? Then, with a sudden, searing moment of realization, Fleur remembered the staff's prophecy and the line about understanding the language of whales and fish. She gripped the rail of the crow's nest to steady herself. Could it be real after all? Maybe more of the prophecy was coming true? Fleur wished that her Uncle William was with her to offer reassurance. Tom had become moody and distant, Arthur was always busy helping Dr Dubois, and she was still slightly wary of Astrid. Fleur had never felt so alone.

Once she had composed herself, she scrambled down the mast and leaped the last few feet down onto the deck. Carlton Bart met her with a huge map rolled under his arm. He tipped his hat as he approached.

'We're making good time, Captain,' he said with a wink. 'Sailin' close to the wind.'

'Thanks, Bart,' said Fleur, flushing. 'Do you really have to call me that though? It feels strange. We both know which of us is the better sailor.'

The sailing master leaned towards her and spoke

quietly. 'If I don't address you properly, what chance is there of the men doing so, lassie?'

Fleur nodded her understanding and he winked again. 'What are your hopes for catching up with the *Triumph* at sea?' she asked.

'I ain't sure, to be honest,' he admitted. 'But we'll give it our best shot.' He smiled broadly before disappearing into the throng of busy crewmen.

Dr Dubois and Arthur were holding morning surgery by the mainmast, and an untidy, noisy queue sprawled around the deck. Fleur stood alone, wondering what to do next, when she spotted Astrid leaning against the ship's rail.

'Hoa, Astrid,' she called out as she made her way over.

Astrid smiled at her. 'I saw you up in the crow's nest.'

'You should have climbed up and had a look around for yourself,' replied Fleur. 'It's the best view in the world.'

Her friend peered up at the tiny perch and shuddered. 'No thank you, I'm no seagull. I belong upon the earth, and when needs must on a stout boat, not up there among the clouds.' She paused and studied Fleur thoughtfully.

'What is it?' asked Fleur self-consciously. Sometimes Astrid's intensity unnerved her.

'Did you see the whales?'

'Aye,' said Fleur, nodding. 'Three of 'em, but I think there were more lurking beneath.'

'With luck they've moved on by now – look.' Astrid pointed over to a small fleet of narrow, pointed boats. 'Whalers.'

Fleur eyed the flotilla with disgust. The boats had stout posts mounted on their aft decks, around which the men would cinch the rope once a whale had been harpooned. It sickened Fleur to think of those great gentle creatures being dragged to their deaths, but for the people of the bay the trade in oil and bones was a precious lifeline.

Astrid continued to peer at her friend curiously. 'And did you *hear* the whales, Fleur?' she asked outright.

Fleur turned and considered the other girl suspiciously. 'What do you mean?' she asked.

Astrid smiled as she stared out at the rolling waves. A gull dived into the sea before soaring upwards again, a wriggling fish held triumphantly in its beak. 'You are not alone in understanding their song,' she said quietly.

Fleur's mouth dropped open as she stared at her

companion in disbelief. 'Did you just say what I thought you said?' she asked. 'Only—'

Astrid giggled and turned to face her. 'Not all the time,' she said, smiling. 'Only when the moon is full and a few days before; which happens to be now. Sometimes I hear the ocean whispering its secrets too, but the song is distant.'

Fleur bit her lip, thinking of the roaring, deafening song she had heard. She let her friend go on.

'At first I thought it was just the wind in the waves. But it's not, is it? I heard the whales telling you there was trouble ahead,' said Astrid. 'Didn't I? Tell me I'm not going mad, Fleur. Tell me you understand them too.'

Fleur could barely speak as excitement bubbled in her belly. If Astrid could understand whale song, then neither of them was mad. More importantly, it meant she finally had someone with whom she could share her strange experiences. Not a bad booty from a floating barrel, she thought to herself.

'Well, if you're a loony, then so am I.' Fleur beamed delightedly. 'Which makes us a pair of mad witches – by Salem standards at least.'

They held hands and jumped up and down with excitement at this remarkable discovery – though they stopped when they noticed the crewmen beginning to stare.

'I hear the voice of the ocean whenever I listen for it now,' whispered Fleur, more serious again. 'It's a family thing, apparently, though I was never able to trust my own ears until now. Understanding whale song is supposed to be one of the prophecy's gifts.' She paused and frowned. 'So why do you have it too?'

Astrid twisted a lock of her long hair in her fingers. 'I don't know. I know so little of myself that I cannot even tell you whether I was born with the gift or not. For all I know it's a new ability.'

'You once said that I had great potential,' said Fleur. 'But so do you. I think there's more that you might be capable of.'

'Perhaps.' Astrid shrugged. 'Although I wouldn't know where to begin.'

'Well, for a start you could try to control those visions of yours,' suggested Fleur. 'Perhaps you could learn to use them to your advantage.' She gasped suddenly and clapped a hand to her mouth. 'Wouldn't it be strange if we turned out to be related in some way?' she said, grinning at the thought.

For a moment both girls stared at each other, their eyes gleaming with possibilities. Astrid reached out and brushed Fleur's tanned cheek with her cool white hand. 'Blood or not,' she said warmly, 'there is something that binds us.'

# CHAPTER 14

The weeks at sea passed quickly for the crew of the *Black Dragon*. But the journey was not a smooth one. Rose struggled to assert her authority over both Fleur and the crew, which made the men increasingly uneasy. Caught in the middle of a fierce power struggle between mother and daughter, they missed the simple authority of William the Heartless. Jack's presence might have been enough to steady their nerves, but he remained hidden away in his cabin, his changed personality a guilty secret. If it hadn't been for the newcomer, Gates, Fleur would have lost control completely. Beneath the bosun's calm exterior was a man as ruthless and intimidating as Captain

Hart himself. Stare into his eyes for long enough and you began to feel like a small boat tossed about in a very large storm. The men accepted his authority without question. But like Carlton Bart, he was obviously uncomfortable with high office; Fleur effectively stood alone. And all the time, Rose lurked in the background, waiting for a moment of vulnerability.

Tom was no support: he had been moody and withdrawn ever since Astrid's vision and, after Fleur's announcement of her intention to sail to England, downright cantankerous. He spent a lot of time tucked away in the crow's nest, whittling driftwood into splinters. He was lost without his captain, and struggled to know how to behave towards Fleur now. Though they were the best of friends, there had always been competition between them. Now Tom was supposed to bow to her without question, and their friendship was tested to the limit. Even worse, Fleur had begun to suspect that he was keeping something from her. The space between them was widening and she found herself missing Tom almost as much as she did William. Arthur and Astrid were a comfort to her, but they were not Tom. His coldness cut her deeply. Fleur's duties left her exhausted, but whenever she lay down, her head whirled with worries, and sleep was impossible.

Some weeks into their journey scarlet fever began to show itself amongst the pirates. Luckily Dr Dubois spotted the infected men and promptly isolated them at the first signs of fever, so it hadn't spread too widely. But still, the shortage of hands was slowing their pursuit. The responsibility that came with leadership pressed heavily on Fleur's slender shoulders. She felt as if she were swimming through tar.

A few weeks into the crossing, Fleur stood at the prow of the *Dragon* staring at the horizon through her eyeglass. It was late, and the bright crescent moon shone in the vast black sky. Grog had wrapped himself around her neck, much as Parsley, the ship's cat, had once done. The lemur had turned out to be a wonderful companion. He liked to curl up on people like a warm teddy bear, exploring faces and hair with his strong little fingers. He was perfectly suited to life on the *Black Dragon*: his opposable thumbs, long toes and tail, adapted for gripping tree branches, allowed him to jump around the old junk as if it was his personal playground. And he loved to sunbathe. Every morning he found a sunny patch on the main deck and lay with his hands outstretched, as if worshipping a sun god. He was sociable like a dog, as cuddly as a cat and as gracefully acrobatic and cheeky as monkey.

Somewhere in the bowels of the ship, Fleur could hear Gates playing his violin, with Astrid's sweet voice accompanying him. Her song told the sad story of a lonely mermaid who fell in love with a man and lured him down to her kingdom of coral, only to learn that humans will drown without air to breathe. So in love was she that she split her tail in two and gave up her golden voice to a sorceress so she might walk beside him on the land. But her love abandoned her for another woman and left her alone for all eternity. Fleur hugged herself against a sudden gust of wind as she listened to the song. She felt sad for the mermaid, but she was cross with her too. How foolish to give up her birthright and surrender her happiness to the needs of another.

Behind Fleur a small group of pirates were huddled in a circle, some playing cards for money. Rose held court there, just as drunk and rowdy as the men around her. Fleur scowled at her mother, then tensed as someone sidled up beside her. She relaxed again when she turned to see Arthur. He stood in a pool of lantern light, looking tired and grey.

'Are you all right, Arthur?' she asked, tucking her telescope into her belt.

Arthur lifted his glasses and massaged the bridge of his nose, yawning. 'I'm fine, but if I drop off, pinch me,' he told her. 'Dr Dubois told me to get some fresh air before I fell asleep on a patient. What with Jack and the fever . . .' The wind carried the sound of Astrid's song to them, and he sighed. 'I love her voice,' he murmured dreamily.

Fleur smiled to herself in the darkness as Arthur gazed up at the moon, a huge star glowing beneath it.

'That star could be one of Jack's big diamond earrings,' he said.

Fleur laughed, but her heart lurched as she thought of Jack raving in his cabin and William clapped in irons aboard the *Triumph*. 'Do you think they'll be all right, Arthur?' she asked in a small voice.

Arthur sighed wearily but didn't reply.

'Arthur?' she prompted.

'I don't know,' he answered quietly. 'Hasn't Astrid had one of her handy visions lately?'

Fleur shook her head and picked at a splinter in the ship's rail. 'We're not going to get there in time,' she worried aloud. 'We're going to be too late.'

'The *Black Dragon* is the fastest ship afloat, Fleur,' Arthur reassured her. 'Even if we don't catch them on the way over, we won't be far behind them when they reach port.'

Fleur nodded, hoping he was right. 'The crew have

started asking more questions about Jack,' she said. 'They reckon he's dying or cursed. But Gates says I can't tell 'em what's really wrong with him in case they think it's a bad omen.' She sighed and looked out at the churning black water. 'And maybe it is.'

They stood in silence, listening to the *Dragon* creaking comfortingly, like an old rocking chair, and the sea lapping at the hull below. Arthur swayed against the rail as he fought to stay awake.

Fleur poked him hard in the ribs. 'Wake up, sleepy-head,' she laughed.

Arthur let out a loud yawn. 'Sorry.' He rubbed his tired eyes with the balls of his fists.

'Forget it.' Fleur grinned. 'I know how you feel. Are your patients getting any better down there?'

Arthur nodded. 'Jack remains the same,' he smiled, 'and the fever has broken; now they've just got these little red sores all over them.'

'It sounds disgusting,' said Fleur, shocked.

'It is a bit,' admitted Arthur. 'But Dr Dubois says that they were lucky to have all survived and the rash means they'll be better soon. A few days at most, he reckons.'

'Well done,' said Fleur, slapping her friend on the back. 'I thought they were goners when those chills came on. White as ghosts, they were.'

Arthur beamed with pride. 'We didn't use liqueur cordials – Dr Dubois reckoned that would fuel their fever,' he told her. 'He prescribed blood-letting.'

Fleur scrunched up her face in disgust. 'What?' she exclaimed. 'Are you sure that was wise, in their condition?'

Arthur nodded enthusiastically and pushed his glasses up his nose. 'Absolutely. All very modern. Very scientific. We've been using it on Lieutenant Jack too.' He raised his left hand and pinched the tip of his little finger with the thumb and forefinger of his other hand. 'Let me remember . . .' he began, warming to his subject. 'The vein above the thumb is bled to lessen all fevers . . . the vein between thumb and the forefinger lets blood for a hot headache, for frenzy . . . and madness of wit, as in Jack's case.' He paused, eyes bright. 'Now that the symptoms are abating we're going to purge the patients with laxatives. That means—'

'I know what it means,' Fleur interrupted, clamping her hands over her ears. 'No more talk of blood-letting or bowel movements, thank you very much, Doctor.'

Arthur chuckled and saluted smartly. 'Aye, aye, Captain Hart,' he said. 'You sail your ship and I'll tend to my patients. Each to their own, eh?'

They shook hands and stared out over the ink-black

water, each one comforted by the other's company. Fleur examined Arthur's familiar profile fondly and thought to herself for the umpteenth time how important it was to keep good friends about her. No matter how wild the journey, your friends would always keep you on course. She only hoped that Tom would remember that too.

As Fleur made her way to her cabin for some much-needed sleep, she decided to drop in on Jack. Perhaps, she thought, he'd be more like his old self now. As she turned a corner in the narrow corridor, she saw Jack's cabin door swing open. Shrinking back into the shadows, Fleur watched as Rose slipped out furtively. What was her meddling mother up to now?

She knocked gently and went into the cabin, gagging on the pungent aroma of boiled herbs and animal fat. Jack lay with his eyes closed, and Fleur noticed with alarm that he was bound to his bed with leather straps. A lump of dried coral sat on his bedside table – a sailor's charm to ward off madness. The candlelight cast flickering shadows on the walls and the burning wick crackled in the silence. Fleur took a tentative step towards her troubled shipmate. The floor creaked and his red eyes flicked open.

'Oh my, another visitor,' he simpered. 'I thought you

were that other girl. She said she'd bring me some lavender water, sweet thing.'

'Did she now?'

'Yes.' Jack nodded. 'And we had the most delightful conversation.'

Fleur stared down at him miserably. His damp white hair clung to his head and his eyes were vacant wells. Jack was still as mad as ever. *And now that Rose knew the truth, what mischief would she make of it?* Fleur wondered. Her mood altogether darker than the soothing face she presented to the rambling first mate suggested, Fleur backed away, smiling and nodding. Jack prattled on to the air as she turned away to find her bed.

The following morning Fleur was in the galley brewing tea for breakfast. She'd never tasted tea before setting sail with William. Back in England it was the preserve of wealthy gentlemen and fashionable townsfolk. Not so at sea, where all were equal, up to a point, and she'd quickly discovered an unquenchable thirst for the stuff. She hummed as she stirred the leaves in the steaming pot.

'Do you want a cup of tea, Toby?' she asked the cook, who was sitting in the corner reading while he waited for a huge pan of eggs to boil.

'No thank ye, lassie,' he replied, without looking up.

'Suit yourself,' said Fleur, pouring a mug for herself. She had just taken a large gulp when the sound of angry voices drifting through the galley walls made her ears prick up. It was Tom and Arthur, and from what she could tell, there was an almighty row underway. She stepped out into the passageway to make out their words.

'Patrick said *I* was to fix these hatches,' Arthur was shouting indignantly. 'I told him it needed doing and that I could do the job. He told *me* to go about it, not you.'

'Yeah, well,' came Tom's angry reply, 'he's probably still delirious with fever.'

'He's as fit as a fiddle, and a good deal of that is down to me too,' said Arthur. 'Anyway, I thought you couldn't work because your arm was bothering you.'

There was a pause, followed by the sounds of a scuffle.

'Let me do it,' barked Tom from below. 'You'll only mess it up.'

'I will not!' exclaimed Arthur. 'You only want to do it because it's my job. Why can't you leave off?'

'Shut up, doctor's pet!'

'How dare you!' Arthur shouted. 'I've had enough of

your snide comments. You've been in a mood ever since we set sail again. Anyone would think you didn't want to rescue Captain Hart. Well, I for one have had enough. If you've got a problem, why don't we have it out now?'

'All right then,' said Tom. 'About ruddy time.'

More scuffling; louder this time.

With Grog close at her heels, Fleur dashed towards the source of the rumpus. As she rounded a corner, she caught sight of the two boys rolling about on the floor beside a broken hatch. They were wrestling fiercely for possession of a boarding axe, and though Tom's arm was still bandaged, he seemed to be getting the better of Arthur.

'Stop it, both of you!' Fleur shouted loudly, startling the boys, who flew apart like repelling magnets.

Tom held the axe aloft victoriously. 'Hah!' he cried.

'What's going on?' Fleur demanded, her hands on her hips and a fierce frown on her face.

Arthur cleared his throat to speak but Tom got there first, as usual.

'Arthur thinks he can fix this broken hatch,' he said, pointing up at the teak door that had almost come off its hinges. It looked like a tooth that needed pulling.

'And I can too,' Arthur cut in. 'It's common sense.'

Tom laughed scornfully. 'It's brawn that's needed, not brains, you codfish. You haven't the strength to do the job properly.'

Arthur snatched the axe away from Tom. 'And you haven't the wits to work out what needs doing in the first place,' he retorted.

Tom puffed out his chest and pushed Arthur hard. Arthur stumbled over the tools that lay at his feet and landed with a painful thump on his behind.

Tom burst out laughing.

'Tom!' Fleur snapped a warning, then turned to Arthur, who was scrambling back to his feet, his face as red as port wine. 'Are you all right, Arthur?'

'I'm fine,' he blustered, embarrassed.

'I don't understand why the pair of you can't work together,' Fleur sighed. 'With your brains, Arthur, and your brawn, Tom, you'd get these hatches fixed in no time. And anyway,' she added crossly, 'this isn't a priority – we have a ship's carpenter to deal with this when he's better. You two should be doing your own work.'

The two boys frowned at each other.

'Oooo, get you, Cap'n,' teased Tom.

Arthur nodded, and for a brief moment the two boys were united against Fleur.

'That *was* a bit stern, Fleur,' Arthur admonished.

Fleur's cheeks burned red and she scowled at them both.

'Anyway, I'd rather work with Grog,' Tom sneered, nodding down at the lemur. 'He'd be of more use to me.'

Arthur gave a strange cry like a cat being strangled, and suddenly hurled himself at Tom again. Tom's eyes widened at the unexpected assault and he stumbled backwards, with Arthur's fists flailing at his chest and stomach. Grog hopped up into Fleur's arms, squeaking and chattering with fear.

'I wish you'd get eaten by a flock of seagulls,' Tom shouted, knocking Arthur to the ground again and leaping on him.

'And I wish I hadn't bothered saving your life that time, back on the Island of Secrets,' Arthur retorted furiously as the two boys wrestled and rolled around the room. 'One more night and that fever would have killed you!' Arms and legs locked together, they crashed into the ancient wood-panelled wall. There was a loud crack, and everyone immediately fell silent.

'What happened?' Fleur gasped, joining the boys by the damaged wall.

They all stared into the huge, ragged hole.

'You broke it!' said Tom, staring accusingly at Arthur.

Arthur glared back indignantly. '*You* broke it!'

Fleur rolled her eyes and studied the damage. 'It was both of you, you idiots,' she groaned, kneeling down to inspect the damage. 'It's completely destroyed. The wood is so old, the whole panel will have to be replaced.'

Arthur sat down beside her and cautiously peered into the hole. Tom tutted and squatted down next to them. He started wrenching away the splintered panel. A handful of creepy crawlies and one oily rat scurried out of their hiding place.

Fleur shuddered involuntarily. 'What *is* in there aside from the wildlife?' she asked curiously. 'I thought we'd bust through to one of the cabins. Only . . .'

Arthur stuck his head in and quickly pulled it out again, a thick cobweb dangling from his nose. 'It looks like a tiny room,' he said, wiping away the cobweb with disgust. 'There are some things piled up in there, but it's too dark to see what they are. Do you think Captain Hart knew about this?'

Fleur shrugged. 'I don't know.'

'I'll get a lantern – hang on,' said Tom eagerly.

'All right.' Fleur nodded. 'But don't tell anyone about this yet.'

Tom dashed off, returning moments later with a swinging lantern. By that time Arthur and Fleur had already removed the rest of the damaged panel and were staring into the small, dark space nervously. The air in there was dank and musty with undisturbed age. Grog peered in too, then scrabbled backwards and darted away.

'It must be a hidden room,' Arthur mused.

'Really?' Tom replied with sarcasm.

Fleur poked him in the stomach and turned to Arthur. 'But what for?' she asked, her eyes widening. 'Treasure?'

Tom strode over and set the lantern on the floor next to the shattered panel. Candlelight flickered over the room and cast strange, spindly shadows on the dark walls. 'I doubt it,' he said. 'Pirates seldom hoard their treasure. It's won, shared out and quickly spent, more often than not. No, I reckon this is for something else.'

Fleur's skin prickled and her heart pounded. What could be waiting for them in that little room?

'I'm going in,' Tom announced, picking up the lantern and checking its flickering flame. Fleur and Arthur nodded, both relieved that someone else had taken the initiative.

'Do you think we should get Gates or Bart?' Fleur asked, gently restraining Tom with a hand on his shoulder.

Tom shrugged her off. 'Once we know what we've

found, aye – but why wait? The harm is already done.'
He snapped another chunk of splintered wood from the
panel and grinned at Fleur. 'If I'm not back in an hour,'
he joked, 'send for help.'

He bent over and stepped carefully through the
missing panel, taking care to avoid the jagged splinters.
The lantern's flame flickered in the darkness, throwing
shadows into the corner of the hidden room. Tom took
a step forward, and another large rat scrambled over the
boards to escape. He held up the light to reveal a thick
curtain of cobwebs.

'Yeuch,' he called back to Fleur and Arthur, 'I think
something big just crawled down the back of my neck.'
He wriggled about uncomfortably as he scanned the
gloom.

'Rather him than me,' Arthur muttered to Fleur.

'Don't be a sissy,' said Fleur. 'Come on.' And she
dragged him through the panel to join Tom.

As their eyes gradually became accustomed to the
dim light, they were aware of many objects heaped up
against the walls.

'What's that?' Arthur asked, pointing at a haphazard
pile of shiny things, layered in yet more dusty cobwebs.

Tom held up the lantern and shuffled towards it. His
bare foot squashed something crunchy and he shuddered.

'Weapons, I think,' he said with interest, 'but like nothing I've seen before. Hang on, there's a mirror.' Tom wiped dust off the glass of an old mirror and set the lantern on the floor before it. Light bounced off the mottled glass to fill the room with a twilight glow. They all gasped as one. They were in an armoury. A vast number of brutal-looking weapons were crammed into the small space. Tom picked up a long spear with a serrated crescent blade attached to the head and a horsehair tassel where the head met the shaft. He swished it through the air, cutting down invisible enemies.

'This is excellent, I want this one!' he enthused. He suddenly looked sad and lowered the spear. 'William would have loved this,' he sighed.

'What's that there?' Fleur asked as the lantern light glinted off something in the far corner of the room.

Tom put down the spear and walked over to where Fleur was pointing. He recoiled, cursing loudly.

'What is it?'

But Tom was already clambering out through the broken panel.

'What is it?' repeated Fleur, scared now and turning to follow him out.

'Bones,' said Tom. 'And I think they might be human.'

★

Fleur dashed away to find Gates and dragged him straight down to the hidden room, ignoring his grumpy protestations about needing to keep the crew in line. His gruffness gave way to slack-jawed surprise when he peered through the shattered panel into the hidden room.

'I'll need a little more space,' he murmured, running a finger along the ragged hole. He pulled a small axe from his belt and raised it high above his head. 'Let's have the rest of this kindling out then.'

'Wait!' Arthur shouted, holding up his hands.

Gates froze mid-swing and glared at him impatiently. 'What now, boy?' he barked. 'Speak up or shut up. I want to know what secrets this ship's carrying before night falls.'

Arthur pointed into the dark space nervously. 'There's men's bones – *skeletons*, sir. They must have been guarding what was in there. They might be diseased, or . . . or cursed. Perhaps you should go about this with more caution?'

Gates looked at him scornfully and swung the axe high again. 'There ain't nothing holy on this vessel,' he insisted. 'And one more curse wouldn't harm me at any rate – I was already among the damned since before I could even grow a beard.' He furrowed his brow and spoke again. 'I ain't afraid of the plague either. I've got too much salty crust for the evil air to reach me. Now, we all know that William would want us to find out, so stand aside while I open up this hole, boy, or I'll open you up too.'

In three swift strikes, the bosun had removed what was left of the wall. Soon he was rooting through the clutter like a prize pig snuffling for truffles, oblivious to the macabre pile of dry bones. The others were more cautious. They stood on the threshold holding lanterns and peering in nervously.

'There *are* good weapons here,' Gates announced as he blew dust from a small, sharp double-headed axe. 'Lethal-looking things,' he chuckled. 'From all over the world, I reckon. They must have been here for years.'

'And what do you make of 'em, sir?' asked Fleur.

The bosun grunted as he poked at the piled bones with his cutlass. Then he reached forward and grabbed a human skull, which he turned in his hands like a merchant examining pottery. 'Hmmm,' he said thoughtfully. 'Now, why would these men hide themselves away in here for a few weapons?'

'There must be something else, sir,' Arthur said.

'Exactly,' Gates agreed heartily, tossing the skull aside.

Fleur winced as he dropped to his knees and started rummaging through the mottled old bones. He showed no respect at all for the men who once owned them. Again she wanted to know what had happened to make him so hard-hearted, and resolved to find out before they reached land again.

'Hold up that lantern, lad,' Gates instructed Tom.

Light swung into the corner and the bosun cried out with delight. 'Got it!' he announced, and grabbed a long, cylindrical bamboo tube that had been covered in a thick mesh of cobwebs.

'What is it, sir?' asked Arthur.

'I'll tell you just what it is,' said Gates, blowing dust from his mysterious find.

At that moment Carlton Bart came bustling down the corridor. He saw the small group huddled around their prize and frowned.

'What's all this then?' he demanded suspiciously. He strode over to the hole in the wall and peered in.

'We found a secret room, sir,' explained Arthur.

'Evidently,' said Bart. He turned to look at the bamboo tube in Gate's hands. 'And what's that, man?' he asked the bosun.

'We're just about to find out,' Gates replied

They all gathered around Gates and the bamboo tube

and watched. The tube was narrow and about as long as Fleur's arm; it looked ancient – the Chinese characters painted on the side had almost entirely faded away. Iron discs were jammed into each end and sealed with a rubbery sap so that it was water- and air–tight, so Gates drew a small knife from his belt to break the sticky seal. A disc fell out, clattering to the deck, but no one bothered to pick it up; they were all too eager to see what the tube held. The bosun peered in and grinned broadly as he gently prised out a large rolled sheet.

'What's that?' Fleur asked, nudging Tom to one side so that she could see more clearly.

'Vellum,' said Bart knowledgeably. 'Rabbit skin – it's more durable than parchment.'

Gates unravelled the roll carefully. It was so thin that the old skin was rendered transparent by the bright sunlight.

Arthur gasped loudly, his mouth flopping open and shut like a landed fish. 'Gosh,' he exclaimed. 'Now I'm starting to feel like a real pirate.'

Tom did little to disguise his scorn. Bart laughed, slapping Arthur on the shoulder as he spoke. 'Right you are, lad. A real pirate always knows a treasure map when he sees one.'

★

Fleur ordered some of the crew to move the weapons out of the tiny room and into the ship's main armoury and fetched Astrid to share the exciting news. Then she spread the rabbit-skin map out flat on a table in her cabin, anchoring the corners with small cannon balls. Carlton Bart stared down at it while Fleur, Tom, Arthur, Astrid and Gates pressed eagerly around him. He pored over the fading pen-work in delight. Tom had seen plenty of treasure maps on his travels with William, but his friends had never seen anything like it before. Fleur stared at the images of skulls, tombstones, sunken ships and jagged mountains: a clear warning to treasure hunters that there was terrible hardship and danger in store for them. The faint drawings seemed to dance beneath the flickering candlelight. At times, Fleur thought, they almost looked as if they were alive. A compass rose in one corner showed them north, south, east and west, and a large cross of gold leaf marked the spot where the treasure was hidden. Carlton Bart traced his finger over the outline of the land, and as he did so, a frown gathered on his face.

'What is it, sir?' Tom asked.

Bart exhaled loudly and looked up from the map with tired eyes. 'I don't recognize the lay of the land, boy. Look' – he pointed to a cluster of islands – 'I know every island from here to Hong Kong and I swear on this ship that this map is false. The headland here – I know it well. But these islands, they simply ain't there. They don't exist.'

'Maybe it's because it's a really old map, sir,' Tom suggested.

Bart shook his head. 'I don't think so,' he said. 'I've seen maps even older than this that charted a truer course. Besides, islands don't vanish in their old age. And here too' – he indicated a large area of open water – 'there should be land here, however old the map may be. Land that ain't there and islands that are when they shouldn't be – this map is for fools. It charts a path to ruin and nothing else.'

'But, sir,' Arthur piped up, 'how can you be sure? No man can know every point on every map.'

Bart slammed his hand down on the table, making them all flinch. 'You dare question my knowledge and experience, boy?' he boomed, happy for the opportunity to vent his frustration on someone.

Arthur shrank away from him, stammering apologies. The sailing master narrowed his eyes and stared at the boy coldly. He was normally a placid man, but with William absent, the stresses of helping to captain the *Dragon* were starting to show.

'I've travelled the whole world over,' he hissed, his voice almost a whisper. 'I've studied maps since before I could read to name the lands they showed. Sea water runs in my veins, boy. So if I tell ye I know every coast and cove, every island and outcrop in the ocean, you'd best take my word for it. Do we understand each other? Do you think a captain as fine as William would let me sail with him otherwise?'

Arthur's cheeks were flaming. 'I'm sorry for speaking out of turn, sir,' he muttered.

But Bart was not to be placated. He turned to Tom. 'Fetch the charts from my cabin, boy. Lay them out here. I'll give young Arthur here a chance to try and prove me wrong.'

'I really don't need to—' Arthur began hopelessly.

'Go on,' he insisted.

'I'll help,' said Fleur eagerly, relieved to find an excuse to escape the tension in the room.

It took her and Tom three trips to carry Bart's extensive collection of maps from his cabin to hers.

'You know,' Tom suggested on the second trip, 'we could just take that one map to your cabin.'

Bart just glared at him. Arthur was set the task of checking the treasure map against the newer charts. It was a laborious enterprise, and the others, Bart included, soon tired of watching him. So they slipped into the armoury for a closer look at the haul of exotic new weapons. There were sabres and spears, swords and staves, stakes, slingshots, daggers and axes, whips and barbed chains and hooked arrowheads, each item spelling pain and death. Fleur eyed Tom discreetly. He had been jolted out of his permanent state of melancholy, and was kneeling in the middle of the deadly loot, as happy as a hippo in a mud hole. Fleur herself felt nothing but sadness at the images of fighting and killing that the weapons conjured up. Tom was reacting much like William would have done . . . She was missing her uncle more than ever. Where was he now? she wondered. She didn't even know for sure if he was still alive. Fleur bowed her head, shut her eyes tight, and tried not to think about the bloody end that threatened all pirates.

It took Arthur a long time to cross-reference the treasure map with every corner of Bart's charts – whereupon he glumly announced his conclusion: the same one that the sailing master had reached at a glance. The map was bogus. The lands it depicted were not real.

'At least, not entirely,' he explained. 'There are bits of it that match real lands here and there, but it doesn't hang together.'

'Like I said in the first place,' declared Bart triumphantly.

'There may still be something in it,' Arthur asserted, a little defensively.

'Aye, lad, there may yet be,' said Gates. 'We'll share it with William – God hope we meet him again. But now there's no more we can do.'

# CHAPTER 15

As their long journey continued, the crew of the *Dragon* began to realize that, barring a miracle, they weren't going to catch up with the *Triumph* after all. Morale plummeted to a new low and Fleur knew that she had to act fast to stave off further trouble. In consultation with Gates and Bart, a new plan was formed, and Fleur gathered the men on the main deck to share it with them. It was a blustery day and the wind was as cold and hard as the faces that stared up at Fleur expectantly. It had been easy to be plucky and carefree around the crew when William was here, keeping them firmly in check. But without his iron hand, they grew restless, quarrelsome and increasingly unpredictable. Rose was a brooding presence, but kept herself to herself, glowering at her daughter when their paths crossed.

Fleur tried to swallow and found that her throat was suddenly dry. She coughed instead and forced herself to speak. 'A new course, men,' she announced firmly, though her voice cracked. 'We sail to Cornwall first.' She stood on the poop deck, looking down on the grumbling crewmen. 'We all know there is little hope of meeting the *Triumph* before she reaches British waters,' she continued. 'So all that matters is that we reach London without running into trouble. We'll need to ditch the *Dragon*, men.'

A mumble of disquiet passed through them. A few called for an explanation.

'Is this not the most feared ship on the seven seas?' asked Fleur, rousing a smattering of 'Aye's and 'Hear-hear's. 'Then how far do you think she would get up the Thames before we were blasted by cannonfire from both banks?'

'We disguised her well enough in New England,' someone piped up from the back.

'Aye, but that was under the cover of night, and anyhow, they might well be expecting us to show up in

London. So,' Fleur began assertively, 'we need to hide the *Dragon* and – ahem – borrow something a little less conspicuous.'

'Why Cornwall though?' Black Matt interjected. 'It will add days to our journey. Days the captain may not have.'

Fleur sought out his face in the crowd and addressed him directly. 'I know a place where we can stow the *Dragon* without fear,' she told him. 'A smuggler's cove cut into the hillside. Nothing so grand as Penance Bay, mind, but my father, Henry Hart, shared its secret with me and I know it will do to hide our ship. If we set course now and waste no time, we'll only lose a couple of days.'

'The child means Pepper Cove, lads,' said Carlton Bart. 'A place that some of us know well.'

'But we'll need to find another ship and capture it!' said Rose from amongst the men. She nudged them aside so that there was a clear line of sight between Fleur and herself. 'A few more precious days added to your rescue plan, *dearie?*' she added condescendingly.

'But if we all work together we can make up the time,' replied Fleur.

Rose narrowed her eyes and smiled slyly. 'Aye, though with a curse on the ship our fate is surely sealed.'

'What are you talking about?' Fleur demanded. 'What curse?'

Rose took another step towards her daughter and met her glare. 'Rumour has it that the first mate has been restrained in his cabin, possessed by evil spirits.'

'Nonsense,' boomed Carlton Bart. 'The man has a fever.'

Rose gave a shrill laugh. 'A fever that has him thinking he's a fine lady?' she scoffed. 'I think not.'

The men all began shouting at once. 'It must be true,' someone called out. 'The lieutenant brought evil down upon himself and all of us when he traded with that Salem witch.'

'What witch?' asked Fleur. 'I know nothing of this.'

One of the men stepped forward. Boneless Bill had been part of the original landing party when they arrived in Salem. He was a quiet sort, most of the time, perhaps because he spent most of his time alone in the rigging, where his flexible climbing skills had earned him his nickname. Bill wasn't slow to speak up when he thought he knew something important, though, and now was one of those times. 'Pardon me, miss, but the witch said she was selling the wind,' he muttered. 'Jack bought a magical hawser from her that she said would bring the wind for our journeys.'

Fleur rolled her eyes in exasperation. A hawser was a simple ship's rope; gullible, superstitious sailors all over the world were often conned out of their earnings by so-called wind-sellers and their magical wares.

'See,' Rose bellowed, turning to the men for support. 'The first mate has brought magic and misfortune to all of us.' She paused to point at Fleur. 'And you, girl, have been lying to us.'

There was uproar, and Fleur waved her arms about desperately. 'Silence at once!' she shouted over the din, and the pirates' roars turned to mutters. 'Bill,' she ordered, 'fetch this hawser. We'll burn it and tip the ashes overboard right now so we can put a stop to this nonsense. As for the first mate, he *will* get better and is certainly not cursed. He took a blow to the head that would've cracked a cannonball, but he's in good hands and on the road to recovery. You were not told about his condition to avoid undue panic, but I assure you,' she said, crossing her fingers behind her back and biting her lip hard, 'everything's going to be just fine.'

Fleur scowled furiously at her mother. She'd been wondering when Rose would start to stir things up. They had barely spoken since their last argument, and there was a wall of resentment between them. She looked to Tom, Astrid and Arthur for support. The three of them were sitting together on empty barrels. Astrid and Arthur smiled back at her, nodding encouragingly, but to her surprise Tom stayed still and silent. Fleur clenched her fists in irritation. What was his problem?

'Anyway, call yourselves pirates?' she snapped at the men, making more than one of them flinch. 'I warrant you'd show less yellow if William the Heartless was at the helm! How can you be scared by a man rambling harmless nonsense? When have you ever feared taking a ship before?'

'And when have *you* ever taken a ship at all, little miss?' purred Rose. 'Do you think it's easy? We could be sailing around the coast till Christmas. And if we pick the wrong target—' She stopped short and drew a finger across her throat theatrically. 'How would that serve my brother-in-law?'

Fleur almost choked with fury. 'Don't you dare call him that!' she raged, shaking a fist in her mother's direction. 'You gave up any claim to kinship when you left us, a lifetime ago.'

Rose thrust her hands on her hips and opened her mouth to respond, but Gates got in first. He stood in front of the poop deck, his arms folded across his chest. 'Till Christmas, you say?' he asked Rose sarcastically. 'What manner of amateur crew have you been sailing with, Lady Pirate?'

The men laughed heartily at that, and for once Rose had the decency to blush. She pushed William's tricorn hat down over her eyes and peered out moodily from under the brim, before quietly backing away.

'Here's how I see it,' the bosun began with an air of authority that Fleur envied. 'William will be tried before the hangman gets his hands on him, which gives us a window of opportunity. We can't be far behind the *Triumph*, and a brief detour won't scupper our plans. Bart here knows the Cornish waters well; we'll cut through the water like a shark and take the first likely vessel. Some of us will sail the *Dragon* to Cornwall. After that, the better half of us will journey on to London under stolen sails and get our captain back, by God.' He turned and nodded curtly at Fleur to continue.

'We've got one shot at saving him,' she said, staring down at the crew with all the confidence she could muster. 'There will be challenges to face, but we shall face them head-on and with the courage our reputation demands. We owe it to Captain Hart.'

A cheer broke out; Gates winked up at her and surreptitiously patted her foot. 'Spoken like a true Hart,' he whispered.

Fleur smiled, but the warm moment withered with the unexpected appearance of Jack – or was it Jacqueline? – Jenkins. Somehow, he had slipped his bonds and was now parading in a sheet wrapped around his shoulders like a shawl, every bit of jewellery he owned glittering at his neck and ears and wrists. Rose appeared behind him, smiling triumphantly. The gobsmacked pirates could only stare as their first mate walked by, babbling to himself in his strange new high-pitched voice and fluttering his eyelashes at them.

'A curse, I tell ye!' bellowed Rose. 'Lieutenant Jack *has* lost his mind and we will be next.' She pointed at Fleur accusingly. 'You've damned us all, you stupid girl.'

The men started shouting again, sending Jack scuttling over to Fleur in a state of terror. He hid his face behind his improvised skirt as she spoke.

'Don't listen to her,' she cried over the roar of noise. 'There's no curse. 'Twas the butt of a gun, not by the blight of a witch, that knocked the senses out of him.'

217

Gates sent up a shrill warning whistle to quieten the crew.

'We'll see,' sneered Rose.

'No, the girl is correct.' The voice had a strong French accent. To everyone's surprise Dr Dubois had appeared above deck. He looked tired and his once magnificent grey moustache and neatly cut hair were shaggy and unkempt, but he remained dignified and composed. He calmly walked over to Jack and gently took his arm. 'Your lieutenant will recover,' he said firmly and nodded at Fleur, 'just as your captain asserts.'

Rose strode over to the doctor with her hands on her hips. 'And how do we know that you're not lying to protect her?' she demanded.

Dr Dubois shrugged dismissively. 'With the captain gone, I owe nothing to anybody on this ship. I was brought here by force, though I have been treated well. Frankly, I do not care if you all tear yourselves to pieces. But I am a doctor, and while I am here I will do my job to the best of my ability, as I would anywhere. That is who I am. If I lose who I am, I will have lost everything to this godforsaken ship.'

Fleur nodded at him gratefully, sorry for the lonely man. He turned to leave, taking Jack's arm.

'Are you satisfied now that you've stirred the hornet's nest, woman?' Gates snapped at Rose. He raised his voice to address the men. 'Don't listen to the hissing of this hellcat, men. She is the true liar here. If any of you have concerns about the lieutenant, come to me. Otherwise the next person who tries to stir up this hornet's nest again will be dunked from the yardarm.'

The sound of the bosun's whistle dispersed the men and normal duties were promptly resumed. Fleur sighed with relief as she watched the activity on deck, but a frown furrowed her brow. The crew had been won round this time, but who knew if it would last? Especially while her scheming mother remained aboard.

That evening Fleur followed the sound of Gates's haunting violin to find him sitting on the poop deck. The atmosphere aboard the *Dragon* remained calm after the earlier mutinous mutterings and Jack's sudden appearance. It had been a long day, but Fleur had kept a sharp eye on everyone, not least Rose, and now she was almost delirious with fatigue. There was a storm rolling in and the boiling black mass of cloud had all but swallowed up the last patches of blue sky. Thunder boomed and lightning flickered, sending Grog dashing below decks.

The bosun stopped playing as Fleur approached and he examined her quizzically.

'Please don't stop on my account, sir,' she said, bowing slightly. 'Your playing soothes me.'

Gates drew his bow smoothly across the strings, sending a pure note skywards like a homesick angel. 'I'm glad you like it,' he said. 'Your uncle did too. He said that a violin sings like a woman's voice.'

'What do you mean, sir?' asked Fleur as she climbed up to stand beside him.

He played a bold, stabbing series of notes. He closed his eyes and his face twitched with the flow of the music. 'How does that sound to you?' he asked.

'I don't know . . .'

He smiled and played again. 'Go on,' he urged. 'Tell me how it makes you feel.'

Fleur thought for a moment. 'Bold,' she suggested. 'Strong and proud too, maybe?'

Gates switched to a gentler tune that darted around like a coney in the shadow of a hawk. 'And this?' he asked.

Fleur grinned. 'Timid,' she replied. 'Small and shy.'

Gates nodded. 'Aye, miss, my fiddle has different

moods just like we do.' He tucked the violin back under his chin and treated her to a dizzying medley of jigs and reels, airs and laments, each one stirring a different feeling in her belly.

She sighed deeply and slumped to the deck beside the bosun, suddenly overcome.

He set his instrument aside. 'I see you have troubles that need sharing, miss,' he said astutely. 'Will you sit and talk a while?'

'Aye. Thank you.' Fleur stared up at the stars; the thunder clouds had suddenly changed course with the wind and the night air felt cool and calm. It seemed they would avoid a lashing from the storm.

Gates pulled a small hemp parcel from his pocket and unwrapped it to reveal a personal hoard of New England peppermint drops. 'From Sarah Wardwell,' he said with a grin, jiggling the sweets under her nose. 'Want one?'

Fleur nodded vigorously. She had long since gone through her own supply. 'Thanks,' she said as she took one and popped it in her mouth. 'I'm amazed you've managed to hang onto them for this long. Don't tell Tom — he won't rest till he finds a way to part them from you.'

Gates chuckled as he took one himself and

rolled it under his tongue. Fleur studied him surreptitiously as they sat in companionable silence, quietly enjoying their peppermint drops. Only a little while ago she had been nervous of George Gates. Now, she thought to herself, she turned to him for practically everything. The gossip had stopped too, though Old Bert remained convinced about their previous encounter. Fleur finally understood why William sailed with him. In her uncle's absence he had remained loyal and kept the men in line. He was happy to hide in a captain's shadow – first William's and now her own – but whenever his mettle was tested, the remarkable Gates proved himself both capable and comfortable in command.

'Thanks for standing up for me,' said Fleur after a while. 'With the men, I mean.' She paused before adding, 'I think they hate me.'

Gates took up his pipe and started filling it. 'Hate is the wrong word, Fleur. They don't respect you entirely, that's all. It takes a fair while for any captain to gain the unswerving trust of his men, and I'm afraid you just ain't earned it yet, miss. Not that you've done anything wrong, but you've not had a chance to prove yourself fully. They admire you for your abilities, but it's not enough. You have to remember that this is a pirate ship, not the family business. Not exactly, anyhow.'

Fleur sighed. 'I just feel so alone,' she admitted. 'I know I'm surrounded by people who are helping me, but it's as if I'm treading water. I work all day, then fall into my bed and snore until I have to get up and start working again. The crew are wary of my promotion, and even my friends don't know how to treat me any more. Not that I'd have time to talk to them if I wanted to!' she added miserably.

'Ah,' said Gates knowingly. 'The loneliness of leadership. I'm afraid that comes with the territory.'

'I miss the captain,' Fleur blurted out. 'I miss him so much sometimes I can barely breathe.' Hot tears spilled down her face and she wiped them away quickly, embarrassed.

The bosun pretended not to notice as he poked tobacco into his tiny china pipe. 'The heart dies slowly,' he murmured. 'Hopes and dreams fade one by one like the sunny days in autumn, until all that is left is darkness and cold. Don't let that happen to you, child. Whatever the outcome of our adventure, promise you'll never close your heart to the world.'

Fleur tipped her head to one side and raised one

eyebrow. 'Is that what happened to you then?' she asked boldly.

Gates exhaled blue smoke and nodded slowly. 'Aye,' he said quietly.

Fleur glanced at the whistle that he always wore about his neck and bit her lip. It was now or never. She pointed at the silver pipe and cleared her throat nervously. 'Does it have anything to do with that?'

She cringed inwardly as the question hung between them. She waited for Gates to chastise her for her curiosity, or perhaps merely to get up and walk away. But to her surprise he closed the pipe in one fist, sighed heavily and nodded.

'I suppose it's only right and fair for you to know my history, seeing as I know yours,' he said. 'Though I'd rather you kept what I tell you to yourself, miss. I have good reason to keep secrets from the men.'

'Of course, sir,' Fleur replied quickly.

The bosun gazed at her steadily, then, satisfied, sat back and began his story. 'I sailed, as you seem to have guessed, with His Majesty's navy. In fact I achieved the rank of vice admiral, just like my father before me. This silver pipe, as I believe you already know, is used by high commanders as a badge of office.'

Fleur tried not to gasp out loud as Tom's suspicions

were proved correct. No wonder Gates always spoke like a gentleman.

'Like yourself, young Fleur,' he went on, 'the sea is in my blood and has been for generations. My father sent me up to Oxford, and I rather fancied a career in politics when I left.' He chuckled darkly. "Twas not to be. So I ended up at sea, and for a while it was fine. In fact, I grew to love the life of an officer. But we treated our crew worse than animals, and that preyed on my conscience.' He frowned as he thought back. 'Men and boys were pressed into service from drinking taverns and docksides. Forced to come aboard and worked half to death, with barely any food in their stomachs. If they flagged for a moment, we whipped them with the cat o' nine tails . . . or worse' – he shook his head solemnly – 'we threw them overboard.'

'But that's terrible,' exclaimed Fleur. 'I thought men of the navy would be treated with more respect. They fight fiercely enough to suggest the loyalty of those who are well looked after.'

'Aye, well, you thought wrong,' said Gates curtly. 'Even those who stayed clear of the cat would like as not be cheated of their wages. If the navy fights fiercely, Fleur, it's because the men need every coin and crumb they can take from the fallen. I won't make any excuses for my former self, but it was the navy that made me a hard and cruel man. I ignored my conscience for so long that there came a time when I felt no shame for my inhuman actions. That was a dark time in the life of George Gates, I can tell you.'

Fleur shivered. He reminded her so much of William at that moment. No wonder the pair of them understood each other so well. Both had looked into the face of the Devil and seen themselves.

'At length I grew sick of navy life and greedy for more money,' Gates continued. 'So, knowing that slavery was a profitable business, I resigned my commission, made my connections and set sail on a slave ship carrying human cargo. We sailed from Africa to America to fill the New World with children stolen from the Old and called it holy work because the Church saw fit to support us in our labours. And well they might, for their own coffers swelled with gold through the trade in human souls.'

Fleur thought about Gates's angry reaction to the religious fervour in Salem. 'Is that why you are so scornful of the Church, sir?' she asked.

'Aye,' he said. 'In my experience, God is often as not a convenient reason to do harm to others.' He screwed up his face with anger. 'War, theft, murder, enslavement. There's nothing Christian about any of it, Fleur. Those ships are hell on earth. Men, women and children crammed into spaces the size of coffins, with nothing to eat and barely enough air to breathe. The stench . . .' Words failed him for a moment. 'Death sailed with us. The slaves believed that when they died they would return to their homeland. Those who were not lucky enough to be taken by sickness would often cut their own throats with a ragged fingernail or jump overboard in their heavy chains at the first opportunity. We had to put netting around the rail to stop them.'

'That's horrible!' cried Fleur. She eyed Gates apprehensively. How could this man whom she thought she knew have been part of such a despicable trade? 'Did you feel no guilt?'

Gates nodded in the darkness. 'Of course I did, child,' he said. 'As soon as we'd collected our cargo on my first trip out, I knew that I'd made a mistake. But I would never have survived the journey if I'd shared that opinion. The crew were drunks and madmen and murderers, Fleur, made more dangerous by the power they wielded over the slaves in the hold. Our ship carried nigh on six hundred souls. They were branded like cattle and shut up in the tiny space between decks, manacled and chained together like spoons in a drawer. When the sea was rough, they'd tumble about – some were crushed to death. We left their bodies to rot, or hacked them free of their chains and tossed the bits to the fishes. I'll never forget the shrieks and groans of the dying . . .' He winced and swallowed hard as the guilt clawed up his throat. 'As for the children, most died of dysentery in the first week of the voyage. It was a mercy.'

The bosun fell silent again, memories overwhelming him, but Fleur sensed he had more to tell. Finally he cleared his throat and looked out across the black waves.

'I was employed by a consortium of merchants – the owners of a fleet of slave ships,' he explained, his voice barely audible above the sloshing of water against the ship's sides. 'My wages were handsome, and there were additional privileges. As a ranking officer, I was granted a *privilege negroe*.'

'A what?' asked Fleur.

'A slave put at my own disposal for the duration of the voyage. Someone I could sell for profit when we reached the New World. It was a practice meant to encourage us to look after the slaves well, so that they would go on to fetch a good price . . .' Gates's voice broke when he tried to continue. 'I was given Esi.'

'Esi?' said Fleur.

'A young woman, Fleur, as beautiful, sweet, clever and kind as any I ever met, despite the horror her life had become. We fell in love at once.'

Fleur gasped out loud. 'Love, sir? You could hardly even have known her.'

The bosun smiled sadly to himself. 'Love doesn't work how we expect it to, miss. It shines its light when least expected.' He stroked his beard thoughtfully. 'I'd never let anyone lay claim to my heart before. I didn't dare to hope that a man like myself was worthy of such a thing. But love crept in and altered me, girl, before I even noticed it was there.'

'Goodness,' said Fleur, reeling from this heartfelt confession. For a moment she found her thoughts straying towards Tom, but she quickly pushed them away. 'What did you do?' she asked the bosun.

'As my servant, Esi was treated better and given more liberty aboard ship than the other slaves. Still, it was hard for us to speak openly, except when I was giving her orders. She had known Christian missionaries before she fell prey to slavers, so she had a reasonable command of English. But there was never a time when we could be together unobserved. Though each knew the other's desire, we were forced to wait until we reached dry land – whereupon I vowed we would find a place to settle together. Not as master and slave, but as husband and wife.'

Gates's face darkened and he coughed, misery choking his words off as he tried to speak. Fleur waited until he was ready to go on.

'As we neared the shores of New England, we grew bold, certain that liberty was at hand. With land in sight, we stole a kiss. The slave driver, a vicious man if ever there was one, saw our embrace and told the captain,' he said in a hoarse voice. 'He seized Esi and decided to make an example of her.' The bosun drew a deep shuddering breath and rubbed his hands over his face. 'They tore her apart, limb from limb, and nailed the parts of her body about the ship as a warning to all. I was thrown in the brig and told to prepare myself for judgement when we landed. I was to be tried for my crime – for the crime of loving a woman . . . a slave.'

'I'm so sorry,' Fleur said. She reached out and laid a hand on his arm. 'Life was cruel to you, sir.' She stared at his broken face and thought of William. 'Do you ever wish that you'd never met Esi in the first place? Then you would never have had to lose her.'

Gates covered her hand with his – it was large and warm and softer than William's callused paw – and shook his head. 'No, miss, I would give up my whole life for the short time I spent with her. Loss is the price we pay for love.'

Fleur nodded. 'So how did your path cross my uncle's?' she asked.

The bosun stretched out his legs and smiled. 'Well, miss, as you know from the motley crews you've sailed with, any rogue is free to become a pirate – if he's got the stomach for it, that is. No man has power over another's liberty, whatever Church and Crown might tell you. They fear us, and rightly so, for we go about our business with brutal intent; but it is the injustices of a world ruled by class and money that spur us on, girl. We're rebels and revolutionaries as well as rogues. We make our decisions and choose our course collectively, without bullying and plotting against one another; we share our bounty out fairly and free any man we find living in slavery.'

Fleur shivered with a sense of pride and purpose. She remembered how the notion of her pirate bloodline had once scared her, when she had only the horror stories of landlubbers to go by. There was more honour and equality among her pirate shipmates, she mused, than aboard any of His Majesty's warships.

'Soon after I was thrown in the brig,' Gates continued, 'chaos broke out above. I heard the commotion, but of course I could not know that the *Black Dragon* was bearing down on us. There was an almighty battle, but soon William's crew were storming the deck. They took that rotten slaver with barely a scratch.'

'But what did my uncle want with human cargo?' asked Fleur.

'It's sport for William,' said Gates. 'A chance to stick two fingers up at a class of merchant that he rightly detests, and perhaps to recruit a few of the unfortunate passengers.'

Fleur thought of the Africans who had been sailing with them since her return.

'The slave ship was sent to the bottom of the sea with the worst of its crew still aboard,' continued the bosun. 'The captives were set ashore, and a handful chose to sail with William as free men – myself among them, for I had been clapped in chains too, remember.' He tapped out his pipe and nodded at Fleur. 'And there you have it. My sad story – to date at least.'

Fleur gazed at him steadily. 'Aye, well, sir,' she said. ''Tis not the end of your story, only the beginning of a new adventure. Life ain't over till we're six feet under, as my uncle says.'

Gates chuckled warmly, then picked up his violin and held it under his chin to play again. 'Wise words, miss,' he said. 'Ones I hope you'll remember yourself.' He drew his bow tenderly across the strings of his instrument and closed his eyes.

The conversation was clearly over, so Fleur settled back and let the music sweep over her. A chord here, a note there, and suddenly she felt her heart flood with happiness and hope.

# CHAPTER 16

The *Dragon* finally reached English waters on a dismal grey September afternoon. Fleur searched the ship for Astrid, Tom or Arthur, desperate to share the thrill of journey's end with a friend, but she couldn't find them anywhere. Finally she trudged back to her own cabin, only to find them all sitting on her bed, their heads together as they studied something. Even Grog was curled up on Astrid's knees, purring like a contented cat. It was a cosy scene, and jealous pangs shot through Fleur like shards of glass as she took it in.

'What are you up to?' she snapped as she entered the room.

All three heads bobbed up at once. Astrid smiled over at her. 'Hello, Fleur,' she chirped. 'We were just trying to figure out that mysterious map you found in the hidden room.'

'Why didn't you ask me to join you? I'm good at map-reading.'

Astrid's smile fell and Tom tutted. 'What's the point?' he said grumpily. 'You're never around any more.'

'Well, that's not my fault, is it?' Fleur sat on the edge of the bed and glanced at the map. 'Any luck then?' she asked sharply.

'Not yet,' said Arthur meekly. 'But we're also teaching Tom to read. And he's going to teach me some sailing stuff in return.'

Fleur met Tom's eyes, and despite the recent chill between them, they exchanged a brief knowing smile. Arthur was always desperate to pick up pirating skills. The problem was, he was never any good at them. An awkward silence fell and Astrid sat forward, tucking a strand of silky hair behind one ear.

'How's it going up there anyway?' she asked.

Fleur shrugged as she stared down at the vellum map. 'Fine,' she said. 'We're approaching the Cornish coast, and if all goes according to plan we'll be in London within days.'

Tom's smile faded as Fleur stole a glance at him. He looked stricken, as if the very mention of that city terrified him. She was on the verge of asking what was wrong when Gates appeared at the door.

'There you are, miss,' he said, slightly out of breath. 'You should know that we're pulling aside a ship.'

Fleur felt a swell of nervousness. This is what they had been waiting for – the plan was about to be put in action; it was time for the battle. She stood up abruptly. 'Do you think we can take her, Gates?' she asked.

He met her solemn stare. 'It's a lone navy flute,' he replied.

Fleur frowned. 'Are you suggesting we capture a navy ship, sir?' she asked in amazement. 'Why face more danger than we must?'

'No navy ship will be expecting trouble in home waters,' he said. 'Any more than they'll be expecting us to roll up the Thames in a navy boat.'

'Surely any onlooker would question a navy ship overflowing with pirates, wouldn't they?' Arthur piped up from the bed.

Fleur narrowed her eyes and stared at Gates thoughtfully. She understood what he was implying, and it was a daring proposal. 'Not if we're in uniform,' she replied. 'We steal their clothes and have ourselves a little game of fancy dress. Gates here could easily play our captain – I'll never pass, not even from a distance – and Bart can be his second in command.'

Gates gave a thin smile and nodded. 'A dangerous plan, but a good one, I think,' he said. 'Most of the crew won't need to change out of their slops, mind, just tidy themselves up. Only the officers wear the King's cloth.' He paused to look from Fleur to Astrid. 'And while I'm thinking about it, we'll have to disguise you as a boy, Fleur, as I know we've done before. You too, Astrid.'

'Fine by me,' Astrid agreed bravely.

Fleur grabbed her bow and arrows from their resting place against the cabin wall and slung them across her back. Duty called. She nodded briskly at her friends, who got up to follow her. 'Arthur, gather up medical provisions and take Astrid to the cockpit.'

The cockpit was a cramped compartment below the water line where they would be able to tend to the wounded during battle.

'Aye, aye,' said Arthur, his face pale.

Then Fleur picked up the narwhal staff and gestured for Gates to lead the way above decks. 'The game's afoot,' she said firmly. 'Let's ready the men for attack.'

★

Fleur immediately sent Tom up to the crow's nest to get a good look at the flute as the *Dragon* closed the distance between them. Grog scampered up the mast after him. The ship, a broad-beamed, stout little vessel, flew a flag bearing the St George cross on the starboard yardarm. From the nest, Tom checked her length and the disposition of her gun ports and cannons, and guessed at crew numbers by how she sat in the water. He clambered back down to report to Fleur and, confident that they could take the vessel, they filled the sails and bore down hard. While the crew readied themselves for battle, Dr Dubois dashed in between them, sprinkling great handfuls of sand onto the deck. This was always done before a battle so the surgeon didn't slip on all the blood as he tended to the wounded.

'Let the Jolly Roger fly!' Fleur shouted from the poop deck. 'Make ready at your battle stations! Stand by the bow cannon!' Her legs wobbled but her voice was loud and true. She was determined to win the ship and prove herself as captain. 'Fire!' she bellowed as loudly as she could.

The forward cannons blazed and found their mark. Smoke billowed from the flute's stern. The *Black Dragon* rode in her churning wake and gained fast.

'Reload!' shouted Fleur.

More cannonballs soared through the air, puncturing the other ship well above the water line, and to Fleur's surprise the navy ship hoisted a white flag of surrender. The battle could not have been won yet, surely? But, sure enough, their target had slowed, and the white flag was fluttering in the chilly wind as clear as day. Fleur signalled to the gunners to hold fire. Gates leaned in close. 'Something feels wrong,' he whispered.

'Aye,' she said. She stared across at the bobbing ship: they were close enough to read her name without a spyglass now: the *Adventurer*. There was barely anyone visible on board. Fleur tried to listen to her instincts, but fear flooded in, blurring her judgement. She turned back to Gates, shaking slightly. 'I don't know what to do,' she admitted.

And suddenly there was Rose. She arched an eyebrow and curled her lip. 'Scared, are you, daughter?' she taunted. ''Twould be better if you made your move!'

Fleur snarled at her furiously, then turned, her mind made up. 'Prepare to board, lads,' she hollered to the crew, holding the narwhal staff high above her head. 'To arms, men.'

Gates breathed out wearily and shot Rose an icy glare. Then he disappeared among the men as they readied themselves to fight, while Rose slipped away unseen. They drew alongside and were readying their lines and grappling hooks to board, when dozens of sailors suddenly popped into view on the *Adventurer* like a row of jack-in-the-boxes.

'It's a trap,' Carlton Bart bellowed from the wheel. 'Hard to port!'

But it was too late. The *Adventurer* opened fire, splintering the *Dragon's* side. Fleur's eyes darted from ship to ship in a wild panic. The men were waiting for their orders, and she had no idea what to do. 'Um . . .' she stuttered. 'Make ready the stern cannons – we'll try to overtake.'

Crew dashed hither and thither as they took their positions, and Fleur felt as if she was conducting an orchestra without ever having learned how to play an instrument.

'Stand ready, lads,' she ordered more confidently than she felt. 'Let's give them a proper fight.'

But before they could pull ahead, the *Adventurer* opened fire again with a full broadside attack. The noise was deafening and the impact made the *Black Dragon* lurch so violently that Fleur almost fell off the poop deck. Adrenalin pumped around her trembling body, making her nauseous.

'Hard to port!' she yelled, clinging to the rail as the

*Dragon* dipped beneath her. 'Load and run out the swivel guns. Fire at will!'

Peter Fenn, approached her doffing his cap, his white face smeared with black gunpowder. 'Beggin' your pardon, miss,' he said nervously, 'but if we fire at will we risk tearing the ship to shreds,' he told her. 'Which would be a shame as we mean to sail her to London.'

Fleur nodded at him miserably. 'I'd sooner lose our prize than our lives,' she said gravely.

Peter nodded and ran back to his station, leaving Fleur to stare down at the bedlam on the main deck. There were pirates rushing everywhere as the smaller ship gave them a thrashing. What would William have said about this disaster? she wondered. Tom raced by carrying charges of powder and Tiny Joe followed him with an armful of cannonballs. They knelt down by the gunners and set about loading the heavy guns as they slid and slithered about on their great wooden wheels. It took eight men to load and run them out, and the scene was one of organized chaos. As Fleur watched, cannonballs arced between the two ships. The *Dragon* swung about hard and the cannon attended by Tom snapped free of its chains and rolled over one of the gunner's feet. The man yelled out in pain as Tom and the others struggled to drag the cannon off him. But as they wrestled, the ship lurched again and the gun slid off on its own, freeing the gunner but scattering the crew like skittles as it mowed down everything in its path.

And still the *Adventurer's* attack continued. Iron hand grenades exploded against the wood and musket balls rained down around them. The *Adventurer* was coming alongside now and the sailors were preparing to board. A sob of fear and panic coursed through Fleur's body from top to toe, her knees buckled and she let the Hart staff clatter to the boards. If they were beaten in battle, all was lost. William would be hanged, and the rest of them would follow close behind.

'Fleur,' said Gates urgently. In the midst of the madness he was back at her side, though she had not noticed him. 'Are you savvy, girl? Think fast. What are your orders?'

Fleur covered her mouth with her hands and stared back at him blankly. For all her combat experience, she had no idea how to win a battle like this.

Gates reached for her hand. 'It's not too late to turn this battle, miss,' he said firmly. 'Do you want me to take control?'

Fleur nodded at him hopelessly, unable to meet his eyes. The bosun was turning, ready to bark his commands to the men, when Rose leaped back up onto the poop deck and a shot rang out from her musket. The men of the *Dragon* turned to her at once.

'Time for the double-bluff, lads,' she hollered over the sounds of battle, glaring down at Fleur with contempt. Underneath the brim of William's hat her green eyes were hard and determined. 'There's no time to argue about this, girl. I have a plan and work to do.'

'Woman, this is not your ship,' snarled Gates.

'Nor yours neither, *bosun*,' hissed Rose icily. 'Nor anyone's unless someone acts to turn the tide of this sorry scrap.' She lifted her head and addressed the crew again. 'Men, if you fancy me for captain in your hour of need, say aye.'

There was a loud chorus of cheers, and Rose eyed Gates triumphantly. He nodded coolly and stepped back, knowing that it was foolish to argue at such a crucial time. 'We'll speak of this later, sea-hag,' he muttered, before dashing off to help lash down the runaway cannon.

Fleur slipped down from the poop deck and stood aside, watching her mother with something like awe. Rose was in her element. She stood as solid as an oak tree, hands on hips, as she rapidly snapped out orders to the willing men. Fleur was hardly surprised when it became clear that Rose had been preparing for the navy's trickery since before the first cannon was fired. While she had been hopping about on the poop deck, it seemed her mother had quietly crammed the *Dragon*'s tender with William's best fighters, then hidden them in the portside shadow of the junk while the battle raged above. Now, with a thick wall of smoke drifting between the rival ships, the men in the little boat slipped silently between them, then slunk up the starboard side of the *Adventurer*. Another thirty or so men lurked below decks, waiting to overwhelm any boarders foolish enough to think that the *Dragon* would be a push-over, though for her part Fleur hadn't even noticed their absence.

'Prepare to receive boarders,' cried Rose, underlining her urgency with a burst of musket fire.

Grappling hooks were tossed over the *Dragon*'s starboard side, followed by the navy's boarding party.

'Fight to the death, lads!'

Screams and cries of pain filled the air as the two crews clashed on the slippery deck. Even Grog had joined the battle. He swung from the rigging like a trapeze artist, knocking weapons from enemy hands and pulling the hair from their scalps. As one navy man bore down on Fleur, the lemur swooped down to snatch a primed pistol out of his hands, landing clumsily on the boom. There was an almighty bang as his clutching fingers found the trigger, and he gave a screech and toppled backwards in a puff of smoke. The pistol clattered to the boards, besides the groaning body of its owner. Grog screeched with triumph, before darting away to safety below deck.

Fleur crouched, coughing, in the acrid smoke as broad swords, hatchets and axes swung about below her. However much it galled her, the ray of hope her mother had delivered had brought her back to her senses. While she had failed to capture the *Adventurer*, she reasoned, she could still fight to keep the *Dragon*. Fleur thought quickly as she stood up, slipping her bow and arrows from her back. The helmsman of the *Adventurer* was at the wheel, struggling to keep his ship steady as her crew boarded the *Dragon*. Fleur shook out an arrow, drew back her string and took aim. The arrow spun through the air and plunged into the man's arm, just as she had planned. The wounded helmsman staggered and let go of the ship's wheel, and the *Adventurer* swung about madly. Several of her crew were tossed into the churning water between the two ships. Rose, seeing what she had done, nodded down at her daughter, but Fleur turned away. With a weary sigh, Rose waved up at the man she had placed in readiness in the crow's nest. He in turn signalled for the men in the concealed boat to launch their counter-attack. There was an almighty roar from the far side of the navy ship, and soon the *Dragon*'s snarling warriors were swarming all over her.

'All able-bodied men on deck,' ordered Rose as she fought off a two-sided attack with her trusty cutlass.

The pirates who had hidden below decks stormed into view. Now the King's men were caught between two ships full of angry enemies. Despondently, they lowered their weapons and awaited their fate. Aboard HMS *Adventurer* the white flag was raised again, and this time it stayed there. Rose had done it; the battle was won.

# CHAPTER 17

With the flute in tow and her furious crew roped
together in the hold of the *Black Dragon*, Rose sailed on
to Pepper Cove.

Fleur hid in the crow's nest. She was grateful to her
mother for saving the day, and had even gone so far as to
thank her, but handing over power was humiliating,
and what little authority she had enjoyed on board
was quickly leaking away. The crew were now turning
to Rose for their orders and Fleur felt like a fool.
How could a mere girl ever have considered herself
worthy of a captain's rank? The idea was ridiculous.
And why did William ever foist the job on her in the

first place? Grog clambered up the mast and wound his warm, furry body around her ankles. He'd spent the rest of the skirmish locked in a fight of his own with the rats in the hold, and he looked rather the worse for wear. Fleur picked him up gently and tickled his soft tummy. He chirped and cooed back at her happily. *At least someone appreciates me*, thought Fleur, sighing to herself as she stared out over the rugged Cornish coast. She had often wondered when she might see the shores of her native land again. But instead of the emotional homecoming she had expected, she felt only numbness. So much had happened since William had come for her. And there was so much still to do if she was ever to see him alive again.

'Fleur,' bellowed Gates from the deck. 'Come down, will you? We're reaching the cove.'

She abandoned Grog and skimmed quickly down the mast.

'You savvy?' the bosun asked.

She stared at the men bustling about her and felt overwhelmed, and suddenly very small. 'Aye, I am,' she lied, 'but I'm ashamed that I almost risked everyone's lives like that. To have failed the way I did . . . I could have got everyone killed.'

Gates shrugged and ran a hand through his thick

beard. 'That's the way it is,' he mused. 'A captain has to learn his – or her – trade somehow, and that can only be done through experience. If you make a mistake, learn the lesson.'

'Yeah, well,' replied Fleur miserably, 'I don't want to be captain any more. It's too hard and too lonely.'

He looked at her in astonishment. 'And do ye think that William was any good at it when he first took charge of a ship, miss?' he said, smiling at the thought. 'I dread to think what mistakes a man of his temperament might have made.' He winked. 'Just you wait, Fleur. With skills like yours, one of these days you'll make a finer pirate captain than even your uncle.'

Fleur tried to smile but she couldn't seem to move the right muscles. The bosun's words were kind but she simply didn't believe them any more. As she stood there feeling sorry for herself, Carlton Bart strode towards them.

'We're cutting the sails and preparing to enter Pepper Cove,' he announced. 'Do ye want to guide us in, lassie?' He nodded over at Fleur.

She looked at the rocky inlet with a sigh and shook her head abruptly. 'I'd rather pump out the bilges,' she muttered – then caught sight of her mother nearby, hauling on the lines along with some of the riggers.

Fleur stuck a thumb in her direction. 'Why don't you ask her, since *she* seems to know what she's doing?'

Gates and Bart exchanged glances over her head.

'But she's not our captain, now, is she?' Bart reminded her curtly.

'And neither am I.' Fleur folded her arms defensively across her chest.

Gates sighed wearily and reached for his whistle. 'Well, someone needs to take charge of these ships,' he said, frowning at her. 'Pull yourself together, girl. I didn't figure you to be the sort to give up.'

'Well, you were wrong,' she snapped, meeting his steadfast gaze.

'Hmm,' he said doubtfully. 'We'll see.' And with that he turned and marched briskly away.

Bart cleared his throat and reached out to pat Fleur awkwardly on the shoulder. 'You've done well, lassie – your uncle would be proud,' he said kindly. 'But I hope you don't mind me givin' you a bit of advice.'

Fleur shrugged sullenly.

'I'm a man of maps, as you know,' he began, and pointed to his own weather-beaten face. 'Why, this here wrinkled mug of mine alone shows you the many chart lines of my life. And what I've learned, young 'un, is that there's many ways to get to the end of a journey. If you find the tide's taking you the wrong way, change your course and keep on going.' He stared down at her with obvious fondness. 'You just took a bad turn, that's all. So shake out a reef and run before the wind. You're born for this, Cap'n Hart.'

Fleur opened her mouth to object, but Bart held up his hand to silence her. 'Give yerself some peace, girl,' he said finally. Then he turned and strode purposefully back to the wheel, leaving Fleur alone with her troubled thoughts.

Unlike the subterranean grotto of Penance Bay, Pepper Cove was a snug smuggler's hideaway carved into the pretty Cornish coastline. A reef of slate ran across the deep-set bay, threatening to snarl up anyone who didn't know how to clear it. The cove's entrance itself was narrow and fringed with cruel, jagged rocks, but once inside, a ship, or even two, was totally hidden by the high cliffs.

And so, with some careful sailing, both the *Adventurer* and the *Black Dragon* were stowed safely away in Pepper Cove's rocky hideout. Not a moment was wasted, for time was against them. Gates split the *Dragon's* crew so that most travelled to London, but a handful remained to look after the *Dragon* and its brig full of prisoners. They were all to be liberated, but not until William was free. Dr Dubois and Jack were to stay as well, and Arthur was to step up as chief medic on the *Adventurer*. Jack's condition was improving, but not quickly enough, and Fleur didn't want anything to distract the crew. As for Rose, although Fleur was desperate to leave her behind in Pepper Cove, she didn't want to give her an opportunity to steal the *Dragon*. That was something else that William had taught Fleur: keep your enemies close. So on they sailed together, with barely a word between them.

'It's like walking on clouds,' said Arthur as he clomped around the busy deck in a smart pair of leather shoes.

'You look like an idiot,' said Tom scornfully. 'They're so big you can't even keep 'em on.'

'You're just jealous I've got them,' snapped Arthur, stumbling over his oversized footwear.

Tom burst out laughing. 'I ain't jealous of the boats on your feet,' he said, looking down at his own new heavy-knit sweater. 'This'll keep me nice and warm up in the nest. Anyhow, I can't wear no shoes up in the rigging, you dunce,' he added, wiggling a bare foot at his friend. 'No grip.'

'Well, I think you look very smart, Arthur,' said Astrid, smiling warmly.

Arthur grinned at her with delight.

'And if the ship starts sinking,' Tom muttered under his breath, 'the left shoe is mine.'

The pirates were enthusiastically raiding the *Adventurer*'s slop chest. Discarded pieces of clothing littered the deck as the crew replaced their filthy old clothes with dry, clean ones. Gates had explained that those who were press-ganged into the navy usually only had the clothes on their backs, which were often dirty and ragged. The navy clothed their recruits from the slop chest, docking two months' wages to pay for them. But now the pirates were helping themselves for nothing.

As the *Adventurer* cut steadily along the Channel towards London, the atmosphere on board was tense and volatile. Fights kept breaking out amongst the frustrated shipmates. They all wanted their rightful captain back at the helm, but they were exhausted from weeks at sea and divided as to the best way forward. Luck was with them though, and the wind was their servant as they raced across the waves. But each man knew deep in his heart that despite all their efforts, they might still arrive too late. There were some who muttered, uneasily at first and then more boldly, that Rose should take control of the *Adventurer* at once. Others stayed loyal to Fleur. More dangerously, a third group had started to whisper about

Astrid, claiming that she had brought misfortune with her and that only her removal, or worse, would set things right. And of course, every last man on board the stolen navy flute knew that if they were caught, they would hang for sure, which hardly helped the atmosphere.

And yet on they sailed through English waters fraught with peril and teeming with the King's men. Ever superstitious, the pirates poured wine onto the deck and fastened a silver coin beneath the masthead in the hope that this would cement the success of their endeavour. Fleur kept to herself as far as possible, while Rose slipped further into the role of acting captain. Not even Gates seemed to have the energy to challenge her, so while they continued to make good progress, it was a far from happy ship.

# CHAPTER 18

On their second evening after leaving Pepper Cove, Toby cooked them all a piratical delicacy called salmagundi, which was a dish made from chopped meat, eggs, anchovies, onions and any other scraps he decided to throw in. The hearty feast helped calm the troubled mood.

It had been a long, horrible day. A storm had rolled in on the sharp north wind; a boiling black mass of cloud that had swallowed the sun and brought booming thunder and forked lightning that sent Grog cowering below deck. A brilliant rainbow had blazed in the troubled skies before everything vanished in the shafts of heavy rain. Fleur had tried to assert her authority again, but her mother was more experienced in dealing with weather like this, and it was she who gave the orders. The pirates were kept busy hauling in the sails, which meant climbing wet ropes to the top of slippery masts on a ship that bucked and fell beneath them like a swing. The canvas sheets already weighed several hundred pounds, but sodden with rain they became an unwieldy burden. Meanwhile, at the wheel, it took three men to fight the wind to hold their course. And down below, the *Adventurer* was leaking like a sieve. A line of crewmen took turns to man the pump – a device like a pair of bellows – in the cold slimy bilge water deep inside the swaying vessel. It was backbreaking work. Fleur, of course, had thrown herself into the task; now she wished she had kept a lower profile. Every bone in her body ached and her hands were covered with blisters.

Tom was particularly delighted with Toby's efforts: salmagundi was his favourite. His mood lifted as he sat shovelling it into his mouth. Grog sat between Fleur and Astrid, delicately picking weevils out of a ship's biscuit. The long trestle tables they ate from were suspended from ropes and rocked when the *Adventurer* did. Rose sat a few yards away from them, entertaining the drunk men with her limitless supply of tall stories.

Astrid frowned and leaned closer to Fleur. 'Is she still being horrible to you, Fleur?' she asked quietly.

Fleur shoved her uneaten dinner aside and looked over at her mother coldly. 'No, we're just ignoring each other now,' she replied.

'That must be difficult,' said Arthur.

'I know,' Fleur snorted. 'But if we tried talking again, I think we'd kill each other.'

'But those unspoken words will surely boil over at some point?' Astrid said with concern. 'Don't miss the chance to make things right.'

Fleur shrugged and folded her arms across her chest. 'I wouldn't know where to start,' she snapped. 'Anyhow, she was the one who left me so it's up to her to try and make things right!' She glowered over at Rose again. 'Though I doubt that's possible.'

'But if she leaves, Fleur, you might never get another chance,' said Arthur urgently. 'You pushed her away once so she probably expects you to do it again.'

'So what! She should try harder. Like I just said, *she* left *me*. It's up to her.'

Arthur looked perplexed as he pushed his glasses up

his nose. He opened his mouth to say something and then clamped it shut again.

'What is it, Arthur?' Fleur turned on him furiously.

'It's just that . . . well, you've been given this chance to have your mother back in your life again,' he replied reluctantly and his bottom lip wobbled dangerously. 'I'd love to have that opportunity.'

'But your mother loved you, Arthur,' she retorted crossly. 'This is a completely different situation.'

They all sat in a tense silence while Grog chattered away happily to himself on Arthur's lap.

'What do you think, Tom?' asked Astrid suddenly. 'You haven't said much.'

All eyes turned to Tom, who was now slurping up the remains of Fleur's dinner. He swallowed his mouthful before shrugging. 'It's up to her,' he said, his eyes flicking over at Fleur. 'Maybe some parents ain't worth knowing.' He shrugged and licked his fingers. 'No sense chasing after more rejection, is there?'

'Exactly,' said Fleur.

Astrid looked from Tom to Fleur in amazement. 'But a mother's love is the oldest, strongest magic,' she said gravely. 'It's more powerful, more precious, than any charm.'

'There ain't nothing as precious as gold,'

snapped Tom. 'You can't buy naught with love, can you?'

'And equally, material objects don't always bring you happiness,' Astrid argued.

Tom scowled while Arthur exhaled with exasperation. 'Can't we talk about the weather or something?' he muttered.

At that moment Grog spied a fleeing rat and all hell broke loose. The lemur gave a piercing warning call and shot off Arthur's lap in pursuit of the oily rodent. As he scrambled across the tables, he knocked over Rose's bottle of rum with a flick of his writhing tail. Cups and plates clattered to the floor. With a howl Rose grabbed the animal by the scruff of his neck.

'Why aren't we tossing this parasite into the pot?' she roared as she rose to her feet. She poked the lemur's fat little tummy and he squealed in alarm. 'Seems to me he's ripe for dinner.'

Fleur leaped to her feet immediately and stormed over, fists clenched. The whole room fell silent. 'That's enough!' she bellowed. 'Grog is the ship's mascot and a friend to us all.'

Her mother burst out laughing and held the grunting lemur above Fleur's head. 'And I say he's nothing but meat with a personality,' she goaded cruelly.

As Rose's admirers sniggered, Fleur tried to jump up and grab the terrified lemur. But every time she reached for him, her mother laughed and whipped him out of reach. He wriggled furiously, desperate to escape her steely grasp, but she held him like a vice. She knew that she was humiliating her daughter, but pushed the knife in further still. 'Who says we pickle this thing tomorrow?' she taunted, turning to the men around her.

'No!' shouted Fleur so furiously that even Rose looked stunned. 'William said that we could keep him as a pet. How dare *you* say otherwise! You have no rights on this ship!'

'But I'm the one who seems to be giving the orders around here now, young miss.' Rose raised her eyebrows in challenge. 'And maybe I'll try to claim the *Dragon's* treasure too, once I've figured out the secrets of that damned map. 'Twould be a pity to waste such promise.'

'I'll kill you first,' shouted Fleur. 'That map ain't none of your business. Who told you about it?'

Rose smiled slyly and tapped the side of her nose. 'I make it my business to listen out for any interesting gossip, and you've just confirmed my suspicions.'

'That map was found on my uncle's ship and belongs to him.' Fleur met her mother's gaze sternly.

Rose stared down at Fleur in genuine surprise. 'Do you honestly think we'll be able to save him, you naïve little fool? He's probably already dangling from the Tyburn tree.' She turned to the crew, shaking her head with mock concern. 'And yet you've got us all on this suicide mission, just so you can see his corpse with your own eyes.'

'He's not dead, I know it in my bones.' Fleur was adamant. 'We *will* save Captain Hart.'

Rose opened her mouth to reply, but then changed her mind and instead lowered her arm and handed over the trembling creature. 'You've got until we reach Tyburn,' she said. 'If William is hanged, the lemur goes in the pot.'

Fleur held the whimpering Grog protectively as her mother's cronies sniggered. She swivelled around slowly, glaring at the men with steely eyes. 'I will not forget this,' she warned them. 'If you push me any further, you will feel my bite.' There was something in the intensity of her stare that made them fall quiet at once: something that reminded them of their true captain.

Then she turned to her mother and looked her up and down with such contempt that Rose's cruel smile vanished at once.

'I hate you,' said Fleur calmly and deliberately. 'I guess

William was right: it was kinder to believe that you were dead.'

Rose gasped and turned pale as she watched her daughter storm away.

Fleur sat sobbing on her bed for a long time. It had all become too much. Rose's unexpected appearance had been a cruel shock, but with William captured, Tom acting weirdly and a mad plan that might get them all killed, Fleur was struggling to cope. The *Adventurer* was an unfamiliar ship and didn't feel like home. The cabin she had taken was sparsely furnished, and aside from the staff and her father's bow she had nothing to remind her of who she was any more. Fleur automatically reached for the locket around her neck for comfort, but of course it wasn't there. Her fingertips fluttered over the empty space and another huge sob tore through her. Everything seemed impossible.

At that moment the cabin door burst open and in tumbled Tom, Astrid and Arthur like a litter of excited puppies. They were all grinning from ear to ear and Arthur was triumphantly waving the tube containing the vellum map above his head. On seeing Fleur's red eyes and tear-stained face, the smiles disappeared.

Astrid dashed over to the bed. 'Fleur, what's wrong?'

she asked, slipping her slender arm around her friend's shoulders.

Tom and Arthur stood in the middle of the cabin, looking horrified. When Fleur cried, they knew things were bad. Arthur cleared his throat nervously as he quickly lowered the tube and hid it behind his back. Fleur furiously wiped away the tears with the palms of her hands.

'William asked me to look after his ship and I'm losing control of everything,' she gasped in a shaky voice. Her words came thick and fast. 'I almost got us all killed too. I'm not ready to be a pirate captain and I'm not sure if I ever will be now. And I hate my horrible mother for wanting to steal the *Black Dragon* – and in general, really – and I miss William. I want him back.' Her bottom lip wobbled threateningly. 'I want things to be how they were.'

Fleur's friends stared at her in stunned silence.

'It's all going to work out all right,' said Tom suddenly and firmly. He came over to the bed and plonked himself down beside Fleur, eliciting a squeak of protest from the aged bed-springs. 'Don't worry, Claw-cat, this is what we're good at.'

Fleur looked at him warily and gulped back the tears. 'Hang on, I thought you hated me,' she spluttered.

Tom looked confused and shook his head. 'Of course I don't hate you, stupid.'

'But you've been acting so strangely, Tom,' she said, frowning. 'Sometimes I don't think you're on my side any more.'

'What do you mean by that?' He jumped up, his cheeks red.

'You don't seem too bothered about rescuing William for a start,' she said accusingly.

Tom gasped indignantly.

'Fleur's right, old chap,' Arthur interjected before Tom could speak again. 'Ever since we decided to go to London you've been really moody.'

Tom shot him a sharp warning look before turning his attention back to Fleur. 'I'm always on your side. And of *course* I want the captain back. And about London, well . . . I've got good reason for not wanting to go there, but I can't talk about it.' He searched Fleur's eyes. 'Come on, Claw-cat, you know I'm rubbish at all that talking stuff. I'm not a girl . . . or Arthur.'

'Oi,' Arthur protested.

'But we always talked about everything before,' said Fleur, ignoring Arthur. 'I knew something was wrong – why can't you just tell me what's going on?'

'Some of it is jealousy,' Tom admitted. 'But I believe in you as much as your uncle does — you're a natural at this pirate lark.' He shrugged. 'But come on, Fleur, you know how much I want to captain a ship too. And, like you, I know I ain't ready yet, but one day I will be and it stings that the captain'll always pick you over me because you're family and I ain't.'

'But you're our family too, Tom,' Fleur argued.

Both Astrid and Arthur nodded but Tom shook his head, then reached over and tapped the ruby ring on Fleur's finger — the same ring that every true Hart wore. 'Not in blood,' he said. 'And that's all that matters in the end.'

'No it's not. Look at Rose — blood means nothing to a woman like that. Why, I feel closer to the rats on our ship, Tom. Family is who we care about.'

'Hear hear.' Arthur perched on the edge of the bed and looked from Tom to Fleur. 'And I don't know what the pair of you are worried about anyway. I think you'll both make terrifying pirate captains one day.'

'Only if we survive this journey,' replied Fleur bleakly.

Arthur sighed and sank his chin into his cupped hands. A heavy silence descended over the cabin. Guiltily, Fleur studied her friends' crestfallen faces. It wasn't their fault she was in this situation.

'What were you lot so excited about anyway?' she prompted, eager to change the mood.

Arthur straightened up and grinned. He held up the map and waggled it in the air. 'We've worked out how to read this,' he said proudly.

Fleur gasped with delight. 'Holy crabs, that's brilliant! How did you do it?'

'It was Arthur,' said Astrid, shifting into a kneeling position. 'Go on, Arthur, you tell her!'

'I can't take all the credit,' he mumbled, 'Astrid was—'

'*You* worked it out,' she insisted.

In the background, Tom let out an exaggerated groan. 'Unless one or the other of you tells her quick, *I'll* do it,' he said impatiently. 'I've heard it three times already,' he muttered under his breath.

'It was driving me mad,' Arthur began, not wanting Fleur to hear Tom's version of events. 'I knew that any map that had been tucked away so carefully like that must contain something special, so I wasn't about to give up easily.'

'Get on with it, you twerp,' teased Tom, sounding more like his usual self again.

'All right, all right ... Carlton Bart entrusted me with—'

Tom burst out laughing. '*Entrusted!*' he teased. 'Sorry, Dr Big Brains, but Bart only let you have it 'cause it ain't no use to anyone if we can't work out its secrets.'

Arthur glanced at Astrid, his cheeks red.

'Go on, Arthur, ignore him.' Fleur was grinning broadly now.

Arthur narrowed his eyes at Tom, then turned back to Fleur and continued. 'So, I was studying the map on deck when Astrid came over to see if she could help. And she saw something, didn't you, Astrid?' he prompted.

'I was holding the map,' said Astrid, 'when everything went black.'

'She did that weird, blank, starey thing again,' Arthur explained authoritatively.

'In my mind's eye, I saw the map sinking through water; sinking to the bottom of the ocean as if it were made of lead,' Astrid continued. 'As it fell, coins and precious jewels poured from it like bubbles.' She shrugged. 'That is all. I didn't have a clue what it meant – but Arthur worked it out.'

'The message in Astrid's vision was actually quite simple,' said Arthur modestly. 'It was telling us we needed to get the map wet.'

Fleur frowned. 'Eh?'

'Look . . .' Arthur thrust the map towards her. 'There's invisible ink between the lines we can see. It reacts with salt water to reveal the hidden map beneath. It's definitely a *treasure* map.'

Fleur placed the map on the bed and stared at it with wide eyes. It was covered in dense script, and the path to the promised treasure was now fringed with strange, inky monsters; mighty frost giants in the mountains, ugly trolls, giant serpents and, at the heart of the map, a great snarling wolf chained to a rock.

'The writing is mostly in Old Norse,' Arthur told her. 'I can pick out a few of the more German-sounding words but we'll need to study it more closely.' He pointed to a cluster of snow-capped mountains that rose like a great claw pointing north. Above their jagged peaks hovered the sun, surrounded by myriad stars. 'I think this part is called the Land of the . . . um . . . something . . . um, something.'

'The Land of the Um Something Something!' said Tom sarcastically. 'Brilliant. I always wanted to go there.'

'Well, you figure it out then if you're such an expert in extinct Germanic languages,' snapped Arthur.

'Where is this place?' interrupted Fleur quickly. 'I've never seen land like it.'

'The frozen North,' said Tom. 'A snowy wasteland, Fleur. A desert of ice as far as the eye can see. No place for sailors, that's for sure.'

'*Viking* country,' added Arthur wistfully. 'I've wanted to see it ever since I was little and my father told me stories about it. We *have* to go. We *have* to figure out this map. Imagine it: Viking treasure!'

Astrid, who had been silently studying the map, suddenly sat up. 'It says midnight,' she murmured softly.

'What did you say?' asked Fleur.

Astrid's eyes shone. 'The writing at the top. It says the Land of the Midnight Sun,' she told them matter-of-factly, tracing a finger over the feathery coastline to the east. 'And these are the Howling Fjords . . .' She shivered involuntarily.

There was a moment's silence before the other three erupted with questions. Fleur shushed the boys and turned to Astrid. 'How do you know these things?' she asked suspiciously.

Astrid shrugged, blushing. 'I don't know,' she insisted, apparently as bewildered as the rest of them. 'But when I concentrate hard on the words, it's as if a mist clears and I'm suddenly able to see their meaning.'

'What does this say then?' asked Tom, pointing to a random word.

Astrid stared at it for a moment. '*Hnoss*. That means treasure, I think, or possibly beauty.' She pointed to a phrase at the foot of the claw mountains. '*Rótlausum viði* – that means rootless tree.' Then she smiled as she circled another word with her fingertip. '*Sjöfn*,' she said. '*Love*.'

Tom folded his arms and frowned. 'Love?' he said doubtfully. 'On a map? Are you sure you're not getting mystically mixed up, Princess?'

Astrid shook her head firmly. 'I promise you,' she said. 'I cannot say how, but I know this tongue as if it were my own.'

Arthur cleared his throat and they all looked at him expectantly. 'Has it occurred to anyone else yet,' he asked, 'that Astrid's name is Old Norse?'

'Well, it had crossed *my* mind,' said Tom sarcastically. 'But I didn't want to steal your thunder, you being the clever one and all.'

Astrid gasped. 'Arthur, if what you say is true,' she said, trembling, 'then this map might lead me home.'

'Maybe,' he replied, 'but that would be a pretty massive coincidence, don't you think?'

'Aye,' said Tom. 'But we're no strangers to coincidence.' He pointed at the narwhal-horn staff, propped up against the cabin wall. 'Let's not forget that thing.'

'Leaping limpets!' exclaimed Fleur. 'Of course, the ruby heart.'

'What about it?' asked Astrid.

'According to the legend,' Fleur explained, 'the ruby heart in my staff was fired in Heaven and cooled in the ice of the frozen North.' She stared at the jewel, which glittered in the gloom of the cabin. 'If we follow the map, yours may not be the only homecoming, Astrid . . .' she said solemnly. 'Between the lot of us, we can figure this out,' she added after a pause. 'Coincidence or not, for now we must put this map aside and focus on matters at hand.'

'Aye,' said Tom earnestly. 'Let's get our captain back.'

Fleur beamed at her loyal and determined friends. 'And won't he be happy to have a treasure map to come home to?' she joked.

Tom shifted forward on the bed and placed his fingertips on the map. 'Aye, but in the meantime let's hide this so Rose can't get her slippery mitts on it.'

'A wise precaution,' Fleur agreed. She rolled the map up carefully and handed it to Astrid. 'You take it. You're the one who can unlock its secrets.'

She smiled at her friends and hugged herself with relief. Just a little while ago everything had seemed bleak and impossible, but now, buoyed by Arthur and Astrid's discovery and Tom's reminders of her uncle's faith in her, she was suddenly determined to assert herself over the crew – and over Rose in particular. Tom was right: the *Black Dragon* was her bloodright; no one could take it from her. She slipped off the bed and tucked her rapier into her belt.

'Where are you going?' asked Astrid nervously.

Fleur winked as she headed for the door. 'To deal with some unfinished business.'

Up on the deck, in the cold night air, Fleur searched around for her mother. She found her near the bow, doling out a punishment to one of the men on watch.

'You can sit there and unpick this old rope,' Rose was telling him as Fleur approached. 'And may your fingers blister and bleed, you scurvy layabout.'

She turned at the sound of footsteps on the boards behind her. She spun round and, noticing Fleur's grim expression, her face hardened at once. 'What's wrong with you?' she asked, dripping sarcasm. 'Fallen out with your playmates again?'

Fleur said nothing, but drew her rapier. The pirate on rope-picking detail looked warily at the rival Hart women, then picked up the rope and slunk away.

'This ain't your ship,' said Fleur in a bold, clear voice.

'You're a stowaway, nothing more. William gave me the wheel and his orders will be respected.'

Rose burst into peals of laughter. 'You ain't ready to captain a ship,' she spat. 'You've proved as much already. I'll admit you've some interesting talents, but you're no pirate queen, lassie; just a little girl with a lot to learn.'

Anger boiled in Fleur's belly, but her words were cool. 'Aye, I am. One with – what did you call 'em? – *talents* you've scarcely seen. I will be the greatest pirate captain ever to sail the seven seas . . . and you *will* fear me.' She held her sword aloft.

Rose looked at her in astonishment. 'You want me to fight you?' she asked. 'You really want the crew to witness the thrashing your old mum will give you?'

Fleur nodded, planting the tip of her sword in the deck. 'You can try,' she growled.

'Stand down, child,' exclaimed Rose, angry now. 'I'd like as not kill you, and I won't have the death of my own child on my conscience.'

Fleur narrowed her eyes and pointed her rapier at the sword in Rose's belt. 'You ain't my mother,' she spat, screwing up her face as if she had a bad taste in her mouth. 'Defend yourself or pay the consequences.'

Rose's green eyes flashed as, with a single fast, fluid

movement, she drew her sword and brought it clattering against Fleur's. Fleur staggered backwards with the unexpected weight of the blow, then launched herself at her mother with everything she had. Rose blocked and returned every attack, and the sound of clashing swords rang out above their cries.

'Why did you ever save me if you hate me so much?' Rose grunted as she just caught a well-aimed lunge with the flat of her blade.

'No idea,' snarled Fleur, twirling her rapier in a fresh attack. 'Everyone makes mistakes, I s'pose.'

Rose ducked under the arc of her sword and hopped up onto the poop deck, scattering a handful of spectators who were exchanging wagers over the outcome. The newer members of the crew were clearly betting on Rose to win, but those who had served with Fleur in the battle against the Bloods were not so quick to write her off.

'Or maybe you do love me, deep down?' said Rose. She grabbed the rail and spun her body round in a wide arc, kicking the sword from Fleur's hand.

Fleur executed a backflip, plucked her rapier from the deck and leaped back up onto the poop deck like a squirrel on a tree trunk. Rose's eyes widened in surprise and her mouth dropped open. She stood facing her daughter, breathless and furious. 'Where did that come from?' she asked.

'Talent,' said Fleur. 'And training.'

Rose swung her sword with more anger than aim and Fleur hopped out of the way. Adrenalin was coursing through her, and now she laughed at her opponent. Rose cried out furiously and lunged at her again and again. Fleur merely stood there, her blade parrying every desperate strike.

Rose howled with frustration. 'What witchcraft is this?' she gasped. 'Are you reading my thoughts, child?'

'Witchcraft? Hah! Have you learned nothing from your trip to Salem, Mother dear?' asked Fleur. She stepped nimbly forward and snatched her mother's sword right out of her hand, leaving her blinking in disbelief.

'I'm born for this,' said Fleur confidently. 'You're just an early chapter; it's *my* legend.'

Rose dropped to her knees and bowed her head, defeated. 'You're the one, aren't you?' she whispered, her face turning pale. 'I knew in my heart that there was something special about you when I saw you fight with the staff back in Salem. *It's said that should the right soul find the ruby — the right combination of talent and true spirit — they'll not just beat their foes in battle.'* She paused before completing the prophecy of the ruby heart in a whisper: *'They'll be able to harness the power of the ocean itself.'*

Fleur nodded slowly. '"Fraid so,' she replied.

Her mother let out a strangled sob and sank her head into her hands. 'When did you find out? Has it . . . ? Is it . . . ? Are you all right?'

Fleur shrugged dismissively. 'What do you care?'

'I do care, Fleur, of course I do,' Rose replied defensively. 'That blasted prophecy sent William crazy and helped to destroy the bond of love between him and Henry.' Tears swam in her eyes suddenly. 'All that power. All that potential, Fleur. It could destroy you too . . .' Her voice cracked. 'You're only a child.'

Fleur stamped her foot. 'Stop saying that,' she demanded. 'My childhood was stolen from me a long time ago.'

'I know,' Rose admitted quietly. 'And I'm sorry.'

'Hold your tongue,' Fleur shouted, furiously wiping away the tears that betrayed her vulnerability. 'How could you have left me behind?'

Rose could only stare at her furious daughter speechlessly. Fleur snorted and backed away, waggling the tip of her sword at her mother. 'You've a split tongue and you ain't worth ship room,' she snapped.

'There's nothing you could say to make me feel worse than I do already,' Rose replied sadly.

Fleur lowered her sword, frowning.

'Fleur, can we talk privately?' her mother asked.

Fleur sighed and reluctantly nodded her consent. 'Five minutes,' she replied. She reached down and snatched the captain's tricorn hat from her kneeling mother, sending her red hair cascading over her shoulders. The hat was far too big for Fleur, but she would never let anyone else wear it again until William's return. She lifted her sword above her head and glared down at the men watching from the main deck. 'Let it be known,' she bellowed, 'that if anyone threatens my captaincy again, they will be leaving this ship at the first port . . . Or possibly earlier.'

And with that she turned and led Rose silently to her cabin.

'I'm still not sure if I am the one to fulfil the prophecy, or even if I believe this whole legend business . . .' said Fleur warily. Her thoughts returned to the whales of New England. 'Although I will admit that things do seem to be pointing in that direction.'

'No child — begging your pardon — could fight

like you,' said Rose, 'without some kind of magic at play.'

'Father trained me since I was a young 'un,' Fleur explained. 'I could already fight with sword and staff before I ever heard of the ruby heart.'

'You fight like the spirit of war, Fleur,' said Rose. 'Henry was gifted in combat, but you . . .' She looked her daughter up and down again and her eyes shone with pride. 'You're a goddess.'

She stood up and reached for the Hart staff, propped up against the wall. Fleur bristled as her mother laid her hands on it, but she said nothing.

'I haven't seen this thing for years.' Rose's voice was sad and faraway. Her fingers ran over the huge ruby in its golden setting. 'Did you know that Henry and I had to hide it from William?'

'Aye.' Fleur nodded. 'I know the whole story.'

Rose raised an eyebrow. 'But I bet you didn't know that your father had to hide it from himself too. He was a strong man, but he knew that the call of the sea would grow too much for him to bear otherwise.'

'*You* weren't strong enough to ignore it though, were you?' hissed Fleur.

Her mother sighed and propped the staff back against

the wall. 'No, I gave in to it . . . in the end,' she admitted, coming back to sit on the edge of Fleur's bed.

Hot tears burned in Fleur's eyes and she wiped them away, furious to find herself crying over her wretched mother yet again. 'You left because you resented me?' she said quietly. 'That staff has a stronger hold on you than I ever had.'

Rose laced her hands together and rested her chin on them. 'Resented is not the right word,' she replied. 'I loved you in my own way, and your father too. But I blamed you, Fleur, for the end of my days at sea with the Hart brothers.'

'That wasn't my fault,' snapped Fleur. 'Father chose to hide you, with me in your belly, because he was scared that the Blood clan would murder us as they had William's wife and baby.'

'I know, and 'twas a noble deed. But that was always his decision, never mine.'

'What?' asked Fleur, stunned. 'You'd've preferred to be murdered, I suppose.'

Rose sank her head into her hands miserably. Her auburn hair tumbled around her shoulders like falling autumn leaves. 'Of course not, but I was only ever happy with the sea beneath me, Fleur.' She looked up again desperately. 'Surely you can understand that.'

'I do,' said Fleur. 'But to win happiness at the cost of your own flesh and blood . . .' She placed her right hand over her heart. 'I couldn't do that. Family is important to *me*.'

Rose looked at her daughter sadly. 'It wasn't to me,' she whispered. 'At least, I didn't think so.'

Fleur hung her head, feeling drained and sad. All she wanted right now was to run away – from the truth, from everything. William had been right: lies were easier to bear.

'You have to know, Fleur,' said Rose miserably, 'that I've missed you every day of my wretched life.'

'You should have tried harder to stay then . . . We've been through all this before.'

'Fleur, I was like a fish stranded on the shore,' Rose replied passionately. 'The song of the ocean never stopped calling to me.'

Fleur blinked back her tears with surprise. 'What? You can hear the ocean's voice too?' She frowned, thinking of Astrid's similar claim. 'I thought only a true Hart could hear it. You've hardly been loyal to the name.'

Rose smiled, and her sharp eyes softened. 'I heard it first when I was carrying you, child,' she explained. 'After that it never left me. And the pull of it, Fleur . . .'

And suddenly Rose was sobbing too, the words pouring out of her. 'I tried to stay, I swear it,' she said, her voice cracking with emotion. 'I never wanted you in the first place, and I'm sorry for that. You felt like a stranger when you were born, Fleur. I thought . . . I hoped I might feel like a mother when I first laid eyes on you; instead I felt like a fraud. I felt nothing.'

A sob escaped Fleur but she sat ramrod straight, listening. 'A black cloud almost swallowed me,' Rose went on. 'I became blind to my responsibilities and began to fear what I might do if I stayed. I used to climb up onto the rocks and stare out across the sea and wonder what it would be like to just let myself fall.'

Her eyes pleaded with Fleur, desperate for her to understand. But her daughter simply sat in silence, chewing on her fingernails.

'The day I decided to leave was the day I began to feel like living again,' Rose continued. 'But that same day my heart froze over; that was when I realized what I was leaving behind. I remember taking you into our bed that last night. You were so small and you smelled of summer meadows.' Tears spilled down her face. 'I held you and Henry so tightly. I even prayed, for the first time in half a lifetime. I would have done anything to break down the wall between us. But God wasn't listening. I left before dawn, knowing it was the right thing to do. I wanted you to grow up right, girl, and I knew you'd have more of a chance without me. I knew that I couldn't be the sort of mother you needed.'

'Any sort of mother would have done,' said Fleur indignantly. 'Weren't you worried that one day we'd meet again and I'd hate you?'

Her mother looked at her steadily. 'I loved you enough to *let* you hate me,' she replied.

They both fell silent. After a while Rose reached out to take Fleur's hand in hers and Fleur let her.

'Henry was a good husband, he adored me,' she said. 'But the sea was his true love.'

'He gave it all up for you,' said Fleur.

'He gave it up for *us*, Fleur,' Rose reminded her gently. 'You became his whole world, even before you were born. I tried to ignore it when you came along – but he stopped seeing me the way he used to. I was invisible, really. You and he were like a team, and I felt left out.' She stood up and started pacing around the small cabin. 'That's when I decided that the two of you would fare better without me.'

'That's not true,' said Fleur. 'William has told me how much Father loved you.'

But her mother nodded, her lips pressed together in a tight smile. 'William doesn't know everything, Fleur. You have to remember that it was a dark, confusing time for us all. He'd lost Anna and his baby boy, Robert, and I became another thing for him to hate and blame for his world falling apart. You were just a wee thing and didn't see what was happening. How could you?'

They sat in silence until Rose could bear it no more. 'Fleur, tell me what's in your mind,' she pleaded. 'I've told you all there is. I'm sorry for the lies and hope that one day you might forgive me.'

Fleur nodded, staring blankly at her lap. 'I understand that you had your reasons,' she replied quietly. 'But I'm not ready to forgive you. Especially after your behaviour on the *Dragon*.'

Rose bit her lip and nodded back. 'Fair enough,' she replied. 'I deserve no better. I actually have a ship that needs its captain; I left it in good hands off American shores. Maybe I went about it wrong, but in my own way I was worried about you taking on too much responsibility. I still think you're too young to captain a pirate ship.'

'For whatever it's worth, so do I,' admitted Fleur. 'I don't really know what Uncle William was thinking.'

Her mother chuckled at that and Fleur couldn't help smiling too.

'Well, *that* we can agree on at least,' said Rose. 'William can be a reckless fool but there's often a grain of sanity in his actions. He must have thought he was doing the right thing.'

'Aye.'

Without warning Rose leaned forward and clasped her daughter in an awkward hug. Fleur tensed, then relaxed, allowing her head to sink against her mother's shoulder.

'I tried to stop loving you because I thought it would be easier,' whispered Rose, squeezing Fleur tightly and stroking her hair. 'But I thought about you all the time. I missed you and Henry but I knew I could never return.' She sighed. 'So I never stopped moving – it was better that way.'

'It must have been lonely,' said Fleur.

Her mother pulled away and stared into her eyes. 'It was a fitting punishment,' she replied. 'Fleur, I know I can't expect too much from you, and I'm not sure what I can give you either. But I hope that time will change that.'

Fleur frowned. 'And you promise to stop trying to take over the ship?' she asked.

'I promise. In fact I'll help you from here on in, however I can ... Though don't expect a happy family reunion when your uncle claps eyes on me. It may be that he'd rather ride the cart to the Tyburn tree than sail with me again.'

Fleur stared back at the familiar green eyes and nodded slowly. 'Then you can stay,' she said at last, and suddenly she leaned forward and kissed her mother softly on the cheek.

# CHAPTER 19

'Well, I'll be blowed,' said Tom, shaking his head in disbelief.

Arthur pulled a face. 'Does that mean *we* have to be nice to her too now?'

Fleur and her friends were sitting below deck in the stuffy mess room. Dinner was over, and most of the crew had returned to their duties, though a few still sat talking quietly on a bench nearby. Grog sat grooming himself in a corner.

Fleur had just told her friends about the showdown with Rose.

'I never knew about any of this,' said Tom.

'I'm surprised Rose didn't confide in you too,' replied Fleur sarcastically.

'You know I make it my business to listen out for anything I can,' Tom snapped back with a scowl. 'And don't give me that bilge, Claw-cat. You're first in line for any bit of juicy gossip on board.' He folded his arms and leaned on the swinging trestle table so that it rocked like a hammock.

'How do you feel now, Fleur?' asked Astrid, reaching out to stop her cup from rolling off.

She stabbed a piece of cornbread with her small pearl-handled dagger. 'Confused,' she admitted. 'I loved her, and then I hated her, and now . . . I'm not sure about anything any more.' She puffed up her cheeks and blew out. 'I think I understand her reasons for leaving, but it still hurts. I think it always will.'

'Not always,' Astrid said solemnly, 'If you've let go of the hatred that consumed you, the pain will fade with time. It needs a cold climate to survive.'

'I hope you're right,' replied Fleur. 'Hey!' she exclaimed, sitting up suddenly, her eyes wide. 'I don't suppose you've had any visions along those lines, have you? Me all happy and grown up, I mean?'

'No,' said Astrid. 'And I wouldn't tell you if I had. It doesn't do to know one's future.'

'I thought you'd say something like that,' sighed Fleur, slumping onto her folded arms.

Astrid glanced over her shoulder to make sure the men sitting nearby weren't listening, then leaned in close. 'I do have an update on the vision front though,' she whispered to her friends.

Arthur clapped his hands together in delight. 'Excellent!'

Astrid chuckled at his enthusiasm and tucked her hair behind her ears. 'I'm learning how to control them, just as you suggested, Fleur,' she explained. 'I didn't think it was possible, but apparently I was wrong.'

'Well, split my skull!' Tom exclaimed, slapping a hand down on the table. 'That could be useful.'

'I hope so,' agreed Astrid. 'Though it doesn't always work yet.'

'So how do you do it?' asked Arthur.

Astrid waited while the group of men got to their feet and shuffled past on their way out.

Tom swivelled on the bench to face her. 'Come on then,' he demanded. 'Spill!'

'I have to really concentrate on what I want to see,' Astrid began, laying her palms flat on the table. 'At the moment it's easier to go back and view the past; the future is harder to reach.'

'That makes sense,' said Arthur, nodding authoritatively. 'The future isn't fixed like the past is.'

Astrid smiled at him, making him blush. 'Exactly,' she said. 'I start by sitting quietly, trying to blank out everything around me, until my mind is empty of everything except the thing I am trying to conjure up. Suddenly the world drops away completely and I'm standing right in the middle of the scene I need to see. Sometimes it changes, but no one ever knows I'm there. I'm always invisible.'

'Probably a good thing too,' murmured Arthur.

'But then the whispers begin,' Astrid continued, squeezing her eyes shut. 'They start like an eerie wind, almost like a huge collection of sighs. And then I'm plunged into a great howling wilderness and the answers are screamed at me from every direction.' She opened her eyes. 'That's what happens when it works anyway. Sometimes nothing happens at all.'

They all sat without speaking for a few moments, taking in what Astrid had told them.

'Rather you than me,' said Fleur finally. 'It sounds terrifying.'

Astrid nodded. 'It is,' she said quietly. 'Before I started trying to control my visions, I only heard whispers, but now I feel like I'm prising something open by force.' She

289

lowered her head. 'Sometimes I feel like I'm standing on the edge of Hell. I've told you before that I call my gift a curse.'

'But it's not a curse,' said Arthur firmly. 'Not when you're trying to use it for good.'

She looked up at him. 'I suppose you're right, and I do want to see what I am capable of,' she admitted. 'Although so far I've only concentrated on trivial things, like where Bart's best pipe disappeared to, or who ate the leftover goat's meat.'

'That's not trivial,' grumbled Tom. 'Who did?'

'Tiny Joe,' Astrid replied with a smile, 'when he was three sheets to the wind on rum the other night.'

'I knew it,' said Tom indignantly. 'That great mountain of blubber would eat the rotten fish out the bilges if we let him.' He paused and grinned at Astrid mischievously. 'Hey, let's see if you can do one now ...' He held his hands together as if in prayer. 'Go on, Princess, we'll be in London soon – try and see how the captain is doing.'

'But only if you want to,' said Arthur quickly.

Tom rolled his eyes at him as Astrid furrowed her brow, thinking hard. 'All right, I'll try,' she agreed at last. 'But remember, it might not work. It doesn't always, and I've never performed to an audience before.'

'The pressure might help,' joked Tom.

'Would you rather we left?' asked Arthur. 'We could wait outside.'

Astrid shook her head. 'I don't think it will make any difference,' she said, licking her lips and taking a deep breath. 'Remember not to disturb me though, whatever happens.'

Fleur and the two boys nodded eagerly, and Astrid lowered her head and closed her eyes. Her silky hair spilled down over her shoulders, and after a while her breathing fell into a slower rhythm.

As the minutes passed, Tom grew bored and started to fidget. Fleur poked him in the ribs and held a finger to her lips. He sighed loudly. 'Do you think she's having one yet?' he mouthed. 'Only, she's been at it for ages and I'm due on watch soon.'

Fleur only shrugged, but Arthur leaned over and gently held up Astrid's hair so that they could see her face. Her eyes were wide open, staring at some scene inside her head. Her pupils darting around wildly, and her brow was hot and clammy, as if she had a fever.

'I think that answers your question,' murmured Fleur.

'I don't like it when she does this,' said Arthur nervously. 'I worry that we'll lose her completely.'

Astrid suddenly sat up straight, and Arthur fell off the bench in shock, landing on the floor with a yelp. She stared at him blankly. Her violet eyes were empty voids, but fire burned somewhere deep beneath.

'I say . . .' Arthur began as he got to his feet, but his voice trailed away.

Astrid pointed at Tom. 'A choice for the cabin boy . . . ' she said in a strange faraway voice that was deeper and older than her own. 'Between the ones for whom he lives and the one to whom he owes his life.'

Tom's mouth opened and closed and the colour drained from his face. Astrid blinked a few times, then seemed to come to her senses, frowning as if the dim light were too bright. Her body went slack and she rubbed her forehead with trembling fingers. As her eyes regained focus, she looked over and reached out for Tom.

'I'm sorry,' she said sadly.

He slid off the bench and backed away from her. Fleur looked from Tom to Astrid in confusion. 'What did you see, Astrid?' she asked.

Astrid swallowed nervously and her eyes didn't leave Tom for a second. 'I saw the captain's trial . . . it hasn't happened yet . . . And more besides,' she said.

Tom held up a finger in warning. 'Whatever you think you saw about me is wrong,' he told her in a ragged voice.

'As you wish, Tom . . .' She lowered her head.

Fleur jumped to her feet. 'Hell's bells, Tom, what's going on? Talk to us,' she demanded.

But Tom's expression was dark, his eyes as cold as a shark's. 'You're unhinged!' he snarled at Astrid. 'Stop making up all these lies about me. Why don't you do us all a favour and go back to the Devil.'

Fleur gasped with shock while Astrid sank her head into her hands and began to sob.

'I say,' said Arthur, rising to his feet. 'You can't talk to a lady like that, Tom.'

Tom squared up to him, his fists clenched tightly. 'Shut up, you lubberly idiot,' he screamed in his face. 'Astrid is a swivel-tongued liar and I ain't putting up with no more of this nonsense.'

Fleur grabbed Tom by the arm, but he shook her off roughly. She stumbled backwards against the swinging table, and the razor-sharp knife she'd been using to eat with slid off and nicked Astrid's calf before clattering to the floor. Blood started seeping through Astrid's breeches, and Tom's eyes widened as he realized what he had done.

'I'm sorry . . . I didn't mean to . . .' he said, backing away like a cornered tiger. 'Please . . . leave me alone . . . all of you.'

And with that, he turned and ran out of the room.

Later that evening, Gates, Bart, Rose and Fleur stood on the bridge discussing Astrid's vision.

'So you're telling us that the cap'n will be tried on the same day that the harvest moon is first full?' asked an extremely suspicious Carlton Bart. 'And we're to trust these visions, are we?'

'That's about the shape of it,' Fleur replied. 'I know it sounds like nonsense, but Astrid ain't been wrong about nothing else yet, and William was always keen to use her skills.'

Gates scratched his bearded chin and frowned. 'But that's tomorrow,' he said.

'Aye, that's right, man,' Bart agreed solemnly.

'So we need to get ourselves to the Old Bailey, and sharpish,' said Rose firmly.

Bart spread a parchment map out on the chart table and pointed to the big river that wound its way through London like a giant ribbon. 'Look, we're nearing the mouth of the Thames now. We can dock somewhere up here' – he pointed – 'near the city; in the morning some of us can take the tender further upriver and walk the rest of the way to the Bailey.'

'So are we to try and rescue him there then?' asked Fleur. She stood with her hands behind her back, fidgeting nervously.

'If we get the opportunity, yes,' replied Gates. 'Though the whole place will be crawling with guards. Once he's been tried he'll be sent back to prison to await the hanging, and that will give us time to work out what we're going to do.'

Bart leaned over the table and snatched up the map. 'It's time to pretend we're the navy.' He shuddered at the thought. 'And may God rest our souls.'

The *Adventurer* boldly sailed into the River of Thames that very evening with the flag of Saint George fluttering from the mainmast. Now each man, woman and girl upon the ship was united in determination to save the captain. Bart, Gates and the others pretending to be of high rank had changed into the blue embroidered dress coats worn by navy officers when ashore. Fleur was in her boy's slops. The winds and tides were favourable so the river was thick with seagoing vessels. The Thames was the passageway to growing colonies all over the world, and incoming ships queued from Blackwall to

London Bridge to unload their exotic cargoes: tobacco, molasses, sugar and dyes from America and the West Indies; bright silks and pungent spices, printed calico and pepper from India. Food and wine ripened beneath the warm Mediterranean sun, and tea leaves and delicate porcelain from the East.

Darkness soon fell over the river, and lanterns began to blaze all around the *Adventurer* as she cut through the busy waterway. It was a fine autumn evening, and men from other ships waved and called out to them as they passed. The camouflage worked, and no one questioned them when they finally anchored on the south side of the river. The hour was late and the moon glowed through the wispy clouds. The first part of the plan had been successful, but the mood was tense. Now the pirates were right in the lion's den and no one would sleep well that night.

Fleur felt restless and went to stand at the prow of the *Adventurer*, hoping that the briny breeze would help to clear her troubled mind. Moonlight poured down over the water and made it glisten like polished steel. After a while she was joined by Arthur. 'I can't sleep,' he said with a wide yawn.

'I'm not sure that I'll ever sleep again,' Fleur murmured.

They leaned against the ship's rail, shoulder to shoulder, staring down into the water below. Grog hopped down from the rigging and settled himself at Fleur's feet.

'Bit of a scene with Tom earlier, eh?' said Arthur.

Fleur exhaled loudly. Tom had been silent and withdrawn since Astrid's second revelation and bluntly refused to talk to Fleur about it. In fact he'd pretty much stopped talking altogether unless it was to respond to an order.

'I wish Astrid would tell us exactly what she saw,' Fleur muttered. 'All these secrets – it's so frustrating. I'm not sure who to believe.'

Arthur cleared his throat nervously. 'About Astrid . . . Have you noticed anything odd about her lately?'

'Well, let's see . . .' said Fleur flatly. 'There's the magic powers – does that count? Oh, and she's got purple eyes and I swear her hair looks silver sometimes. Apart from that . . . um . . . what sort of odd?'

Arthur ran a hand through his shaggy fringe and shrugged. 'I dunno. It's nothing . . . probably.'

Fleur turned to face him and Grog yelped indignantly as she trod on his long bushy tail. 'Sorry, Grog . . . Come on, spill it, Arthur,' she demanded. 'We both know you'll tell me in the end.'

He stared at her for a few moments, then pointed down at the murky brown waters of the Thames. 'The more I sail with William the more I am forced to question what I thought I knew about the world,' he began. 'When Tom said you can't learn everything from books, he was right. The ocean holds lessons no book could ever have taught me.' He looked up. 'No doubt the heavens do too. I'm unlearning and relearning everything, Fleur. And these new truths . . . well, they are even stranger than I thought possible.'

'Are you planning to make sense at any point in this conversation?' asked Fleur, one eyebrow raised.

'I might. Bear with me,' said Arthur. He stood on tiptoe and peered over the side of the ship again. 'I wonder what secrets are hidden in the world's darkest depths,' he mused, 'where no light ever shines . . .'

Fleur rolled her eyes and groaned. 'I still don't know what you're saying, Arthur. Either get to the point quickly or else keep going, and maybe I'll be able to get some sleep after all.'

'It's Astrid,' said Arthur abruptly. He scrunched up his face, as if his words were a betrayal.

'Go on,' urged Fleur, suddenly interested.

He sighed and scanned the deck to make sure no one was listening. 'Earlier on,' he murmured conspiratorially,

'I asked to see the wound to her leg, where Tom stabbed her.'

'He didn't stab her, Arthur, you idiot,' said Fleur. 'It was an accident.'

'Well, anyway, she didn't want me to look at it. Wouldn't let me near it.'

'And?' said Fleur. 'Maybe she doesn't like doctors.' She bent down to pick up Grog, who scampered up her arm to lie across her shoulders like a cat.

Arthur sighed again. 'The thing is, the wound wouldn't stop bleeding, so in the end she had to come and see me. And when I examined her . . . this will sound strange, but there was this sort of pattern on her legs.'

'A what?'

'Like I said, a pattern. Like fish scales. I thought it was a tattoo at first; but, Fleur . . . it's not a tattoo.'

Fleur snorted loudly. 'Fish scales! Don't be daft, Arthur. You're over-tired. You're seeing things that ain't there.'

'You see?' moaned Arthur indignantly. 'This is exactly why I wasn't going to say anything to you about this. I knew you'd mock me.'

They froze suddenly and stood in tense silence as Black Matt staggered past, clearly with a little too much rum in his belly.

'Look,' sighed Fleur, when they were alone again. 'Are

you sure you're not imagining this? Only, I've seen Astrid's legs — we were sharing quarters, remember? And I'm sure I would have noticed if she was covered in . . . in "not tattoos".'

Arthur puffed out his cheeks and shook his head. 'I'll admit it does sound peculiar,' he said. 'But the markings — whatever they are — were as clear to me as the nose on her face, Fleur. She tried to hide them from me, but of course she couldn't.'

'So what did she have to say about these . . . um, markings?'

Arthur shrugged and scratched Grog's head. 'Well, nothing — I mean, I didn't ask . . . Not gentlemanly . . .' he mumbled, embarrassed.

'Blimey, Arthur, get over it. You're a doctor, ain't you?' Fleur frowned thoughtfully. 'Assuming for a moment that you did see something . . .'

'Which I did.'

'Assuming you did, are you sure it wasn't some sort of disease? I don't want her spreading a fever among us when we need all hands on deck.'

Arthur shook his head firmly. 'I have certainly never read of a medical condition that could make skin shimmer like a shoal of herring.'

'So what do you make of it then?'

'Let's look at the facts,' said Arthur. 'Astrid says she knows nothing of her past, not even her full name. She denies witchcraft, but exhibits both clairvoyant skills and an ability that, frankly, goes way beyond the natural appeal of a pretty girl . . . She can read ancient Norse . . . . Her singing voice can reduce our whole crew to tears, which is a bit weird when you consider the bloodthirsty rabble we're talking about . . .'

'And she can hear the song of the ocean when the moon is full,' said Fleur casually.

Arthur's mouth dropped open in astonishment. 'Really? Are you sure? Are you absolutely certain?'

'Aye. I found out as we were leaving New England. What does it matter?'

'I'm just going to say what I'm thinking,' Arthur blurted out. 'Oh God . . . you're going to think I've gone loony.'

'Just tell me.'

'OK, OK.' Arthur took a deep breath and fixed her with a level gaze. 'Astrid's a mermaid.'

'What?' said Fleur, bursting into laughter. 'But that's madness, Arthur. Folk saw mermaids all the time back in Cornwall. My dad used to say it was amazing what too much rum and a seal with seaweed on its head could conjure.'

Arthur shrugged defensively. 'There've been sightings of mermaids all over the world, Fleur,' he told her stiffly. 'There are reliable accounts . . . well documented ones. There's a reference to a mermaid sighting in one of Christopher Columbus's journals.'

'Christopher who?'

'The explorer,' Arthur explained patiently. 'My father had copies of all his journals.' He sighed with exasperation. 'Look, I'm just putting it out there. You don't have to believe me, but I would urge you, of all people, Fleur, to keep an open mind. And look again at her legs, if she'll let you.' He pushed his glasses up his nose and coughed nervously.

'You realize what this means – if you're right,' said Fleur seriously.

'What?' said Arthur.

'You're half in love with a fish.'

# CHAPTER 20

At dawn Fleur, accompanied by Gates, Bart and Arthur, slipped into the ship's tender and rowed up the Thames. Fleur had asked Tom to join them but he had refused point blank and gone to hide in the crow's nest instead. Arthur, on the other hand, was desperate to join the landing party, thrilled at the prospect of seeing the Old Bailey. As no one expected any trouble on this outing, his wishes were granted, with Rose left in charge of the remaining crew.

At first, Fleur and her landing party had to grope their way carefully through the spooky river mist. All was quiet, except for the *drip-drip* and *splosh* of the oars in the water. Fleur perched nervously on a narrow seat at the stern, thinking back to her strange conversation with Arthur and the even stranger events that had followed.

She had gone back to her cabin and found Astrid studying the map they'd found on the *Dragon*. Seizing the bull by the horns, she had shared Arthur's preposterous mermaid theory, expecting to share a good laugh at his expense. Instead, Astrid had gone quite pale. And when Fleur had pushed her, she finally exposed the skin of her wounded leg – mottled, just as Arthur had suggested, with a delicate silvery pattern like shimmering scales. Fleur had shrunk away, until reason and Astrid's quiet pleading helped her to regain her senses. The two girls talked: Astrid clearly had no more idea why the strange markings had appeared than Arthur had, though she could at least testify to feeling healthy and fit in all other regards.

'I don't think I'm a mermaid, for what it's worth,' she told Fleur with a weak smile. 'Or getting thrown overboard would have been less of a problem for me.'

'You were nailed into a barrel,' Fleur reminded her. 'It looked pretty mermaid-proof. Do the marks on your legs hurt?'

Astrid smoothed her nightshirt down again and shook

her head. 'No, but they shine like this for a few days before and during the full moon, same as when the song of the ocean calls to me.' Her eyes widened with fear. 'Please don't tell anyone else about this, Fleur. They'll think me even more of an oddity.' Tears began to run down her cheeks, and Fleur had stroked her hair and soothed her.

'Flesh or fish, you're friend to me,' she said. 'We're sisters of the sea.'

As the tender made its way up the Thames, Fleur couldn't stop thinking about Astrid and how fate had brought them together. And however fanciful the mermaid notion, in the back of her mind a bigger story was forming: one where all these questions would finally be answered. And she had a sneaking feeling that it had something to do with the treasure map. For now, though, she had to put that aside. All that mattered was William.

The wide river was already teeming with ferries and merchant ships groaning with heavy loads. Soon the morning sun burned through the haze and the scenes around them sharpened. Fleur had never been to London before and was amazed by the sheer size of the magnificent city. Christopher Wren's skyline rose gracefully above the other densely packed buildings. They took the tender beneath the shadow of London Bridge, marvelling at the houses and souvenir shops that sprawled along it. Below that, at the Port of London, ships were already lining up to unload cargo from every corner of the world. The four of them stared at their surroundings in silence, lost in their own thoughts.

'We'll get out here,' Bart announced suddenly, making Fleur jump. 'It's as near as we can get by river – we can walk the rest of the way.'

The small boat was tethered to a post in a small inlet and her crew waded the short distance to dry land. As they did so, a huge officious-looking man came charging towards them. His straggly brown hair was scraped back into a greasy ponytail and his eyes were like two small currants set in a mound of dough.

'Uh-oh – trouble,' said Bart under his breath. He stood up straight and adjusted his hat. 'It's the parish beadle.'

'Oi, where do you lot think you're going?' the man demanded. He leaned on his stout wooden cudgel and scanned the group suspiciously.

In two strides Gates was next to him, eyeballing him with contempt. 'Who do you think you're talking to, maggot?' he snapped. 'How dare you question me!'

The beadle's face fell as he took a second look at

Gates and backed away nervously. 'Beggin' your pardon, sir,' he said, pointing over at the Thames, 'but we've been told to watch these 'ere waters for pirates, sir.'

'Pirates, you say?' said Gates theatrically. He turned to Fleur and the others. 'Have you seen any pirates, men?'

'No, sir,' Fleur replied, trying not to laugh. 'Not since we was in Cornwall anyway.'

The beadle frowned as he studied Fleur, but then thankfully turned back to Gates. 'They're 'olding a famous pirate in Newgate,' he replied. 'Right monster, so they're sayin'.'

'Really?' said Gates, with an eyebrow raised. 'Monsters?'

'That's right, sir. A merciless savage who speaks in tongues. The guards reckon there might be a rescue attempt.' The man shook his head and scratched his flabby chin. 'Though why anyone would try that is beyond me.' He suddenly frowned at the pirates before addressing Gates again. 'With respect, what *are* you doing here, sir?'

The bosun sighed and stalked away with his hands behind his back. 'What do you *think* we're doing at this time of the morning?' he retorted, turning to glare at the beadle. 'We're out to press a few men into service, if you must know,' he snapped. 'We've drained the docks of

**307**

likely scum to serve on my ship, and I'm hoping to find a few more flotsam littering the streets outside the taverns.'

The beadle nodded eagerly. 'You'd be right, sir,' he said. 'I've seen some meself this very morn. Passed out in their own waste, sir. And for a couple of shillings I'll point you in the right direction.'

Without a word, Gates pulled out a small leather pouch, shook out a single shilling and handed it over. The beadle's face fell and he left his open hand outstretched. 'I've named me price,' he cried.

Gates raised an eyebrow haughtily. He was putting on a fine performance and Fleur wondered whether he was revealing something of the man he'd once been. The beadle was a big man, but Gates was bigger and towered over him menacingly.

'I'll pay you a single shilling, and if you don't tell me what you know, I'll carve your gizzard into strips and boil it for my supper,' the bosun threatened.

The beadle winced and quickly pocketed the shilling. He pointed with his cudgel to a dark, narrow alleyway behind him. 'Follow that passage to the end, then head right – you'll find the Bell Tavern,' he said. 'There was a brawl last night and you'll find 'em still lying drunk on the street outside.'

Gates nodded and allowed himself a thin smile. 'You've done well, man.' He pointed to the tender bobbing up and down in the muddy water of the Thames. 'And if you do see any of those nasty pirates, make sure you keep them away from my boat.'

The beadle nodded again, eager to keep the navy captain happy, and even saluted before they parted company.

Gates led the group along the alleyway, past the Bell Tavern, stepping over the drunken men lying outside, and in amongst the densely packed houses. Fleur hurried to catch up with him.

'I never thought I'd see the day when I'd be wearing this uniform again, miss,' he muttered to her ruefully as they fell in step. 'It reminds me of a time I'd rather forget.'

'Aye, sir,' replied Fleur. 'I can imagine.'

He sighed and glanced down at her. 'And worse still,' he said sadly, 'it reminds me of the old George Gates.'

'But you're not that man any more, sir. I don't think you ever could be again.'

'What makes you say that?' demanded Gates gruffly. 'You barely know me, child.'

Fleur cleared her throat nervously and spoke up. 'Perhaps not,' she said, 'but with respect, sir, to go back would mean betraying your heart, betraying Esi – and I know in my own heart that you could never do that.'

Gates nodded, clearly surprised. 'Aye, child, there's truth in that,' he agreed; then his face hardened. 'The very thought of serving alongside those who took her from me churns my stomach with bile.'

'I just hope we don't run into any old friends while we're here,' said Fleur as they marched past a group of men loitering at a street corner.

'If we do, Fleur,' said Gates darkly, 'run away from me, as far and fast as you can, for I won't be shown any mercy. And nor will you for knowing me.'

Fleur shivered and pulled her coat around herself protectively. Danger threatened them from all sides; she could almost feel its icy fingers on her neck.

The city was a maze of streets, each one different from the last, that crawled on for miles, though open fields with grazing livestock stretched out towards the north. Some of the dank narrow alleys were little more than open sewers. Fleur stared in disgust at the squalid housing and decaying tenements that littered the city like open sores. The air was thick with sulphurous coal as smoke belched out of chimneys, and hogs and vermin roamed the streets, living off the rotting waste.

As the city began to wake up, Fleur felt ever more

exposed and fearful, hurrying along with her head bowed low. She stayed close to Arthur, who'd barely spoken a word since they'd left the *Adventurer*. It was the first time he'd been away from a ship in months, and he seemed nervous. But that was how it was for most of those who spent a long time at sea. It was all too easy to believe that the ship you sailed in was the whole world.

The cityscape soon began to change. Gates explained that after the Great Fire investors had begun pouring money into rebuilding the city. Fashionable areas were springing up from the ashes, and some of the houses even had running water. But the solid brick of the new buildings and the comfort they offered still couldn't persuade Fleur that a landlubber's life was preferable. The view from a porthole suited her fine, and the open sea was the only address she would ever need.

The pirates turned into a narrow alley that ran north from Ludgate Hill, and suddenly found themselves at their destination. A great crowd had gathered at the Sessions House of the Old Bailey, hoping to catch a glimpse of the celebrated pirate whose trial was about to start. Gates had to barge a path through the throng of spectators, litigants, witnesses and court officials who filled the Sessions House Yard, and up the stone steps to the terrace of the courtroom itself. Not wanting to attract attention, he was careful not to provoke a quarrel, so their progress was torturously slow. At last, however, they took up positions in an observation gallery above the courtroom, with a good view of the judge's bench and the dock – a sort of topless wooden cage where William would be kept throughout his trial. The atmosphere in the room was tense and the crowd, packed as tightly as a shoal of herring, was growing louder and more excitable by the minute.

'It's like a giant Punch and Judy Show,' Arthur whispered in Fleur's ear.

They stared down at the yard as more spectators pushed their way in. Nosegays of flowers and aromatic herbs were routinely spread about the courtroom to counter the stench of the prisoners, but the whole place reeked. With a rap of his wooden hammer, the King's justice called for silence for Judge Joseph Fielding and, amazingly, the mob obeyed immediately.

The dreaded judge made his entrance in silence, his black robes sweeping like giant bat wings around his bulky frame. He was a striking, fierce-looking man with a magnificent bushy moustache; a large white ceremonial wig perched on his head. He took his seat and nodded solemnly. Next, a wretched assortment of terrified-looking men and women in heavy chains were brought into court. A roar went up as William appeared at the end of the line. His bearded face was pale, and there were dark shadows beneath his bloodshot eyes. His clothes were dirty and torn and it was clear that he had been badly beaten – yet still there was pride and rebellion in his stiff shoulders and the set of his jaw. Fleur gasped as she took in his sorry state and had to restrain herself from vaulting over the gallery rail to rescue him at once.

As if he could read her thoughts, Gates placed a firm and reassuring hand on her shoulder. 'Not yet,' he whispered. 'All in good time, miss.'

Fleur bit her fingernails nervously as the court proceedings got underway. One by one, the prisoners were led up to the dock to protest their innocence, or else hang their heads and dully admit their guilt. Either way, it seemed to Fleur, the outcome was the same. The stern jury pronounced a guilty verdict on every soul brought before them, and Judge Fielding clearly took pleasure in handing down his sentences, from branding with hot irons – which was done on the spot, to the crowd's delight – to transportation or death by hanging. The cases were tried in order of severity. Thieves followed beggars; highwaymen followed thieves. Next came the trial of a repentant murderer, caught red-handed beside the body of his mistress, and eager to assuage his terrible guilt. Judge Fielding was, of course, only too happy to oblige, donning his black cloth cap to deliver the death sentence.

At last only William remained. He was pushed and kicked into the dock, where he stood, defiantly meeting the judge's steely gaze.

Judge Fielding stared at him with cold blue eyes. 'Aha, the infamous Captain William Hart,' he said, leaning back in his chair and lacing his fingers together theatrically. There were hoots and cries from the watching rabble, until he hushed them with a call for order.

Arthur leaned towards Fleur. 'I've been looking at that judge . . .' he murmured. 'Does he seem familiar to you?'

Fleur stared hard at Fielding's angry face and saw a glimmer of something – or someone – that she thought she recognized. She nodded slowly. 'Aye, Arthur, there's something about him—' She broke off as the judge started to sum up the case against Captain William Hart.

'Your crimes against Church and State are too numerous to recount here today,' he barked. Unfurling a scroll, he scanned an apparently endless list of crimes, shaking his head with disgust. 'You have pleaded guilty to piracy, robbery and murder, among many other heinous misdemeanours. I see no reason for delay in pronouncing sentence upon you.'

'Hear, hear,' came a cry from the balcony. The men of the jury nodded their approval and Judge Fielding smiled broadly.

'Very well' – he placed the black cap on his white wigged head – 'you shall be taken from this place and carried to the cell from whence you came, and from there to Tyburn, there to be severely hanged by the neck until you be dead. Your body will be gibbeted in irons and hung at Cuckold's Point as a warning to all pirates of the fate that awaits them. God save the King.'

Fleur's knees gave way as she listened to the sentence. Gates steadied her with an arm about her waist as they watched their captain. He was straining against his shackles with every ounce of strength in his battered body and there was a wild look in his eyes that Fleur knew well.

'Don't think it's over, you lily-livered shrimp!' he yelled with a maniacal laugh.

Judge Fielding's eyes bulged and his cheeks flushed angrily at the prisoner's insolence.

'I've been in tighter spots,' William went on, 'and lived to sail off into the sunset, Fielding.'

Some of the crowd cheered the brave captain, which made the judge go redder still.

'And if by some mistake I am brought to Tyburn without finding the moment to slip my bands and be off, take heed, your honour: I'll haunt you till your hair falls out; I'll haunt you till you're driven mad by it and end your own worthless, hateful life. When I've finished with you, Fielding, you'll wish your mother had stayed a pup and never spawned you!'

The spectators roared with laughter.

'Silence!' screeched Fielding, and the black cap slipped off his head as he shook with rage. 'I've waited a long time to see you hanged, William the Heartless, and I will not allow you to escape again.' He stood up, his robes flapping around him. 'I shall drive you to Tyburn myself and watch you dance at the end of the rope.' He slammed his hammer on the bench so hard that the handle snapped. 'Take them away and let them rot in Newgate jail until the gallows are ready for them,' he hissed, before collapsing back in his seat.

William laughed as the guards dragged him away. Then Gates led a shaky Fleur, along with the others, back through the crowds to the nearest coffee shop.

Women weren't allowed inside such establishments, but any male who was reasonably dressed and prepared to obey the rules was welcome to come in and drink a dish of coffee. Gates paid a penny for each of them and they sat down at a table by the hearth.

Fleur was still shocked from what she had just witnessed and she couldn't stop shivering. She and Arthur warmed their hands before the fire and gradually began to take in their surroundings, while Gates and Bart brought out their clay pipes and smoked. Men swarmed in and out, some scribbling notes or reading quietly, others debating or taking snuff from dainty boxes. The walls were lined with books, advertisements and signs listing the house rules. The whole place smelled of tobacco, sweat and burned coffee.

The coffee was finally brought over in a Turkish pot and poured into bowls. It was as black as soot and tasted bitter, but they sipped it eagerly. Fleur scalded her tongue but she barely noticed. All she could think about was William.

After a few moments Gates got to his feet and wandered over to speak to a group of men. He returned to his seat looking satisfied. 'It's hanging day on Monday – three days' time,' he said sombrely. He nodded over at the men he'd been talking to. 'The condemned prisoners will be collected from Newgate at seven in the morning and taken to Tyburn.'

'If they survive that long,' said Bart darkly.

'What do you mean?' demanded Fleur.

'I had the misfortune to spend some time there once, lassie,' Bart began, shuddering at the thought. 'The little box they locked me in was nothing but a waiting room for death – as cold as a tomb, it was. There was a body rotting in the cell next door and the stink almost drove me mad.'

'Why didn't they remove it, sir?' asked Arthur, wrinkling his nose in disgust.

'Because you have to pay a departure fee when you leave there son, — dead or alive. The family of that stinking corpse in there were still saving up. There was probably nothing left when they finally came to take him away.' Bart downed the dregs of his coffee and grimaced. 'It's hell on earth in there – even if you survive the ordeal, the mind never forgets the horror.'

They all sat in silence, taking in what Bart had told them. Finally Fleur forced herself to smile. 'William will be all right,' she said firmly. 'But it's up to us to think of a plan to free him.'

'Well said, miss,' replied Gates, and patted her hand reassuringly. 'Now I say we return to the *Adventurer*.' He glanced over at the door nervously as a couple of naval officers entered. 'There's nought more that we can do here and I don't want to run into anyone who might remember me.'

'Fair enough,' said Bart. He turned Fleur and Arthur. 'Are you both savvy?'

They nodded miserably and followed him through the busy streets to their little boat.

# CHAPTER 21

'So how exactly are we going to rescue him then?' demanded Rose.

Fleur and Gates had gathered the crew on the *Adventurer*'s main deck to inform them of their plans. It was mid-afternoon, and the Thames was teeming with sailing vessels and hungry, shrieking gulls.

'I could go into Newgate with my staff and fight our way out,' suggested Fleur. She was pacing around the deck, rubbing her hands together as she thought.

'No, child,' said Bart. 'Even with your abilities there will be too many guards for you to fight. Remember what happened in Salem.'

Fleur sank onto a bollard and rested her chin in her hands. 'Can't we just blow the whole place up then?'

'I wish we could,' Bart replied bitterly. 'It's a miserable cesspit.'

'Who was the judge who sentenced William anyway?' Rose said, briskly changing the subject. 'I like to know who's in my bad books.'

'Fielding,' replied Bart as if the name were a bad taste in his mouth. 'Joseph Fielding.'

At that moment Tom, who had been listening from the rigging above, lost his hold, tumbled down the hempen ropes and crashed heavily to the deck.

'Tom, are you all right?' asked Fleur with concern. He was usually as nimble as a monkey in the rigging. '*Tom?*'

But he scrambled to his feet and ran off without a word.

It took Fleur more than an hour to discover his hiding place. He was tucked away in a corner of the hold, tickling an ecstatic Grog under the dull glow of his flickering lantern.

'Tom, what's going on?' asked Fleur as she picked her way over bales of spices and barrels of rum to reach him. 'Everyone's worried about you.'

Tom set Grog down and leaned against a barrel with

his knees tucked under his chin. His eyes were red. 'Go away,' he muttered, wiping his cheeks.

'Shan't,' said Fleur, plonking herself down in front of him. 'Tell me what's wrong or I'll have the men nail up the door and leave you down here for ever.'

Tom sighed and suddenly punched the floor. Grog immediately shot up to seek the safety of Fleur's shoulder.

'Astrid was right,' said Tom, nursing his knuckles. 'She was right all along but I couldn't admit it. Not to anyone.' He took a deep breath. 'I'm not an orphan.'

Fleur's eyes widened. She inched closer and put a reassuring hand on Tom's knee, though in truth her own mind was reeling. She bit her tongue and waited for him to say more. He struggled to control himself before continuing.

'Joseph Fielding is my father,' he blurted out at last.

This time Fleur's jaw dropped open. '*What?*' she exclaimed, so loudly that Grog nearly jumped out of his skin for a second time. He leaped off her shoulder and headed for the door, barking indignantly. 'Joseph Fielding, the hanging judge?' she asked incredulously. 'The one who condemned William to death?'

Tom nodded and hid his face with shame. Fleur sat there, dazed, while the pieces fell into place in her head.

No wonder he had been so secretive. No wonder he'd wanted to avoid the very place where his father held court. She gasped, remembering how Fielding's features had seemed familiar. Father and son were cut from the same cloth.

Tom groaned and peered at Fleur through his fingers. 'I s'pose you hate me now that you know who I am, eh, Claw-cat?'

'Of course not, stupid,' Fleur answered quickly. 'You're Tom the cabin boy, not Judge Joseph Fielding Junior. You ain't a split-tongued, bilge-sucking, black-hearted chuckle-head like him, are you?'

Tom groaned again. 'That's my dad you're talking about,' he said, smiling weakly. 'But you're right of course.' He reached for her hand and gave it a squeeze. 'I'm sorry I lied to you, Fleur.'

'Don't worry, I understand why,' she said, shuddering as Fielding's cruel face loomed large in her mind's eye. 'I would have lied too if he were my father.'

'I ran away from home after my mother died,' Tom explained. 'He was always a cruel, spiteful man, but my mother made it bearable there. He used to beat us both, and when she died, he was set to put all his energy into the raising of his son.' He laughed bitterly. 'All he ever wanted was someone to follow in his footsteps and rain

**323**

down righteous fury on London's ne'er-do-wells. For my own part, I longed to go to sea, right from when I was a young 'un.'

'How did you get away?' asked Fleur.

'It was on the day of my mother's funeral. My father got horribly drunk and started blaming me for her death.'

'How so?' asked Fleur in astonishment.

Tom's blue eyes welled with tears and he looked very young and vulnerable. 'She'd been standing up for me,' he explained. 'I'd broken one of his precious oriental porcelain figures. His pride and joy. Mother found him beating me with his cane . . .' His voice trailed away as he remembered the angry words and blows. 'She took the beating for me,' he whispered. 'He almost killed her. The following day a fever set in . . . it finished her off.'

'And so your father blamed you?'

'Aye . . . He's not the forgiving kind. 'Twould never have happened if I hadn't been so stupid. Of course he told the rest of the world that she'd taken a tumble on the stairs. Only he and I — and now you — know what really happened.'

'But it's murder,' Fleur exclaimed. 'He murdered his own wife. And he's . . . he's a judge.'

'I know, and yet he condemns people to death for

lesser sins,' Tom replied bitterly. 'I ran away that very night and stowed away aboard Captain Hart's ship. I'd heard all the talk about William the Heartless and was desperate to join his crew. And even though my father had no idea where I'd gone, I took comfort in the thought that it would anger him to know that I had chosen to sail with his enemy. I left without a single souvenir to remind me of who I had been or where I'd come from ... I wish that I had kept something of my mother's though,' he admitted, his eyes suddenly watery. 'I've forgotten what she looks like.'

Fleur chuckled suddenly, surprising them both.

'Which was the funny bit?' demanded Tom defensively.

'Sorry,' she said quickly. 'It's just ... well, when we first met we were both penniless orphans, and now look at us! You're practically high society. A judge's son, no less.'

Tom laughed, but his face soon fell again. 'I always feared that Captain Hart would have to face my father one day. I know they've had their run-ins, but I never thought the law would catch up with your uncle.' He looked deep into Fleur's eyes, and for a moment she glimpsed all the pain, fear and self-loathing that he felt. 'I'd do anything to get William back, Fleur,' he added.

'He's been more of a father to me than Judge Fielding ever was.' He swallowed and blinked away fresh tears.

They both sat in silence for a while, lost in their thoughts. After a while Fleur straightened up and stared at Tom, a daring idea just beginning to form in her mind. Perhaps there was still a chance of rescue for William, she thought – though the plan she was now considering would test Tom's loyalties to their limits.

'What's wrong?' He wiped his nose on his torn shirt. 'You look like you're having one of Astrid's visions.'

'Tom,' said Fleur, grabbing his arm, 'would you really do anything to get the captain back?'

Tom nodded firmly. '*Anything!*' He ducked his eyes down shyly. 'As I would for you,' he murmured softly.

Their eyes met again before Fleur continued: 'I've got a plan. But it won't be easy – for you in particular.'

'You want me to go back, don't you? To him, I mean?' he mumbled as realization dawned.

Fleur nodded. 'I'm afraid so. It's the best – perhaps the only chance we have to free William.'

Tom exhaled heavily then, much to Fleur's surprise, a broad smile crept over his face. 'Back in Salem,' he told her 'the captain gave me a bit of advice. He told me that we must all face the thing that we fear most in the world, because once we've done that and come out the other side, there's nothing left to scare us ever again.' He got to his feet and held out a hand to help her up. 'Don't worry, Fleur. Whatever it takes, we'll get him back.'

# CHAPTER 22

Fleur's plan was bold, daring and very risky. After she had laid it all out to Tom, and he had agreed to it, they had gone to tell the others. Now it was dusk and the crew gathered again on the deck of the *Adventurer*.

'I still can't believe that Judge Fielding is your father, boy,' said a shocked Carlton Bart. 'He's a nasty piece of work.'

Tom hung his head. 'Why do you think I never said nothing?' he muttered. 'I was ashamed of my own kin.'

'Well, I think you're very brave, Tom,' said Astrid kindly.

'Aye,' Gates agreed. 'It must have taken courage to

walk away from wealth and privilege and begin a brand-new life with nothing but the clothes on your back.'

Fleur glanced at the bosun and they shared a small, knowing smile: he himself had done the very same thing.

Tom shrugged and dug both hands deep into his pockets. 'I might as well have been locked up in Newgate for all the freedom I had,' he replied dully. 'Running away was the best thing I ever did.'

'And now you're planning to go back?' Gates stroked his beard thoughtfully. 'Are you sure you can do that, lad? From what I've heard, your father is a violent man and he *will* make you pay for what you did.'

Tom swallowed nervously. 'I'll turn up at his door and beg for forgiveness,' he said. 'That might lessen the punishment.'

'Oh, come on!' Arthur exclaimed. 'We all know he'll beat you black and blue.'

Tom winced. 'Aye, he'll use his fists to welcome me, I'm sure, but I can take it. It's time for me to face him again.' His eyes locked with Fleur's. 'I ain't scared of him no more.'

'But what happens if he beats you to death, Tom?' asked Rose. 'How will that serve us?'

'He won't kill me,' said Tom, though his voice shook.

'He's a proud, vain man and always wanted his son to follow in his footsteps.' He forced a smile, although he wasn't fooling anyone. 'I'll lie like a flat fish at the bottom of the sea and make him believe I'm back to do his bidding.'

Rose looked at him with new-found respect. 'It's a dangerous game you're playing, young Tom,' she warned. 'Remember, once you're in his home, none of us will be able to look out for you.'

Fleur began to wonder if her plan was too ambitious. Rose was right: if Fielding beat his son to death, accidentally or otherwise, Fleur would lose him too. But she could tell that his mind was made up. His jaw was set and his brilliant blue eyes blazed with purpose. He was determined to make the plan work and save his captain, and Fleur knew that there was nothing anyone could do to stop him.

Tom soon confirmed her thoughts. 'I *have* to do this,' he said passionately. 'I owe Cap'n Hart my freedom and I'll gladly give my life for him. All I have to do is gain access to my father's house and make him believe that I'm sorry for running off.'

'Don't go telling him you've been sailing with William the Heartless for all these years, lad,' said Gates. 'It'll lead to nothing but trouble.'

'Aye, sir, he'd kill me on the spot.'

The bosun laid a hand on his shoulder. 'And do you honestly think you can do what you have to when the time comes?' he asked. 'It will mean you can never go home again.'

Tom nodded. 'Aye, sir.' He smiled darkly. 'I think it will give me great pleasure.'

That very night Tom left the ship alone. Just as when he had left all those years ago, he was returning to his father with nothing more than the clothes on his back. He said his goodbyes quickly, though Fleur hugged him as if she would never let him go. He apologized to Astrid yet again, and then Arthur shook his hand and gave him two little china pots containing foul-smelling concoctions.

'This one is a salve for bruises,' he explained as he handed over the first pot. 'You only need a little bit to ease the pain.' Then he handed over the second one, and smiled at Tom conspiratorially. 'You know what this one does . . .'

Tom nodded as he slipped both pots into his pocket. 'And it will definitely work, right?' he asked his friend.

Arthur tapped his nose and winked. 'Definitely. I doubled the usual dose.'

Tom patted him on the back and grinned with as

much bravado as he could muster. But nobody could miss the ashy paleness of his face or his trembling hands. Fleur climbed up to the crow's nest to watch Gates drop him ashore. It wasn't long before the little boat vanished in the darkness, and then he was gone. Below, down on the deck of their stolen ship, the lanterns looked like fireflies. Suddenly Astrid's beautiful voice soared upwards, soft, pure and haunting. And then . . . there it was, the soft low song of the ocean; pulsing through Fleur, calming her senses. But as she gazed out at the glittering city, she wondered if the ache in her heart would ever go away. All she could do now was wait: everything depended on Tom.

# CHAPTER 23

At first light on that bleak Monday morning, Newgate's bell rang out hollowly. Eight times a year the bells were muffled to alert the city that it was time for the hanging march. Fleur, Gates, Bart, Rose and a handful of William's best men were already crossing the misty Thames as the first chime sounded. Fleur shuddered and pulled her cloak around her more tightly. No one mentioned the common superstition that if you heard church bells at sea, someone from your ship was going to die.

Fleur had ordered the remaining crew to sail the *Adventurer* back to Cornwall immediately and wait in the hidden cove; Carlton Bart was to take control of the ship. Gates knew that as soon as the authorities learned that a pirate had been freed, the waters around London would be swarming with officers of the law. Once they had rescued William, it would be safer to make their way back to Cornwall on horseback.

Fleur had put on a brave face to say her goodbyes. Her mission was incredibly dangerous – they all knew that this goodbye might be for ever.

'I know you'll get our captain back, Fleur,' said Arthur, hugging her tightly. 'Come back in one piece, won't you?' he added in a wobbly voice.

'I'll try,' she promised.

Astrid stepped forward. 'There's something you should know,' she said quietly, checking over her shoulder to see if they could be heard. 'Watch out for Rose – I'm not certain you can trust her. I caught her creeping out of my cabin earlier.'

'Really?' said Fleur confused. 'She's on our side now – *isn't she?*'

'Yes, of course,' said Astrid quickly. 'But she tends to act in her own best interests.' She sighed heavily. 'Fleur, I'm sorry, but I think she was looking at the map. It wasn't put back properly and the vellum was still damp. Only you, me, Tom and Arthur are supposed to know where it's hidden.'

'Bilge rats!' Fleur cursed loudly. 'Just as well she's coming with us to rescue William. At least I can keep an eye on her that way.' Panic suddenly ran through her veins like ice. 'You said the map was wet . . . So she knows how to read it too!'

'Maybe, but she didn't go so far as to take it,' said Arthur. 'She might have been able to copy some of it down, but she wouldn't have understood the Old Norse.'

'That's probably more than enough for a pirate queen,' muttered Fleur darkly.

Gates nodded at her from the prow. It was almost time for them to leave. Fleur took a deep breath. 'Look, if it comes down to it, we'll just have to beat her to the prize. For now I have to trust her – I have no choice.'

'Fair enough,' said Arthur. 'But watch her slippery fingers around the Hart staff. It's obvious she's taken a fancy to it.'

Astrid leaned in to embrace Fleur and whisper in her ear, 'I've seen the end of this.'

Fleur pulled away at once as she realized what Astrid was saying. 'Tell me,' she begged. 'Not everything – I know you won't do that – but give me something that will offer me hope, Astrid. Please.'

Astrid stared into her friend's desperate, haunted eyes

and nodded once. 'We will be together again when angels dance with the *Dragon*,' she said solemnly.

Fleur blinked. 'Is that all I get?'

'It *is* a bit vague, Astrid,' Arthur chipped in.

Astrid looked at them both with an odd smile. 'It's all you need,' she said firmly. 'If I say any more I might alter the path of things. Follow your instincts, my friend, and all will be well.'

Fleur eyed her doubtfully. 'Is this a real vision or are you making things up to make me feel better?'

Astrid laughed softly. 'What does your heart tell you?'

'That we will get my uncle back safely,' said Fleur firmly. 'And that Jack will recover.'

Astrid rested her hand on Fleur's shoulder. 'Let it be so.'

The girls smiled at one another warmly.

'I'm so glad you've found your home with us, Astrid,' said Fleur sincerely.

'Then hurry back to us, Fleur,' Astrid replied softly, 'and make it a happy one.'

Fleur's rescue party soon reached the shore. They tethered their boat to a post, hurried up the banks of the Thames and into the streets that led to Newgate. A couple of crewmen set off to find some horses so that they would be able to make their escape when the time came. Fleur felt the weight of her father's bow, slung over her shoulder beneath her cloak. She feigned a limp so that she could walk with the Hart staff without attracting undue attention. She rubbed her thumb against the ruby heart, hidden beneath the rough material, and it seemed to give her the strength she needed for the task ahead.

Fleur was horrified by the festive mood of the crowds thronging the streets around the prison.

'Everyone looks forward to hanging day,' Gates muttered ruefully. 'It's like a holiday. Even the shops have shut.'

'I'll never understand those who find sport in killing.' muttered Fleur.

'Nor I, miss,' he agreed. 'But then we're pirates, not barbarians.'

They found a spot beside the heavy prison gates where the air was thick with the cries of street hawkers offering ballad sheets and refreshments, and waited. The air was cold but the sky above was a bright peacock blue. Suddenly a huge roar swept through the crowd and everyone surged forward.

'What's happening?' asked Fleur, jumping up and down in an effort to see over people's heads.

'They're bringing out the condemned, Fleur,' Rose hissed. 'It's starting.'

The pirates pushed and shoved their way to the front of the mob just in time to see the condemned prisoners being brought into the Press Yard. The cries grew louder as William appeared and was thrown to the ground alongside the others. Fleur gripped her staff tightly and ground her teeth as her uncle's chains were hacked off by the blacksmith. Then another guard, the Yeoman of the Halter, tied the prisoners' hands in front of them with a cord that wrapped around their bodies and was knotted at the elbows.

'What's that for?' asked Fleur.

'So that they're able to pray when they reach the Tyburn tree,' muttered Rose grimly. 'Too little too late for these rogues, I'd say – with all due respect to your uncle, girl.'

There were eleven prisoners sentenced to hang. One was a young boy no older than Fleur. He wept openly as his hands were tied, and begged the guards to show him mercy. They closed their ears to his entreaties and bundled him into a cart with the others. Rose tapped Fleur on the shoulder and pointed at another cart that held William on his own. Holding the reins, just as he had promised in court, was Judge Fielding in his gown and periwig. He was both scowling and grinning as he prepared to drive his old enemy to the gallows.

The journey was three miles, and for Fleur the pace was torturously slow. Led by the city marshal and his under-sheriff, the carts made their way through the jeering crowd under a hail of rotten fruit and worse. William stood proudly, dodging the missiles rather more successfully than the judge. The boy on the cart behind him, though, sobbed louder still and clung to his despairing father, who was jogging along beside him, screaming at the mob to leave his poor child in peace.

At St Sepulchre's they stopped to the sound of the church bells; here the prisoners were given posies of flowers and cups of wine and invited to ask forgiveness of the Lord. Most drank heartily but refused to beg for salvation. Then they went on, over the River Fleet and up the hill to High Holborn. There was another stop at the Bowl Inn, where prisoners and guards alike were plied with gin and ale, and yet another at the Mason's Arms, accompanied by raucous songs.

William was in his element, singing lustily and downing several large jugs of ale drawn from the Mason's cellar. 'I'll pay for 'em on my way back,' he promised the landlord with a laugh – to great cheers from the crowd.

Fleur watched the strange procession closely. The

lawmen – with the exception of Fielding and the marshal – were as drunk as the prisoners, and for a moment she thought about attacking the cart at once and vanishing into London's maze of winding alleys. Her fingers tightened around the shaft of the Hart staff and she started towards the convoy.

'Not now, miss,' whispered Gates in her ear, sensing her impatience. 'Stick to the plan.'

Fleur nodded miserably as the carts trundled off again, on the last leg of their journey.

As the terrible shadow of London's great three-sided gallows came into view, most of the prisoners, drunk as they were, fell quiet and slumped against the sides of the cart, their eyes wide with fear. A highwayman of some repute continued offering kisses to the prettier girls in the crowd, and William still shouted out a steady stream of jokes and threats, but for most the hopelessness of their situation was enough to silence them. Fleur stared at the gallows: each of the long oak beams was capable of holding the weight of eight men; an instrument of mass murder. She shuddered.

Suddenly Gates's hand shot out to snatch the wrist of a skinny, ragged urchin who was dipping his quick fingers into the folds of the pirate's coat.

'Ain't nothing in there for you but trouble, boy,' he said fiercely, and the pickpocket yelped, shook himself free and vanished into the crowd.

Glancing again at the carts, which were now trundling right under the scaffold itself, Fleur thought of Tom. What would happen if he failed in his mission – to him, to William . . . to all of them? Her heart raced. She had to do *something*! Desperately she searched for a route through the crowd to the captain. Someone had to act. And at that moment, almost as if he'd heard her thoughts, William turned and somehow found her among all the thousands of spectators. Their eyes met and Fleur remembered his words during their sparring session:

*'You rush into everything like a dog among rats, Fleur. Slow down . . . think about your next move.'*

He nodded at her sharply with a brief toothy grin, then turned away. Fleur's grip on the staff relaxed and she let out a sigh. For once she would be patient.

Overlooking the gallows was a large house with iron balconies from which the sheriffs of the city and their invited guests could watch the executions in comfort. In the space below, wealthier spectators paid two shillings for seats in Mother Procter's Pews, large open galleries with a good view of the grisly proceedings. The rest jostled and squeezed around the gallows, waiting eagerly for the macabre entertainment to begin. Broadsheet sellers advertised the criminal exploits of the condemned. Needless to say, the legend of William the Heartless was very popular.

'Hats off!' the shout went up, not out of respect for those about to die, but for a better view of their death dance.

The hangman, who was as drunk as anyone else, uncoiled the rope's free end from each prisoner in turn and threw it up to an assistant balanced precariously on the beam above. Each was tightly fastened, leaving very little slack. When the moment came, the carts would be driven out from under the prisoners, leaving them dancing the Tyburn jig, their legs paddling helplessly in the air.

Each prisoner was given a chance to say a few last words. Some repented; the hapless young boy proclaimed his innocence; but William used his time to entertain the crowd with his black humour and bold manner. He bent his knees as if testing the strength of his rope and shrugged doubtfully. 'Are you sure this string is strong enough to hold us, Fielding?' he bellowed. 'I'd hate for it to break and leave me a cripple for the rest of my days!'

As the crowd roared with laughter, the prison ordinary stepped forward and began praying earnestly with the condemned. Gates nodded at Fleur and the rest of their group, then led them down a narrow side street, where their fellow crewmen waited with the horses.

'We nicked 'em from a coaching house in Southwark,' said Black Matt with a toothless grin when Fleur enquired.

'Good work, men,' said Gates approvingly.

'The captain will hear of this,' added Fleur. 'Once he's free, your loyalty will not be forgotten.'

They all mounted their horses and made ready. Fleur shrugged off her cloak, revealing her father's bow and the quiver loaded with arrows. She stripped the sacking from the narwhal-horn staff with trembling fingers. The ruby heart glowed brightly as she polished it on her sleeve.

Rose nudged her horse forward alongside Fleur's. 'Take care,' she said, smiling. 'I never thought I'd see the day when we'd be fighting side by side.' Then her smile faded and her eyes glittered with tears. 'I'm so proud of you, daughter,' she blurted out suddenly. 'And I know that Henry . . . your father, I mean . . . well, he would've been too.'

Fleur could only nod and blink back the tears that welled up in her own eyes.

'Ladies, are we ready?' interrupted Gates, pulling back

on the reins of his eager mount. 'Only there'll be plenty of time for family affairs when we've saved the cap'n.'

Rose grinned and nodded at him. The bosun drew his sword and held it high. 'It's the world against us and us against the world. We fight for friendship's sake and for better days ahead!'

'And curse the King and all the higher powers!' added Boneless Bill.

With a grim set to his jaw, Gates spurred his horse into action, and they charged out of the narrow street and into the mêlée beyond.

# CHAPTER 24

To begin with nobody noticed the small band of pirates carving a path towards the gallows. The guards were too busy breaking up brawls. But as Fleur, her mother and the men approached the mob, their clashing blades and the cries of the panicking spectators finally drew the attention of the authorities.

'Stop that rabble!' bellowed the under-sheriff as Fleur and her party bore down, but his cry could barely be heard over the general din.

Every guard still sober enough to swing a blade sprang into action at once, but the pirates fought them off. It was as if some hungry foxes had been released into a chicken coop. The pirates were vastly outnumbered, but the speed and boldness of their attack more than made up for that. The guards desperately began firing their pistols into the dense, unruly crowd and everything went mad. A woman was shot and the mob around her turned on the guards and fights began breaking out everywhere.

Fleur used her staff to knock aside anyone who got in her way, eyes firmly fixed on William. Spotting her approach, the city marshal jumped up and shoved the drunken hangman aside, signalling to the drivers of the prisoners' carts.

'Drive away, men,' he shouted urgently; and, to the driver of William's cart, 'Judge Fielding, your honour, quickly! These villains must be hanged at once.'

Fleur stared at the back of the judge's head, where he sat hunched over the reins of William's cart and pulled sharply on the reins. Nearby, Rose was bravely fighting off three constables with her blood-smeared cutlass. For a moment Fleur thought about Astrid's warning . . . But she could trust her mother, couldn't she?

'Mother!' She held the Hart staff aloft. 'Take this!' She threw it over and Rose caught it deftly, then promptly used it to knock the last constable to the ground. 'And make sure no one gets in my way,' Fleur added as she spurred her horse into action.

'With pleasure,' Rose yelled back with a grin.

As she galloped towards the Tyburn Tree, Fleur pulled her bow over her head and drew back an arrow. She aimed at the noose around William's neck and let it fly. It sliced neatly through the thick rope and thudded into one of the heavy oak posts just as the carts began to move away from beneath the scaffold.

'Tom!' she shouted at the top of her voice. 'Now!'

And at that moment the dreaded Judge Fielding stood up in his cart and threw off his wig, whipping his horse fiercely and letting out a mighty, 'Hyaah!'

William tumbled backwards as they shot off, flanked by their pirate cavalry, and his eyes widened with joy and amazement as his driver turned to address him for the first time since leaving Newgate.

'All right, Captain?' said Tom, wiping away the sooty lines that had made do for wrinkles when passing for his father. 'Hold on, we're in for something of a bumpy ride, I'll wager.'

'Tom, you magnificent boy,' roared William. 'However—?'

'Tell you later,' Tom interrupted, whipping his horse to greater speed. 'All Fleur's idea, to be honest.' And they rumbled away, the shocked spectators parting before them like wheat in a cornfield.

In amongst the crowd, Gates was desperately urging Fleur on: but she had turned to watch the other prisoners dangling helplessly at the ends of their ropes.

'What are these rogues to you?' yelled Rose, as she pulled her horse up beside her daughter. 'We have to leave before the authorities are upon us.'

'Rose is right,' agreed Gates. 'We haven't time to save every soul.'

'But they don't deserve to die for the crimes they are accused of. I can't leave them like this.' Fleur's eyes were locked on the youngest of the prisoners. His father was trying in vain to reach him as he kicked and struggled at the end of the rope. The boy's face had swollen and his eyes bulged alarmingly. He clawed at his throat with his hands. Time was short. Without taking her eyes off him, Fleur drew back her bow once more.

'Go,' she said calmly. 'And remember that we're rogues ourselves!'

She fired the arrow and the boy fell to the ground. His father charged forward, scooped his child into his arms and slipped away into the crowd.

'One down,' said Fleur, pulling another arrow from her quiver.

Her arrows flew clean and true and she didn't once miss her mark. Soon all the prisoners were choking and gasping for breath on the dusty ground beneath the gallows. Rose, Gates and the handful of remaining pirates had stayed by her side, fending off any attackers until the last of the prisoners was free.

'Come on, child,' Gates snapped impatiently. 'You've done your duty and managed to extend our rescue mission to every prisoner in London,' he grumbled, only half jokingly. We've got to get out of here. *Now!*'

Fleur slung the bow across her back, drew a cutlass from her belt and charged along behind William's cart, away from Tyburn and the roars of their appreciative audience. Away to freedom.

They didn't stop till they reached Hounslow Heath, to the west of London. The authorities would no doubt have the Thames locked down to stop the pirates escaping by sea. They were less likely to look inland.

Fleur and her little group galloped towards the northern corner of the heath where their friends were waiting for them. They slowed their horses to a trot as they entered a patch of dense woodland. Sunlight filtered down through the chestnut trees, and autumn leaves drifted idly to the ground. Fleur drew her horse alongside William's cart and they grinned at each other warmly.

A burst of laughter suddenly startled them. They

followed it towards the huge canopy of a massive copper beech tree. As they approached, the laughter stopped abruptly.

'Who goes there?' someone demanded gruffly.

'Your captain,' said William with a smile in his voice.

'Friends,' added Fleur.

Tiny Joe appeared from behind the tree's thick trunk, smiling broadly; the rest of the crew followed him out of the undergrowth. 'Hoa, Cap'n,' said Tiny Joe. 'Good to have you back, sir.'

William leaped out of the cart. 'Good to be back, man. Mark me, you'll all be rewarded for your loyalty,' he replied, to a round of delighted cheers. He strode towards his niece with outstretched arms. Fleur jumped down from her horse and flew into his embrace. As they held each other, she drank in the familiar smells of sea salt, smoke and rum that clung to every item of his clothing. All her tension and sorrow evaporated as she squeezed her uncle with all her might. Finally William prised her from him and set her down on the ground.

'I told you I'd come for you if you ever got taken,' said Fleur, choking back her happy tears.

'And I didn't doubt it for a moment,' said William. He rested a mighty paw on her small shoulder. 'I knew that with you at the helm of the *Dragon*, my crew wouldn't be able to give up on me, neither.'

'It wasn't just me though,' she protested. She looked around at the pirates, slapping each other's backs and sharing their tales of derring-do, and paused to gaze at Tom, who was being held aloft in triumph. 'It was all of us,' she added.

Slipping down from her horse, Rose came over to join them. William watched her approach with cold, hawkish eyes.

'What's she doing here, by the way?' he demanded, pointing at her rudely. 'I told you we couldn't trust her.'

'I know,' said Fleur, holding up her hands in defence. 'But things have changed since you've been away, Uncle. We've reached an understanding.'

The captain exhaled loudly and rolled his eyes. 'Don't be so green, girl,' he snapped furiously. 'She's lying to you.'

Rose inched further towards them. 'I'm not, William,' she said firmly.

'Tell me,' he began, pacing around her. 'Did you try and pinch my ship while I was rotting away in that armpit of a place by any chance?'

Rose bit her lip and looked away uncomfortably.

'I have my answer,' he roared. 'See, Fleur, a leopard

SARA STARBUCK

don't change its spots, and this wildcat ain't nothing but a liar and a cheat. Don't forget what she did to you either, girl. Don't be her fool.'

'You know I had my reasons,' snapped Rose, turning on him. 'Look, William, I'm sorry for how I wronged Henry – and you, for the matter – and I understand why you can't trust me. But many years have passed and I want to try and make things better. Surely I deserve the chance to be forgiven for my sins?' She looked at her daughter fondly. 'Fleur and I have found a new beginning – and I hope that you and I can do the same.'

William snorted and raised an eyebrow. 'There's little chance of that, woman,' he snapped. 'But I won't stand in the way of you and Fleur – she deserves a mother's love, if you can actually give it, that is. And you'll have to prove yourself there too.' He looked down at his niece. 'Is this what you want, child?'

Fleur nodded meekly.

'I'm sorry for my part in all our ill-fated adventures,' said Rose. 'I'm trying to make things right.' She looked at William beseechingly. 'We were friends once,' she said solemnly. 'Can you forgive me enough that we may begin again?'

William's dark eyes narrowed angrily as his brother's widow spoke, but seeing Fleur's troubled expression, he

352

sighed and nodded. 'Aye, Rose, I can try,' he said wearily. 'Though I can't promise anything. You wronged me sorely, and my kin worse . . . but for Fleur's sake, and that alone, I'll give it a go.'

'Thank you, William,' said Rose with relief.

'So what happens now then?' There was a challenge in his voice.

'Now . . . ?'

William folded his arms and tapped his foot, pointing at Fleur. 'The girl, Rose,' he said impatiently. 'Will you take her or do you expect to stay with the *Dragon*?'

Fleur gasped: she hadn't even considered Rose's plans. She looked at her mother in panic. Rose was clearly as shocked as she was. 'I . . . I haven't . . . um . . .'

William raised his eyebrows. 'Well?'

Rose gazed blindly at him, then blinked and turned to Fleur with regret in her eyes. 'Fleur, you understand why I can't stay, don't you?' she said. 'I can't be that sort of mother to you.'

Fleur nodded silently. She felt the rejection like a blow to the stomach, but she did understand.

Rose came to crouch beside her daughter. 'I love you, Fleur,' she began. 'But I have spent so long alone now that I know no other way.' She nodded over at William. 'I wish I had what you share with your uncle. You and

William must stay together. You need each other. It's clear that he loves you as much as Henry ever did.'

'What about you?' asked Fleur as tears rolled down her cheeks. 'Don't you need to be loved?'

Rose's legendary composure almost broke and her bottom lip trembled. 'I have to get back to my own ship.' She squeezed Fleur's shoulders. 'I'm not very good at letting people love me,' she muttered.

Fleur stared at the ground, feeling suddenly small and powerless. After all they had been through, she'd never meant to leave her uncle's side, but it still hurt that her mother was so ready to abandon her again.

'We *will* meet again, daughter,' said Rose, her green eyes sparkling. 'The sea will carry us to the same shore before long. That's the way of things.'

'You don't know that . . .' said Fleur miserably.

A smile played at the corners of Rose's lips. She opened her mouth to speak, then seemed to change her mind. She shook her fiery locks and paused for a moment before continuing: 'Like I said, my girl, the sea has a habit of arranging family reunions for our lot. There are more adventures to come for us, mark me.'

Fleur was about to mention the map, but Rose shook her head and held a finger to her lips. Then she pulled her daughter into her arms and stroked her hair and rocked her gently on the balls of her feet. For a moment Fleur was a little girl again, held in the arms of a loving mother . . . Then it was over.

Rose pulled away brusquely, smiled at her daughter, then leaped onto her horse.

'I think you've forgotten something.' The captain's booming voice surprised everyone as he came swishing through the fallen leaves towards them, with his arms outstretched as if to hug her. As he reached Rose's horse, he clapped his hands together and held them out, suddenly stern. 'Come on, hand it over.'

Rose blushed and gingerly lifted a flap of tarred cloth that hung from her saddle. She reached underneath and unhooked the Hart staff, which she handed, somewhat reluctantly, to her daughter.

Fleur gasped in horror. She hadn't even noticed it was missing.

'Sorry,' said her mother sheepishly. 'Force of habit.' She nodded at her brother-in-law, then grinned mischievously and tugged on her horse's reins. The animal rose up on its hind legs and whinnied. 'It fits best in the girl's hands anyway,' Rose laughed. Then she raised her arm, sword in hand, to salute the men. 'Here our ways divide,' she cried. 'I wish you fair winds, my friends.

Ever and always.' And with that, she dug her spurs into her startled horse and galloped away, to a chorus of raucous pirate cheers.

As Fleur stood there, silent, Tom came to stand next to her. 'You all right, Claw-cat?' he asked, taking her hand in his.

'Aye,' she said. 'At least, I will be now.'

They both watched as the blue of Rose's billowing cloak vanished amongst the distant trees. 'Will you miss her?' Tom asked.

'I have a funny feeling we'll be seeing Rose again sooner than William would hope. But we can handle her,' said Fleur, turning to face her friend. 'So the plan worked, then.'

They grinned at each other in delight.

'Like a dream,' said Tom. 'It was just like Astrid's prophecy. The choice, and all that. I went home — to Judge Fielding's home, that is — and threw myself on his mercy.'

'Did he beat you?' asked Fleur, concerned.

'Black and blue.' Tom grinned, rubbing his buttocks at the memory of his father's cane. 'But it was nothing. I got my own back when he took his brandy at bedtime. Arthur's sleeping drug worked a treat. He was still snoring this morning when I took his wig and robes and hopped onto the cart in his place at Newgate. I've never been so glad of the family resemblance.'

'You looked amazing,' said Fleur. 'I wasn't even sure if it *was* you. Where did you get the moustache? It looked so real.'

'It was,' Tom chuckled. 'Once he was out cold I snipped it off him and stuck it on with treacle.'

'But was it horrible, Tom?' Fleur asked, suddenly serious. 'Going back, I mean?'

Tom puffed air from his cheeks and ran a hand through his mop of sandy hair. 'It was no more than I could stand, Fleur,' he began, his voice a whisper. 'The beating was harsh, but what hurt the most was his reaction when he first saw me after all our time apart. I thought he might be glad of my return – I even felt guilty about what I planned – but there was nothing but victory in his eyes to see me slinking back. He was only happy to have won, happy that I had lost.' He shook his head regretfully. 'That's no kind of father in my book.'

'But you showed him,' said Fleur, nudging him in the ribs.

'Aye, I played my part well, and he was an arrogant fool to underestimate me.' Tom paused to scan the motley collection of crew mates scattered about the copse and sighed with relief. 'It's good to be back among my own, Fleur,' he said, before bursting into a wide smile. 'And look at this . . .' He reached into his pocket and pulled out a small, pear-shaped bottle made from delicate milk-white glass.

'What is it?'

Tom uncorked the bottle and thrust it under Fleur's nose. 'Smell it,' he commanded.

She raised an eyebrow suspiciously, then sniffed cautiously, and the scent of fresh-cut flowers filled her nostrils. It took a moment for her to realize. 'Oh, Tom,' she said, holding back more tears. 'Your mother's perfume.'

'I found it in a drawer,' he told her. 'One whiff of this and I remember her, Fleur. I remember everything.'

The friends were interrupted by William. 'Young Tom, you impress me more and more,' he boomed, ruffling his cabin boy's hair. 'You'll make a fine captain yourself one day, and in the meantime you're the best cabin boy – nay, *apprentice* – any pirate ever had.' He rested a hand on Tom's shoulder and his expression grew serious. 'I know what you were called upon to do to for me, lad, and I appreciate that. That judge is more of an idiot than I thought.' He lowered his voice. 'My own boy was taken from me too young, but by Neptune, if he'd lived I'd've wanted a son just like you, Tom Fielding.'

And with that, he spun on his heels and strode off, leaving Tom speechless and brimming with pride.

Ten long days later, the land-weary pirates ditched their tired horses and picked their way down the smugglers' path to Pepper Cove. They clambered over barnacled rocks and down to the sandy beach: here they found the *Black Dragon*, with the *Adventurer* swaying in the water beside it. The clouds parted and sunlight poured over the scene, glinting off the rippling water and sending golden shapes dancing and sparkling up the sides of the ships and over their fluttering sails. Fleur grinned with delight as she remembered Astrid's words: '*We will all be together again when angels dance with the* Dragon.'

Their shipmates, who were dozing in the afternoon sun, or busily digging for crabs and oysters marooned by the tide, waved and cheered as they approached. Astrid was standing at the rail of the *Dragon*, her long hair blowing in the wind like spider's silk. She caught sight of Fleur and squealed with delight. Arthur came dashing over with Grog coiled around his neck, and they stood waving and yelling like maniacs. Then there was Jack, laughing down at his friends. Fleur looked up at him, hoping that he was restored, but then Dr Dubois appeared beside him and Jack grabbed him in an awkward embrace.

'The doctor and I are to be married,' he called down in a shrill voice.

'Oh no,' said Fleur, but then she saw that Jack was laughing heartily and even Dubois had cracked a smile.

'Just my little joke,' Jack bellowed down. 'Dubois and Master Arthur fixed me up proper.'

More and more pirates joined them at the ship's rail, until the roar of cheering men was deafening.

Fleur and Tom grinned and slapped each other on the back. There were so many more adventures to look forward to. First there was treasure to find, then they had to work out where Astrid had come from – and of course there was always the matter of the Hart staff, which seemed on the verge of giving up its secrets.

William strode proudly ahead of the group, eager to reach his beloved ship. He stopped suddenly on a large flat rock at the foot of the gangplank and turned back to Fleur.

'We're home, lassie,' he said, his dark eyes shining.

Fleur nodded and gazed out beyond the cove and over the wide sapphire sea. William was right. They were home.

# Acknowledgements

Once again this book has been a massive team effort. I am sincerely grateful to everyone who has helped and encouraged me throughout this experience, and also for the patience of my friends and family, who I'm forever cancelling on to meet my deadlines.

A special thank-you goes to the following people:

Toby Starbuck, for some serious front-line editing. His footprints are all over this book.

Lauren Buckland, my editor, for all her hard work, passion for the story and brilliant editorial input.

Sarah Such, my agent, for her constant support and good advice.

Tom Starbuck, for all the hours we spend together lost in his imagination. It's all good stuff for a writer.

Sophie Nelson, my copy-editor. Adam Relf, who has designed another amazing cover image. Niall Stewart Harding, for all the lovely inside illustrations. Kelly Tapper, my publicist, and everyone else at Random House who has in some way helped me with this book.

Ahoy to my M.O.P.s at Mile Oak Primary School in Brighton. Special thanks go to Ben, Ashley, Christian, Chelsea, Jessica and Daisy, otherwise known as the terrifying band of pirates the Black-eyed Wolves, for naming a character in this book, the bendy pirate Boneless Bill. Excellent work, my pint-sized bullies.

I forgot to thank Alice Such for being first-eyes on *The Dread Pirate Fleur and the Ruby Heart*, as she has been for this book too. I rightly deserve to be dunked from the yardarm as was promised if I forgot anyone. Sorry, Alice, you owe me a dunking.